ACCOLADES AND PRAISE FOR
A Royal Guide to Monster Slaying

Winner of the Ruth and Sylvia Schwartz Children's Book Award

Shortlisted for the OLA Silver Birch Award, the Diamond Willow
Award, and the Pacific Northwest Young Reader's Choice Award

A School Library Journal Best Middle Grade Book of 2019
An Ontario Library Association Top Ten Title of 2019

"A fast and fun read, [and] a great read-a-like for
Tamora Pierce's Tortall series."
—Starred Review, *School Library Journal*

"A fresh take on familiar fantasy creatures and situations."
—Starred Review, *Shelf Awareness*

"A rousing romp for monster hunters
and monster lovers alike."
—*Kirkus Reviews*

THE
FINAL
TRIAL

KELLEY ARMSTRONG

PUFFIN CANADA

an imprint of Penguin Random House Canada Young Readers,
a division of Penguin Random House of Canada Limited

First published 2022

1st Printing

Jacket design: Kelly Hill
Jacket art: © Cory Godbey
Manufactured in the U.S.A

Library and Archives Canada Cataloguing in Publication

Title: The final trial / Kelley Armstrong ; illustrated by Xavière Daumarie.
Names: Armstrong, Kelley, author. | Daumarie, Xavière, illustrator.
Series: Armstrong, Kelley. Royal guide to monster slaying (Series) ; 4.
Description: Series statement: A royal guide to monster slaying ; 4
Identifiers: Canadiana (print) 20210330279 | Canadiana (ebook) 20210330295 |
ISBN 9780735270206 (hardcover) | ISBN 9780735270213 (EPUB)
Classification: LCC PS8551.R7637 F56 2022 | DDC jC813/.6—dc23
Library of Congress Control Number: 2021947874

www.penguinrandomhouse.ca

Penguin
Random House
PUFFIN CANADA

THE
FINAL
TRIAL

CHAPTER ONE

I stop in my tracks to stare at the town rising before me, white spires stretching into the midday sky. As we approach the gates, I cannot stop gaping. It's as if we have walked clear into the clouds and found a mystical city there.

"I have never seen such a place," I whisper.

Dain—my fellow monster hunter in training—turns to look at me. "You live in a *castle*, princess."

My twin brother, Rhydd, shakes his head. "She means we have never seen a town like this. Even our castle isn't so grand, and these are just ordinary buildings."

Dain grunts in grudging understanding. He's never been beyond the mountains either. Few people in our expedition have. Our kingdom, Tamarel, is bordered on three sides by monster-infested waters and on the fourth by monster-infested forests and mountains, which we had to cross to reach this nation, Roiva.

Our journey was not uneventful. Dain nearly got trampled by yet another khrysomallos. My jackalope, Jacko, nearly got carried off by a wyvern. And while my party would claim that I nearly got dragged away by a nekomata, I saw it the whole time and was just trying to get a closer look. Overall, though, we made it through easily, and we could claim that's because we're an awesome party of monster hunters, but the truth is bigger. Much bigger—as in, dragon-sized.

For the past few months, monsters have been on the move. Some have completely fled the Dunnian Woods. Others have just relocated within it. There's a mother dragon in the mountains, where there hasn't been a dragon in generations, and the monsters have steered clear. Even the dragon herself has gone silent, tending to her babies.

That dragon is the reason we're here. She's on our soil, and we need to protect her. I may be the royal monster hunter but really, I'm more of a referee. While I will kill monsters if necessary, my real job is finding ways for humans and monsters to live together by relocating the beasts and educating the people. We believe humans can live peacefully with the dragon. We could be wrong, and if so, we'll need to drive her out. What we don't want is for people from other kingdoms to do what they did to the original dragons: kill them and steal their babies and force the beasts to flee to distant lands.

I'm part of an expedition to explain the situation to kingdoms beyond our borders, starting with Roiva. We have good relations with Roiva. Better yet, they're a land of scholars who pride themselves on their universities. Who better to enlist in our dragon-education plan?

We've crossed the mountains, come through a swath of arid scrubland and finally reached this border town. A messenger has gone ahead to announce us. It's not as if those in the guard tower could miss us. We have a giant wolf—a warg—plus a jackalope and a dropbear. A pegasus filly periodically flies over our heads and a ceffyl-dwr—a carnivorous aquatic horse—trots beside me.

We're also a party of over a dozen people. There's my brother and me. Two of our friends, Dain and Alianor, plus Trysten, a kinda-sorta-prince we're returning to his homeland. Dain, Rhydd and I are twelve years old, while Trysten and Alianor are thirteen.

As for adults, there's Liliath, my and Rhydd's great-aunt and a member of our royal council. Having the passage to Roiva clear of monsters provided the chance of a lifetime and she couldn't pass it up. There's also my bodyguard, Kaylein; Wilmot, my trainer and Dain's foster father; and a half dozen guards.

We haven't even reached the town gates before they fly open and a man on a white steed rides to greet us, followed by six more horses. Both the riders and their mounts are dressed in finery that sparkles in the sunlight, as bright as the town's white spires.

The riders are men and women mixed, most with skin as dark as that of my bodyguard, Kaylein. Natives of Tamarel have brown skin, like my own, though there are many families like Kaylein's, who are originally from Roiva, and even a few people as pale as Wilmot, who hails from the kingdoms beyond.

As soon as the riders draw near, the leader dismounts and bows. "Prince Rhydd and Princess Rowan. I am Sir Terryn, lord of this town. You honor us with your visit."

"Did we have a choice?" Dain mutters under his breath. I shoot him a look, but he's right—the only road to the Roivan capital runs straight through town.

"Thank you, Sir Terryn," Rhydd says. "The honor is ours. You do not need fear a royal visit. We are simply passing through, though we may shop for supplies, if that is acceptable."

The man straightens, his chin lifting. "The crown prince and princess of Tamarel shopping like common travelers? Never. We will see you are fully restocked for your journey."

"While that is unnecessary, it would be appreciated."

"You will be my guests tonight."

Rhydd glances at Liliath. As heir to the throne, my brother outranks her, but she's with us for exactly this reason—so Rhydd may seek her counsel in our mother's absence.

"Liliath of Clan Dacre," she says, stepping forward. "Aunt to Queen Mariela and member of the royal council. Your offer is very kind, Sir Terryn, but we did not intend to impose on your hospitality."

"It is no imposition, and I insist. It is already late afternoon. By the time you restock, you would barely pass our western gates before you needed to make camp. Please do me the honor of hosting you this evening. I'm sure it has been many days since you've eaten a proper meal or slept in a proper bed."

Beside me, Alianor whispers, "If he mentions a hot bath, I'm abandoning you and staying here forever."

Liliath nods to Rhydd, turning the decision over to him. He glances at me. Only a half year ago, I'd been heir to the throne. The death of our aunt—the former royal monster hunter—and an injury to Rhydd's leg allowed us to switch future roles. I say *allowed* and not *forced*, because it's what we both wanted.

"Hot baths?" I say to Sir Terryn. "We could be swayed from our path with the promise of those."

The white-haired man laughs. "Yes, princess. I do believe we can provide that."

"Do you mind my sister's entourage?" Rhydd asks. "The warg is her bodyguard, and the jackalope her companion. The pegasus and ceffyl-dwr will be fine with a stable and pasture separated from other horses. Also, Dain here has a young dropbear."

"I see it clinging to him," Sir Terryn says with a smile. "We will happily accommodate whatever you require for both human and beast. I daresay my staff will be delighted to see such wonders, particularly the pegasus." He shades his eyes to look at Sunniva flying overhead. "She is a beautiful creature."

"Just don't tell her that," Rhydd says. "She's more of a princess than my sister. All right, then, Sir Terryn. Lead on."

We have been treated like royalty. Yes, as Dain would point out, Rhydd and I *are* royalty. At home, we live in a castle, and we have staff who cook our food and tidy our rooms. We are extremely privileged, which we recognize and attempt to repay with our service to the country. Still, our treatment at

Sir Terryn's goes beyond what we'd receive at home, and it is miles above how we expected to spend tonight.

Baths are drawn before we even get into Sir Terryn's sprawling manor house. We are offered the choice of assistance or privacy. I select privacy, and Alianor naturally accepts the pampering. Our clothing is whisked away to be washed, and we rise from our baths to lush robes that Alianor threatens to steal—which is more than a threat, considering she's the daughter of a bandit warlord.

We're then shown into our guest quarters, an area bigger than my room at home. A roaring fire chases away the autumn chill, and Malric—my warg—takes up a position in front of it with Jacko angling in to catch a bit of heat.

Trays of food wait in my room, and Alianor and I devour them while Liliath and Kaylein have their baths. Clothing is provided for dinner, along with entertainment. I eat so much I struggle to stay awake for the festivities. My body aches from a week of sleeping on the ground, and I barely sink into the bed before I am soundly asleep.

I wake to fur in my mouth . . . jackalope fur, it seems, as I open my eyes to see a bunny butt on my face.

"Jacko?" I croak.

He gives a semi-apologetic chirp and hops onto my chest before resuming the real cause of my early waking: his alert cry. I scramble up. Alianor groans beside me and Malric snaps at the jackalope, telling him he's done his job and can be quiet now.

"Malric's right," I say around a yawn. "I got the message. Please stop before you wake the entire household."

"Too late," Alianor grumbles as she lifts her head. "What's he going on about?"

At a movement in the room, I glance to see Kaylein silhouetted in the moonlight, sword in hand. Malric is my constant companion, and he considers himself my bodyguard, just as he was my aunt Jannah's. Outside the palace I need a human one, too, at least until I'm older. That would be Kaylein, the youngest member of the royal guard at eighteen. She was supposed to sleep in another room—as was Alianor—but Kaylein insisted on a floor mat and Alianor insisted my bed was big enough for two.

Now Kaylein is at the balcony door, and when she opens it, a roar echoes in the distance. I'm out of bed in a flash, running to the balcony and leaning over the railing as Malric tugs at my nightgown.

"The creature is at least a half mile off," I say, pulling my gown from his jaws.

Kaylein says, "I think he's more worried about you vaulting over the railing to investigate."

Alianor comes out, yawning. "What *is* that?"

"It sounds like some kind of wildcat," I say. "A big one. A lion maybe?"

"Oooh. I've never seen a lion."

"Neither have I. I do know people in other kingdoms keep them in menageries."

I squint into the night. The sound comes again, a wild and angry roar. There's something else in the sound, too . . . a note of fear.

The sound chills my spine, and I shiver. We don't have menageries in Tamarel, and while I've heard there are excellent ones abroad—dedicated to helping injured or rare animals— I've also heard the horror stories that made my ancestors outlaw them. I'd be surprised to find that in Roiva, though. Their nation is known for its educated and forward-thinking ways.

When the door opens, I turn to see a maid standing there, wide-eyed.

"Is that from a menagerie?" I ask.

"N-no, Your Majesty. It is a monster. It came from the mountains, and it has been terrorizing our town for weeks now."

Alianor turns to me. "See? I told you there was a reason Sir Terryn was being so nice. There's always a reason."

"A monster?" a voice says. We turn to see Trysten at the doorway.

"Hey!" Alianor says. "This is our *bed*room."

"Yes, which is why I'm staying out here." He turns to me. "Rhydd's on his way. Did someone say that's a monster?"

Before I can answer, footsteps sound outside the door, and Dain and Wilmot step past Trysten.

"Now we know why they wanted us to stay," Dain mutters.

"I just said that," Alianor says. "Bringing up the rear, as always."

He rolls his eyes and walks in past the maid, who still hovers just inside the door. His dropbear—Dez—clings to the front of a shirt Dain has hastily pulled on.

"Can you see anything?" he says to me as he steps onto the balcony.

I shake my head.

"What can you tell us about the beast?" Wilmot asks the maid.

"Nothing. No one can get close to the creature. It seems to be living in a ruined building to the south." She points. "It was an old guard tower that collapsed in an earthquake."

As she speaks, Rhydd appears.

"Why did your lord not just ask for our help?" Rhydd says. "We're traveling with the royal monster hunter and two members of our monster hunter troop."

"He knew you had urgent business with the king. He feared you would not stop."

Rhydd sighs. "So he put us up for the night, knowing we'd hear the beast. I'll need to speak to your lord about this."

"B-but you must help," she says. "Please."

"We will," I say as I come in from the balcony. "We just aren't happy with how Sir Terryn went about it. Can you tell us anything about the monster?"

"Only that it is a terrible and fearsome creature that roars nightly and steals lambs from our flocks."

"And babes from their cradles?" Wilmot says dryly.

"Not yet, but it will. You must free us from—"

"—this dreadful scourge? Yes, yes. I've been a monster hunter for twenty years. I know the routine." Wilmot turns to us. "Dain and I will take care of this."

"What?" I say. "And leave me here, when there is an unknown beast I may have never seen before?"

He sighs. "It was worth a try. Come on, then. Let's free this land from the dreadful scourge. Or at least get that blasted beast to stop roaring so I can sleep."

CHAPTER TWO

Wilmot doesn't bother rousing Sir Terryn. I'm sure the lord can hear us preparing to leave—kind of hard to miss the clomp of a half dozen pairs of boots. Trysten will stay behind. He has too little experience with monster hunting, as much as he'd like to join us. As for the lord, Wilmot will deal with that matter later. We have a monster to catch.

According to the maid, the tower is a mile away. We could see it from the balcony, so we don't need directions. The only horse we have is Doscach, my ceffyl-dwr, and we don't bother asking to borrow others. I leave Doscach behind, too. This will be easier done on foot.

We make our way along the dark streets, windows opening as people peer out at us. They can hear the beast roaring and now they hear the sound of our passing. If they look out, they'll see a party of foreign-dressed strangers with swords and bows, all of us making our way toward that roar.

Those shutters close quickly as we pass, lest we ask for help. I could grumble at that, but it's not as if we'd accept help even if it were offered. We're Tamarelian monster hunters.

From the balcony, the building had seemed a simple structure: the collapsed remains of a stone guard tower. Now that we get closer, I can see there's also a small garrison among the ruins.

We're still a hundred feet out when we reach a fence. A sign informs us that this is a historic site undergoing archaeological study. That's why the tower and garrison haven't been repaired. They're digging up the ruins to see what lies beneath.

"It's like a mountain," I say as I look at the toppled stone and mounds of dirt. "A cavern, at least."

When Alianor frowns over at me, Wilmot says, "Rowan is right. The ruins of this building could act like a den or cave. The maid said the monster came from the mountains, undoubtedly driven out by the dragon."

"It stopped here," Alianor says. "And holed up someplace that reminded it of home. Poor thing."

"Yeah, you won't be saying that if it tries to devour you," Dain says. "Whatever it is, it doesn't sound small."

We pause at the fence, and I look at our companion beasts. They're all staring into the shadowy ruins. I'd have preferred to leave Dez and Jacko behind, but I know better. Jacko has been known to chew through cages, and Dez escapes into rafters. They're predators, and they consider it their duty to protect us.

"Malric?" I say.

He growls, his chest rippling.

"Yep, whatever's in there is big," Alianor says.

Up close, the roar still sounds like a wildcat but also like the bellow of a bull, and there's something about it that makes my ears ring and my head boom, as if a headache is coming on. That nudges a vague memory from a bestiary, but when I try to pursue it, nothing comes, and there's little point in trying to identify the beast from its roar. I'll see it soon enough.

I glance at Wilmot for instructions—he is my trainer, after all. But he's watching me, and I realize he wants me to lead. This expedition is taking the place of my trials, and to satisfy the council, he'll need to tell them all the ways I proved I was worthy of the ebony sword on my back. Soon I will lead the monster hunters, and so I must begin that now.

I squint along the fence. Then I say, "I'd like to circle the ruins and try to pinpoint exactly where the sound is coming from."

We're not even halfway around before I realize the futility of my plan. That booming roar echoes off everything, and the more I hear it, the more my head hurts. I have no idea where it's coming from except "somewhere in the ruins."

"I suggest we move past the fence and surround it," I say. "Space out, but in pairs—keep someone close enough to see you and come to your aid if the monster charges."

"Would you like to assign pairs, Rowan?" Wilmot asks.

I'd rather let people pair off themselves, but I need to take the lead and assess strengths and weaknesses, as uncomfortable as that is.

"Alianor? Go with Wilmot, please." That puts our most experienced monster hunter with our weakest. "Rhydd? You'll be with Kaylein." Both are expert sword fighters, and Rhydd has had monster-hunter training. "Dain? We'll triple up with Malric."

With the groups set, I assign search areas. Arguably the strongest team is Malric, Dain and myself, plus the two smaller monsters. We'll start at the darkest portion, where our beasts' night vision will help.

Dain and I circle around to the back. There, the tower ruins face the open desert, away from the lights of the city. Then we separate with Malric between us as we advance on the ruins. Our portion is the tower itself, half toppled onto the garrison. When I squint, I can make out several openings where the stone has crumbled enough for a beast Malric's size to crawl through.

That's when the monster stops roaring. The wind has brought the smell of humans, and it has gone silent.

"I like this gap over here," I say, pointing.

"You mean the darkest and scariest one that is also the one the beast most likely used?"

"Exactly."

"One could argue, princess, that we'd be better off going in through a less likely opening and sneaking up on it."

"It already knows we're here."

"Which means it's crouched just beyond that gap, waiting to pounce and devour you."

"Pfft. No. I'm the princess. You're going through first."

He gives me a look. "If I actually thought you'd let me, I'd take you up on that."

"You're the archer. You provide backup for"—I pull the ebony sword from my back—"the royal monster hunter!"

"Yeah, you run through holding that. It'll catch on the stonework and impale you before the monster can eat you alive." He lifts a hand. "Please do not tell me it'd kill you before it eats you."

"Depends on what kind of monster it is." I glance at the gap as we approach. "You should probably stop talking now."

"Me?" His voice squeaks adorably.

"Such a chatterbox." I notice Jacko nearing the gap and hurry to stop him. "Uh-uh. No bite-sized monsters through the hole first."

Jacko glares at me and chitters.

I point at my boots. "Protect my feet. That's your job."

He still grumbles but hops over to stay at my feet. I stop just outside the gap and return my sword to its sheath. Dain's right that the blade is too big for this, so I take out my dagger. Then I pause. When I look over at Malric, he's nearly invisible, black fur against the darkness. Just his yellow eyes show, those eyes fixed on me, waiting for me to figure it out. That's progress. A few months ago if I'd approached this gap, he'd have yanked me back.

"You first," I say with a wave.

That makes sense, as much as I hate putting anyone else at risk. Malric grunts and moves to the opening. He sticks his head in, and I hear him sniffing as his ears swivel. The gap is just big enough for him to pass through with his head ducked— in other words, waist-high on me.

He takes one step through and then another. I wait until his hindquarters are inside. Then I start forward, brushing his tail. He doesn't wheel and snap, which means there's no immediate danger. I follow.

Inside, it's pitch-dark. I blink hard to no avail. Taking out a fire stick, I light it and raise it above my head as Dain lights one behind me.

I step forward. My foot hits something that clatters loudly enough to make me wince. I lower the fire stick and see the leg bone of a full-grown sheep or goat. The beast's dinner. That means we are indeed looking at a large monster, one at least the size of a wolf.

I point it out to Dain, who nods. Then I extend my arm and wave the fire stick. We're inside the tower, with a ruined staircase to my left. The remaining space is small enough that I can tell it's empty. I lift the fire stick and peer up. Nothing obviously hiding there either.

Dain taps my shoulder and points. There's an opening ahead, and it's the only exit. I nod and start forward. When I reach it, I examine the stone sides—it's the remains of a doorway that once led from the tower into the garrison. The falling tower crushed it until only a hole remains, one that we'll need to crawl through. I stick my arm in as far as I can reach and wave the fire stick around.

A screech sounds behind me. I jump up so fast I drop the stick. Something swoops at my head as Dain shouts a warning. A leathery wing smacks my face, and I stagger back, my dagger rising. Another shriek as a dark form flies up into the tower.

"Was that a harpy?" I say, backing against the stonework.

"Looked like a bat," Dain says. "But it was huge. As big as a harpy."

Another dark form swoops. It's coming straight at me and I swing my dagger to slash at it, but before I can, a cry rings out and Dez leaps from Dain's shirt, red eyes flashing in the darkness. The creature starts swooping up, winging away as fast as it can, but the dropbear is faster, zooming up the stonework. Another cry, and Dez leaps clear over our heads. A thud as she smacks into the flying beast in midair.

"Dez!" Dain says.

He runs forward to catch her as she hurtles toward the ground. He's too slow, though, and she hits, landing right atop her prey. She looks up at him, her wide face turning his way as if wondering what all the fuss is about. She's a dropbear. That's how she hunts. She drops. She'd struck the creature in midair and ripped out its throat before it even hit the ground.

"Good girl," I say as I crouch beside her. "Such a good girl."

She looks up, blood dripping from her mouth. Then she glances at Dain.

"She's waiting for your praise," I say. "Yours is what matters."

He tells her she did a fine job, and then she dives into her meal, ripping at what I see now is indeed a bat, much bigger than those we have at home. Its body is as long as hers. Dropbears may look adorable, but they are deadly predators, even when they're as young as Dez.

Using her prehensile hands, she rips a chunk of meat and holds it out to Jacko, who takes it and nibbles delicately.

"You're going to need to stash that," I say. "We can't stop for a snack."

She doesn't understand me, of course, and just keeps eating, but I move back to the ruined doorway, and Dain lets her take another bite before scooping her up. He sets the dead bat aside and tells her she can return to it, and she snuggles into the pouch across his chest.

I light another fire stick. Through the doorway, I kneel to see a room, and I motion to Dain that we're going in. Then I wave for Malric. The warg sniffs the entrance and grumbles deep in his throat at the indignity of needing to crawl on his belly. He does it, and I follow with Jacko.

CHAPTER THREE

I'm barely through when Wilmot's distant voice rings out. "Don't move. Stay right where you—"

A roar cuts him off, and I stumble up into a run even as Malric snaps at me. I race into the remains of a large room. The roar comes from the next section. When I don't see an obvious entrance, I stop short . . . and then I spot a pile of rubble with wavering light behind it. It's another ruined doorway, this one mounded high with debris.

I grab rocks and wood and throw them aside. Dain curses as one hits him, and then he starts helping me dig. Soon, I can see the next room. Wilmot stands across it, and he's looking at something over here. He stands in some kind of pit, the top of his head below me.

I clear a gap big enough for me to fit into and scramble through as Malric growls behind me. I pop out the other side and nearly tumble down. It seems Wilmot isn't standing in a pit—I've come out on a landing over a sunken room.

"Hey," a voice says to my left. "Nice of you to join us."

I look over to see Alianor at the far side of the landing, which is cracked down the middle. It's not an actual landing, I see now. Most of the room has fallen into the space below it, and that's where Wilmot stands. Alianor and I are on the part that didn't collapse, but it did crack and it's sunken in the middle. All of this is not nearly as important as what stands in that crack, having cornered Alianor.

"A nian," I breathe.

The beast turns its head my way and roars, and while I'm sure I should shake in terror, I grin instead. I don't even think Jannah ever got to see a nian. They live in the mountains, but on this side, near the grasslands, and they don't tend to bother people, much less venture into towns.

The roar should have given it away. It's said that a nian's roar can split open a man's skull, which is obviously impossible. As with every legend, you need to dig past the exaggerations to the truth, which seems to be that the pitch of a nian's roar hurts our heads.

I thought that roar came from a big cat. I'm partly right. The nian has the head of a lion, complete with mane. The body is more canine, with a ropy tail that looks like it belongs on a bull or boar. The beast also has boar-like tusks.

"So, Rowan?" Alianor calls. "Do you think you can stop admiring this monster and save my life? It looks really hungry."

I wouldn't say that, but it does seem upset. It's not as big as I expected. Maybe a little smaller than Malric, but still definitely big enough to kill Alianor. Right now, it's settling for roaring at her from the rubble piled in the crack between us.

"Wilmot?" I call.

"I have it in my sights," he says from behind his bow.

"Same here," Dain says to my rear.

"Alianor, would this be a bad time to ask how come you're up here and Wilmot's down there? I thought we were working in pairs."

"He told me to stay here," Alianor says.

"No," Wilmot says. "I told you to stay down here, in a safe spot, while I checked what looked like the beast's den. But you spotted bones."

Alianor is a healer in training, specifically a monster healer, and if she sees bones, it's like me spotting a new monster. She has to investigate.

"Has the beast made any aggressive moves?" I ask.

"Besides snarling and flashing tusks as big as my forearm?" Alianor says.

"That's a threat display. Is there anything near you that it might want?"

"Just bones."

She picks one up, and the nian stops roaring.

"Uh," she says. "That's weird. Does it want the bones?"

"It seems young. You could be in the middle of its toy pile."

"Seriously?"

She picks up the biggest bone and throws it. The nian leaps, and behind me, Dain sucks in breath. Malric crouches,

— 20 —

ready to attack. The nian only chases the bone, picks it up and brings it back to where it started.

"Did it just fetch the bone?" Alianor asks.

I take a step toward the nian.

"Princess," Dain warns.

I nudge Jacko back with my boot. He chitters but moves behind my feet, as I've been teaching him to do.

I take another step. The nian is down in the crack, maybe ten feet from me, its head just above the tilted floor I'm on. I crouch.

"Hey, little nian," I say.

"Princess." Dain's voice rises.

"Keep your bow on the beast," Wilmot says. "Rowan's fine."

"Hello," I say to the nian. It turns its leonine face toward me, bone still in its mouth.

"Where's your pride?" I ask. "Your family? You seem a little young to be off on your own."

She'll have no idea what I'm saying. It's my tone that counts. I'm working this through, too. It's a she—I could tell that when she was facing Alianor. Her size and short mane mean she's young. Nians live in prides, like lions, and females like this one generally stay with them.

The nian stares at me, and there's no fear in her gaze. No confusion either, at this puny prey creature being so bold.

"Dain?" I say. "Can you get the bat Dez caught?"

When Dain hesitates, Wilmot reminds him to listen to me. Dain goes and brings back the bat. I take a moment to prepare the mangled creature. Then I hold it out by one leathery wing and step toward the nian. She waits patiently.

I toss the bat to her, and she catches it in midair and then starts ripping into it.

"The maid lied," I say. "Well, on the lord's orders, I'm sure, so I don't blame her. This nian didn't come from the mountains. No wild predator eats that calmly in front of other predators." I nod toward Malric. "She's barely noticed a warg. She's paying no attention to Jacko. And she's not the least bit fazed by humans."

"So she won't kill me?" Alianor says.

"Mmm, I wouldn't wager on it. Obviously no one has been eager to come fetch her, so she's hardly a house pet. You'll be safe where you are. We need to . . ." I trail off as I turn to Wilmot. "I'm not sure what we need to do."

"What are our options?" he asks.

Before I can answer, Rhydd appears, crawling through a hole in the far wall. I quickly tell him and Kaylein, who's close behind, what's happening. Then I respond to Wilmot's prompt.

"The problem," I say, "is that I don't want to return her to Sir Terryn. I know people keep monsters in menageries, but as the royal monster hunter, I can't condone that. However, this isn't our kingdom. But since Sir Terryn tricked us into doing this for him, that means he doesn't get a say in what happens to her now. She's our responsibility. Yet even if we had the time to escort her back to the mountains—which we do not—she wasn't raised there and likely can't fend for herself. That's why she's hiding here and stealing livestock. We also can't allow her to just keep doing that." I sigh. "It's complicated."

"My head was already hurting from her roars," Alianor says. "Now it's hurting twice as much."

"Rowan is correct," Wilmot says. "I believe she's covered all the possibilities, none of them ideal. We have ourselves a dilemma."

"May I ask what you suggest?" I say.

"That we begin by sedating her. That needs to be done whatever the ultimate solution."

I nod. "Agreed. Alianor, you have some sedative, right?"

She holds up her pouch.

"Excellent. Now Dain will tackle her to the ground, and you'll inject her while I stand guard."

Dain makes a noise behind me.

"Fine," I say. "I'll tackle her, and you stand guard."

"You know what would have been really helpful, princess? If you'd put the sedative into that bat she's eating."

"That *would* have been smart, wouldn't it? However, barring that . . ."

I take two running steps toward the nian. Dain only has time to squawk before the beast slumps to the ground a heartbeat before I hop down beside it.

"You'd already sedated the bat's remains," Dain says.

"It *was* an excellent idea." I gingerly check the nian's breathing while holding my dagger. Jacko noses at the beast's leg.

"She's unconscious," I say. "We should truss her and return her to Sir Terryn's home. Kaylein, please run and tell them we'll need a wagon."

CHAPTER FOUR

A half hour later, the rest of our group has assembled in Sir Terryn's gardens, and when I return from checking on Sunniva and Doscach, Alianor is regaling Trysten and Liliath with the tale.

"Then Rowan leaps onto the nian just as it falls unconscious," Alianor is saying. "I thought poor Dain was going to pass out from shock. Wilmot, on the other hand, didn't bat an eye."

"Because I saw Rowan inject the sedative," he says. "She needs to work on her sleight of hand."

"Or she could just tell us all what she's doing rather than pull stunts like that," Dain says.

"What a boring bard's song *that* would make," Alianor says.

Trysten grins at me. "Nicely done. It *will* make a good bard's song."

Dain grumbles under his breath.

Trysten walks over to me. "Are the equine monsters all right having the nian near? I checked them while you were gone, in case the roars spooked them. Sunniva seemed a little nervous, and Doscach was on guard."

"They're fine," I say. "Thank you for checking on them, though. I appreciate that."

Dain mutters something I don't catch. Alianor crouches beside the nian and assesses her vital signs while sneaking in a few pats. I kneel in front of the beast and run my fingers through her short mane.

"We need to speak to Sir Terryn," Rhydd says.

Liliath sighs. "His family has been good to the royals of Tamarel. This, however, is an insult."

"The insult was that Sir Terryn didn't trust us enough to simply ask for help," Rhydd says. "I'm not even sure he expected us to wake and go after the beast. More likely, he thought we'd ask questions in the morning, and he could confess and hope we volunteered in recompense for his kindness."

The nian stirs, stretching one leg and twitching her tail. I double-check the bindings, which are loose cloths that will give her room to move while keeping her secure.

"I've got this," Alianor says. "You go speak to Sir Terryn. I have sedative and food and water for her. Just leave me a guard in case she wakes up angry."

I glance at Wilmot, and he nods and asks one of our other guards to stay with her. Then we go to confront Sir Terryn.

Sir Terryn is sorry. Very, *very* sorry. That's the gist of the conversation. I stay out of it. I'd rather be back with the nian, but I need to be her representative here. My brother and Liliath handle the conversation expertly. Liliath takes the role of the offended foreign dignitary while Rhydd plays the more sympathetic ear.

It seems Sir Terryn does not—thankfully—own a menagerie of monsters. The nian was bought from a passing foreign trader. Sir Terryn's daughter took pity on the motherless cub and bought it in hopes of freeing it, but scholars explained why that couldn't be done, so they'd been raising it in an enclosure for scholarly study.

What they learned from those studies is that nians require more space. Also, they do not fare well without hunting. Dropping off live animals for her to hunt didn't help—the nian wanted her freedom, and she kept escaping until finally she was too big to lead back to her enclosure. She injured a guard who tried to wrangle her, and she's been living in the ruined tower for the past month.

We'd happened along at just the right time because the townspeople were, not surprisingly, getting increasingly upset about this dangerous beast living in their midst. Sir Terryn hoped to convince us to … Well, we aren't sure what he wanted. He isn't sure either. Not kill the beast. She hurt the guard in self-defense and doesn't deserve to die. So what does he expect us to do with her? He has no answer. Just do something. *Please.*

While the others eat breakfast, I return to the courtyard and find Alianor with a very sleepy nian. The beast is eating meat from her hands and letting Alianor stroke her mane.

"So much for being careful," Dain mutters, appearing behind me.

"I am," she says. "She's made no move to hurt me."

Malric circles around to where the nian can see him as he approaches. She lifts her sleepy head and blinks at him. When he sniffs her, she hisses, but it's half-hearted. Jacko hops over, and she barely looks his way. Same as when Dez climbs onto the pergola to peer at her.

"I think she's more than just sleepy," Alianor says. "Yes, I know we shouldn't give monsters human emotions, but she seems sad. Lonely. She should be with her pride."

"Should be," I say. "Can't be. She's too old for one to accept her. She'd be competition."

"The best thing might be . . ." Dain clears his throat. "No one's going to want to hear this, but if the only alternative is to confine her for the rest of her life, she should probably be—"

"No," Alianor says sharply, surprising us. We know what Dain was about to suggest. Euthanize the nian. Sometimes it's what you need to do, and of the three of us, Alianor is usually the most likely to support the practical solution.

"I don't think we need to go that far," I say. "I would do it if it was the choice between a terrible life and a merciful death. No monster should live in a cage. But I think that she can be kept in her enclosure a little longer. We need to come back this way. If they can properly secure her with suggestions from Wilmot, then we can decide later whether it's possible to rehabilitate her. If so, we'll pick her up on the way back."

"Thank you," Alianor says, her voice uncharacteristically soft as she strokes the nian's mane. She looks up at Dain. "I'm sorry if I snapped at you. I know you were just trying to do what's best for her."

He grunts something and dips his chin.

"I'll go speak to Wilmot," I say. "I'll also grab us all breakfast. We need to leave as soon as possible."

We're on the road before midmorning. That puts us a half day behind schedule, but Wilmot had to check the nian's enclosure and make suggestions, as Sir Terryn agreed to care for her until we come back this way.

The land here is strange to me, and I keep scanning it, looking for any sign of monsters I might never have another chance to see. It's an arid landscape of flat plains that seem to go on forever. It's warmer than Tamarel, but not as hot as the desert lands to the south.

Our ultimate destination is the palace, which lies at the other side of Roiva. When we near the next town, we divert around it. That will add time to our journey, but we don't need another noble family deciding they really need to host us. We're well supplied, and so there's no need to stop. We're passing yet another village when the dipping moon says it's time to stop for the night.

"We should camp closer to the village," Alianor says.

Wilmot shakes his head. "Any closer and they'll see us."

"Yes, but any farther and we risk being set upon by the bandits who've been following us since midafternoon."

"What?" I say. "We're being *followed*, and you didn't mention it?"

She raises her hands in defense. "I've been keeping an eye on them, and they've been staying back. I know a thing or two about bandits."

Kaylein's brows shoot up. "I thought you were the one insisting Clan Bellamy *aren't* bandits."

"We aren't anymore." Alianor ignores Dain's snort. "But I know how bandits operate, and I have been monitoring these ones. They are not yet committed to the course."

"Not yet committed to robbing us blind?" Liliath says dryly.

"Not yet committed to waylaying us. We are a royal party, but also a large and very well-armed one with few valuable goods. There are four of them. They'd only dare strike at night, and even then, it would be a quiet robbery rather than an outright attack. To dissuade them, we should camp closer to the village, if not inside it."

Wilmot sighs. Deeply. Then he shakes his head.

"What?" Alianor says.

"I find your calm quite remarkable, Alianor. As if we were trying to avoid annoying peddlers rather than cutthroat bandits."

"Only the most amateur of bandits cuts a throat. It spills blood everywhere, and the gurgling almost always wakes fellow travelers." She looks at us. "That was a joke. Proper bandits don't need to harm anyone. The trick is to demand all their goods and then tie them up loosely enough that they can escape once the bandits are long gone."

"That is *not* reassuring," Trysten says. "Perhaps you meant it to be, but it's not."

"Would you rather they *did* slit your throat?"

Liliath waves for attention. "Enough of this. I see no reason to hide in a town when we're being pursued by such a small party of bandits."

"I would agree," Rhydd says. "The town won't protect us tomorrow if this group decides to keep following. Better to roust them now and show we are not easy targets." He pulls his sword.

Liliath looks at him. "Your enthusiasm is appreciated, Prince Rhydd, but your mother would not wish you running into battle. We have guards to do that for you."

"All right," Rhydd says, and when he sheathes his sword, I have to smile because both Liliath and Wilmot relax, as if that's the end of the matter. They do not know my brother.

"The guards shall roust them, along with Wilmot, while Rowan and I fulfill the other role."

Liliath's eyes narrow. "Other role, your highness?"

"Why, the innocent targets, of course. Predators need prey." Rhydd glances over at me. "Would you like to be prey, Rowan?"

I grin back at him. "Absolutely."

CHAPTER FIVE

O

f course, no one agrees quite so quickly. Liliath and Wilmot object to any plan that puts the prince and princess at risk. Alianor and Dain object to any plan that they're not part of. Trysten says, "That doesn't sound safe," which proves he hasn't been with us long enough to realize that's pretty much our motto.

I know what Rhydd has done here, so I just lean against Doscach to watch the fun. While I've been trained in these same political tactics, my brother is so much better at them. The trick is to propose something unacceptable, feigning absolute confidence in your proposal, and then grudgingly negotiate to the compromise that you actually prefer.

In the end, Rhydd's plan remains structurally the same. The guards and Wilmot will circle around to confront the bandits from the rear. Liliath will go with them, remaining behind during the ambush portion while ready to step forward and speak on their behalf. This was entirely her idea, which suggests we aren't the only ones looking for a little excitement. Trysten will go with Liliath.

That leaves the four of us—Rhydd, Dain, Alianor and myself—to play bait. Four "children" with only a young jackalope and dropbear for protection. There's no chance of sending Malric far from my side, but I can convince him to go off a little ways, as if he's hunting for his dinner. Doscach will go with Wilmot.

That settled, we strike a temporary camp in what any monster hunter would realize is the worst possible location. Near a creek, yes, but also beside a stand of trees, where bandits could sneak up on us. We're a royal expedition—no one expects us to be sensible about these things.

After we strike camp, Wilmot and the others set off as if riding for the village, which is about a mile away. Alianor has been keeping an eye on the bandits. The last time she saw them, they were about a quarter mile away. They've disappeared behind a ridge to wait for their chance. They can't miss the adults leaving—Wilmot even shouts back for us to stay where we are and keep the warg close. And the moment they're out of sight, Malric lopes off to the creek to fish for his dinner and we wander in the other direction.

Wilmot chose our camp well, despite all appearances to the contrary. The forest will be the obvious point of entry for the bandits. He and the others have left through long grass, where they will soon disappear while seeming on a direct route to the village. Then they can circle back and roust the bandits from the rear.

"Does anyone have any dice?" Alianor asks loudly, twirling her hair. "I'm *bored.*"

"We could practice archery," Rhydd says. "Or sword-fighting. I could go back to camp and get my sword."

"Ugh, no. I am *so* tired of all that. *You need to practice your archery, Alianor. You need to practice your sword-fighting. Why? I'm a girl. I'm going to grow up and marry a handsome prince.*" She sidles up to Rhydd. "What do you think, your highness? Should I marry a handsome prince?"

"You should. I hear Trysten is available."

She smacks him. "You are the worst, Prince Rhydd. The absolute worst. Now those boring grown-ups aren't going to be gone long. We need to take advantage and have some fun. I say we kiss."

Dain sputters in genuine shock. "Wh-what?"

"You get the princess, and I get the prince." She hooks her arm through Rhydd's. "Come along, your highness. We have kissing to do."

Dain glances at me in horror. Alianor looks over her shoulder, bats her eyelashes and makes kissing faces.

"So tell me, Prince Rhydd, when *exactly* will you take over as king?" she says as they walk away.

I turn to Dain. "She's right. I think the only answer is kissing."

His expression makes me chomp on my cheek to keep from laughing. I lift Jacko and bring him to Dez in a mock kiss.

"There," I say. "Isn't that cute? Now it's your turn."

I lift Jacko up for him to kiss, and that makes him laugh and shake his head. Then he glances in the direction Rhydd and Alianor went.

"No, they aren't actually kissing," I say with a sigh. "And if they were, you shouldn't be looking. Let's sit down and play with our beasts, like the innocent children we are."

I lower myself cross-legged to the ground and take a strip of dried meat from my pocket for Jacko. Dain crouches and puts Dez down beside him. She toddles over to sniff my hand. I'm about to find some meat for her when the forest erupts in shouts and the clamor of running feet.

"Mission accomplished," I say. "The bandits fell for the ruse, and Wilmot has them on the run."

I peer over at the forest, tracking the noise. "They're going in the other direction." I rise and stretch. "That didn't take long. Shall we join Malric at the creek while we wait? I could use a wash-up."

Dain nods. "I'll grab my bow first. I don't like being without it."

We'd left our larger weapons at the makeshift camp, though we have our daggers. I consider going back for my sword. On the one hand, it feels odd not having it strapped across my back. On the other hand, it's a very big sword, and I kind of like the break. I decide it can wait and head for the creek. Jacko follows at my heels.

I can hear Malric splashing around. He's realized the danger has passed and so he's actually fishing. The creek is bordered with long savanna grass, and I move in, pushing it aside. I've spotted Malric when Jacko screeches. He leaps past me just as hands grab my boot.

There's a very human cry as Jacko lands on my attacker. I kick free and back up, dagger in hand, as Malric comes running from one direction, Dain from the other. By the time they arrive, my attacker has risen to his knees, hands lifted in surrender.

The man is dressed in a cape with the hood drawn up over his face. I prod it back with my dagger and see a young Roivan, no older than Kaylein. He wears his hair in braids, and he's looking up at me, his brown eyes calm.

"Princess Rowan," he says. "I need to speak to you."

"This is not the way to go about it."

"Perhaps, but it is an urgent matter."

Behind me, Dain grumbles, "Please don't tell me you have a monster problem she needs to solve."

The young man pauses.

"Seriously?" Dain says. "That's how our trip's going to go? Constantly being stopped to fix monster problems? Call your own people."

While Tamarel specializes in monster hunters—because it deals with the most monsters—every country has its own way of handling the few they do see. In Roiva, there are a small number of soldiers with extra training who would be called out to deal with any concerns. With the increased monster population from the migrations, though, I presume they're overwhelmed with calls.

"Unless it's urgent," I say, "I'm afraid you'll need to wait for your own experts."

"He doesn't need a monster problem solved," Alianor says as she walks over with Rhydd. "That's one of the bandits. He must have snuck ahead of the others and tried to grab Rowan. Which was a really stupid move. Now he's going to pretend he has a job for us. Nice try, bandit."

"I take that as a compliment, coming from Alianor of Clan Bellamy."

Alianor's eyes narrow. "How do you know me?"

"Because I know your sister, and you look like her. Sarika also mentioned that her younger sibling was fostering with the princess."

"You know my—"

"Have you seen Sarika?" the man continues without letting Alianor finish. "She left the university abruptly. I received a letter saying there was an emergency at home. I would have ensured she was properly escorted, but she'd already left. I even sent men to catch up with her. Tell me she made it home safely and that whatever emergency took her there was not dire."

Alianor and I look at each other. Sarika had indeed fled the university, leaving halfway through her term to return home. She'd said there was an issue, which she never discussed. I'd gotten the impression that the issue arose in Roiva. It certainly didn't come from her family, who'd had no idea she was returning.

"What business did you have with my sister?" Alianor says. "You seem very concerned."

His eyes flash. "I care for her."

"You're friends?"

He pauses. "Yes, we were—are—friends. She is very important to me. Please tell me that she arrived home safely."

Alianor groans and looks over at me. "My sister fell for a bandit. That's why she ran home so fast. She came to Roiva to escape our family's reputation and become a scientist, and what happens? She falls in love with a bandit."

"Bandit?" the young man says.

"Wait." Alianor peers at him. "*Did* she fall for you? Or did you pursue her? Is that why she fled? That better not be the reason. She came here to study, and if you thought you could gain influence with our clan by romancing her—"

"No, absolutely not."

"Yes, Sarika's safe," I cut in. "Her family, uh, emergency is resolved. Our guards have sent your fellow bandits scattering, and I'd suggest you follow them. We have urgent business with the king."

"Yes, you do."

"Thank you. Now get up and go. We'll be watching you."

He shakes his head. "I cannot do that. As you said, you have urgent business with the king. He also has urgent business with you. Perhaps we should complete the introductions." He extends a hand. "King Estienne of Roiva."

CHAPTER SIX

"You do think us children, don't you?" I say as "King Estienne" rises to his feet. "The king of Roiva is named Guarin. He is twice your age. Also, he does not prowl the countryside in a bandit's cloak."

"He should, though," Alianor says. "Because that'd be awesome."

I glance at Rhydd, who obviously has something to add but is keeping quiet. When I arch my brows, he says, "The crown prince is named Estienne. However, the king is neither elderly nor in poor health."

"He was in excellent health," the bandit says. "Until he died suddenly three weeks ago. I believe he was poisoned."

"You know we can check all this," Alianor says. "We can walk straight to that village and ask whether their king is dead."

"Please do," he says.

Rhydd glances over his shoulder. "And those bandits our guards are pursuing?"

"Those would be *my* guards, asked to lead your people away so that I might approach the prince and princess in private." He takes a whistle from his pocket. "May I recall them?"

Rhydd nods, and the caped man blows a shrill whistle that has Malric growling.

"May I also show this?" The young man puts out his hand. On it is a signet ring. He tugs it off and hands it to Rhydd. "I don't know whether you'll recognize it."

"The royal seal of Roiva."

Rhydd holds it out for me to see, and I might have thought I wouldn't have recognized the seal—I'm much better at recognizing monsters—but I know it immediately. I've seen it on enough letters to my mother, royal missives passed back and forth between our nations.

Rhydd then interrogates the king with a barrage of questions that only Roivan royalty could answer. He responds to Rhydd's satisfaction.

"Wait," Alianor says. "You're the king *and* you know my sister? How's that?"

"We are—were—at university together. I was studying history and geographical politics, but I took a course in geology, and that's where I met Sarika. At the time, of course, I was just the crown prince."

"*Just*," Alianor says.

"Can someone tell me what the king of Roiva is doing here?" Dain says, and everyone turns to him. He's been silent until now.

"If he is the king," Dain continues, "then why's he here trying to talk to Rhydd and Rowan instead of just meeting them at the palace? That's where we're going. Sure, a royal escort would be nice but . . ." He waves at Estienne's outfit. "That's not a royal outfit."

"You asked whether I was stopping you to resolve a monster problem," he says. "I am. As for why I'm doing it this way, it's . . . complicated." His head shoots up. "Here come my guards and yours. I think it's time for a talk."

The first part of the talk is, of course, Estienne explaining who he is to Wilmot and Liliath and then proving it—and proving that we aren't gullible children who believed some random guy in a cape saying he's the king of Roiva. It also helps that Trysten had met Estienne during a state visit to his home country, and he can confirm this is the crown prince.

That done, we set up camp for the evening. Wilmot starts to grumble about a second delay. Then he seems to remember that the person we're going to meet is sitting with us, so there's no longer any rush to get to the capital city.

As for why King Estienne is here? A monster problem. Multiple monster problems, actually. Border towns situated closer to the mountains have been sending envoys to the capital begging for help as monsters fleeing the dragon invade their towns.

"So send help," Wilmot says. "I'm sorry, your highness. I know you're new in your position, but you do have people who can handle this. Your border towns often have monsters, and you have troops trained to deal with them."

"We do," Estienne says. "All those troops are currently in the capital, preparing to wage war on the dragons."

"What?" I take a deep breath. "I apologize for my outburst. But we've come to discuss the dragon situation. There's no need to wage any sort of war on them."

"Tell that to my prime minister," Estienne mutters. "I'm not sure if you understand how Roiva is governed . . ."

"There's a hereditary king or queen and an elected prime minister," I say. "As well as a cabinet of elected officials. The king is head of state, but his position is—sorry—mostly ceremonial and diplomatic."

"Exactly. I have power, but not when it comes to matters of defense. That falls to the prime minister and the minister of defense. My father could make his voice heard because he'd proven himself an able leader, but I'm still young and untested. The collision of events—my father's sudden death plus proof of dragons—provides the perfect excuse for the prime minister to ignore me. My job is to meet with you and your brother and your envoy and say pretty things and calm your nerves . . . while my troops eliminate the dragon and her young."

"I appreciate you telling us this," Rhydd says slowly. "It will help to know what we're facing."

"People who just want the dragon family gone," I say. "Who aren't even willing to hear why that may not be necessary."

"Also people who are going to trespass on Tamarelian land," Rhydd says, his tone deceptively calm. "*Troops* who are going to trespass on our land, which can be seen as provocation for war." He meets the young king's eyes. "Is that what you intend, sire?"

Liliath makes a small noise, and I look over to see her face glowing with pride. Mine is, too, I'm sure. Estienne may be a very young king, but my brother is at least five years his junior and already handling this better than I ever could.

"No," Estienne says firmly. "I may disagree with my prime minister and minister of defense, but I know they absolutely are not using the dragons as an excuse to invade Tamarel."

"They just don't care if we're insulted," Rhydd says. "We are, after all, across the mountains. A quiet country, largely self-contained, and not a major trade partner."

"Bluntly? Yes. I know you will be king someday, Prince Rhydd, and so I'm speaking to you as the ruler of a neighboring country. My father always said to begin things as you plan to continue them. I plan to continue with honesty. The dragon family is a problem. I'm personally willing to listen to Princess Rowan's plans regarding it, as are many in my court. However, at this moment, the dragon is not my primary concern—my people are. My prime minister is ignoring the pleas of the border towns. He thinks that the answer is to deal with the dragons: If we focus all our effort on that, then we won't *have* more issues at the borders. I understand his reasoning, but I also hear the pleas of my people. The monsters are causing deaths and destruction. These towns do not need an entire army to protect them—just a few skilled hunters to kill or drive away the beasts. Yet my prime minister insists on sending all our monster experts to deal with the dragons."

"You want us to help these villages?" I say.

"Please."

"But if we do that, then we aren't able to argue for the dragons. You're setting me two opposing goals, sire. I want to help your people—obviously—but I feel as if you're sending me on a distraction mission. I abandon my aim to advocate for the dragons and head out to border towns, only to discover a few colocolos eating grain, and in the meantime your troops have marched into *my* country and killed *our* dragon."

Estienne smiles. "I met your aunt Jannah once. You sound just like her. My people keep telling me I am far too young to rule. They should meet you and your brother, and they will see that youth is no obstacle to intelligence."

"You're very kind," Liliath murmurs. "Take care that Prince Rhydd and Princess Rowan do not see false flattery."

Estienne goes serious as he nods. "You're right. I apologize. It was not intended as false. I do have a plan, which is why I came to meet you in this disguise—so that we might speak, and I might explain the situation, and we can discuss solutions. Here is what I propose: I'd like to hear Princess Rowan's defense of the dragon and how Queen Mariela intends to handle the situation. I suspect, though, that Prince Rhydd and Lady Liliath can bear that message to my ministers. The princess's passion and experience would stand her in better stead if enough ministers were in any mood to listen to it. Prince Rhydd and Lady Liliath will be better received."

"Because they're politicians," I say. *And I'm just a monster hunter.*

I don't say the second part. It could sound like complaining. It's not—it's frustration. I understand what Estienne means. If his ministers are already set on killing or driving out the dragons, then it will do me no good to fight on the monsters' behalf. This battle is a diplomatic one.

"They need to know that their plan has been exposed," Estienne says. "That they cannot sneak in and kill the dragons with Queen Mariela never the wiser."

"Then you want me to go to the border towns," I say. "Me, Wilmot, Dain and whoever else can help us there."

"Yes, and my goal with that is twofold. I want to start my reign as I intend to continue it—refusing to sacrifice any citizen or their livelihood, however distant they may be, however poor. I also hope to show why we should listen to and trust the experience of Tamarelian monster hunters."

"It will also place your country in our debt, will it not?" I say. "Perhaps your ministers don't see those towns as important, but if we help them, it will be harder to justify entering Tamarel with Roivan troops. Also harder to argue that we do not know how to properly handle monsters."

He nods. "Yes."

Rhydd looks at us and I can see him thinking. Then he says, "We will consider your offer, King Estienne. We'll ask that you provide us with all the details you can—of what you need my sister to do—and then we will discuss it among ourselves."

There's little to discuss, really. If the ministers won't be swayed by my passionate defense of the dragons, then Rhydd is better suited for the diplomatic mission. He respects the dragons as much as I do and will fight for them, but he's better able to hide his concern for the beasts and make this seem a purely diplomatic issue. I am better doing what I do best: fighting monsters.

So my brother and I finally got an adventure together, only to separate once again. It seems as if this is our new life, and I know it's part of growing up, but it really hurts. I console myself with the memories of our week's adventures crossing the Dunnian Woods. There will be more like that. I just need to accept that we won't always be at each other's sides, as we were when we were little.

Rhydd and Liliath will continue on to the capital with King Estienne. All the guards except Kaylein will go with them. Kaylein and Wilmot will come with me, Alianor, Dain and Trysten. There's some discussion about Trysten. He's not a monster hunter, and he's on his way home, but his situation there is complicated.

Trysten's dad is the king. His dad is not, however, married to his mother—they'd been engaged when he decided to marry someone else. His father had told his mom that Trysten was going to Tamarel to be fostered with us. In reality, the king sent Trysten to live in the Dunnian Woods with monster poachers. In other words, fearing Trysten as future competition for his throne, he got rid of him and won't be thrilled to have him return.

The idea was for us to enlist the help of the king of Roiva. That's not going to happen with everything else going on, and Estienne is afraid that if Trysten spends too much time in the Roivan capital, he might suddenly disappear—spies loyal to the Dorwynne king will spirit him away. This all reminds me that while it can be lonely on our side of the mountains, there are advantages to not living close to other kingdoms.

Not surprisingly, Trysten would rather come monster hunting with us. Facing fearsome beasts seems the less dangerous option.

As for the monsters we're going to be hunting, it's not as if the border towns are being ravaged by gryphons and rocs. There was a report of a grootslang sighting, but that hasn't been confirmed, thankfully. The problems are mostly smaller monsters making pests of themselves.

The first town has an infestation of ramidrejus, which are most closely related to weasels. They're like long-bodied, green-furred weasels with pig snouts that help them sniff out food underground. The thing about ramidrejus is that they're really good diggers, capable of tunneling incredible distances in search of food. The village they've invaded is known for root crops—everything from spices like ginger and turmeric to fancy kinds of carrots and potatoes. The ramidrejus are burrowing under the crops and stealing them, which would be kind of funny if it didn't endanger the town's main livelihood. Worse, on their way to the crops, the ramidrejus are also burrowing under buildings and several have collapsed.

We've dealt with ramidrejus in Tamarel, so this shouldn't be too difficult. After that, it'll get harder, but as Wilmot says, we can use these missions as part of my training. To become the royal monster hunter, I'm supposed to perform a bunch of trials, leading up to the final one, where I'm alone in the Dunnian Woods for a week.

The council has decided that my recent adventures are acceptable substitutes for my early trials. As for the big one, well, it doesn't make much sense for me to prove my monster-hunting skills by spending a week alone in a forest where most of the monsters are in hiding. They decided that this trip would take its place: I'd go to Roiva and speak to the ministers and plead the dragons' case. I'm no longer doing that, and so Wilmot hopes clearing the monsters from a few villages will be a reasonable substitute.

"I'm looking forward to the perytons," Alianor says as we walk the next morning. She glances back at Sunniva, trotting along behind us. "Winged deer. Won't that be awesome? I bet they're very pretty. Probably even prettier than a pegasus."

Sunniva stamps and flips her red mane. It flutters down over her pure white coat, and I swear Doscach stumbles. Alianor says he's in love with Sunniva. Personally, I think Alianor is far too interested in love. She spent the morning pestering me to speculate on whether her sister and King Estienne were secretly courting.

"That would make sense, wouldn't it?" she had said. "Sarika and the prince fall in love, and then he becomes king and she panics, which is just like Sarika. She'd be worried about what would happen, how our father might take advantage of the king. She won't talk about why she came home. The answer is obvious. She fell for a king, and he fell for her. Did you see his eyes when he talked about her? Definitely in love."

Yep, that was my morning. Even worse, I eventually started wondering about it myself. How would that work, the Roivan king and a Tamarelian warlord's daughter? Did she leave because he could never marry her? Did she leave because she'd never *let* him marry her, for his own good? What if they were *really* in love, and they couldn't be together? It was like something out of a bard's song.

All things that are none of my business, but maybe it means I'm getting older if I can't stop thinking about it.

As for Doscach and Sunniva, I have no idea if animals and monsters can fall in love. Of course, there are hundreds of legends about exactly that—especially different kinds of animals courting to explain how monsters were created. That's nonsense, of course. While some animals in the same family can mate—like dogs and wolves—animals from different families cannot.

Doscach likes Sunniva, but maybe just as a playmate. They're both herd animals who've lost their herd. Anything more is speculation, and if it seems that Doscach stumbles when Sunniva flips her mane, it's probably coincidence. Same as how it was coincidence that Sunniva flipped her mane when Alianor suggested perytons might be prettier than pegasi. Or Alianor's glance and tone told Sunniva that she was being teased.

As for perytons, they're winged stags, and one of the monsters we'll need to deal with. A herd has invaded another village's crops, and it's hard to drive off deer that can fly away when you chase after them.

"I wonder if we'll really see a grootslang," I say.

Dain glares over at me. Even Wilmot gives me a hard look.

"What?" I say. "That'd be something, right?"

"Yes," Dain says. "As it's swallowing you whole, you can say, 'At least I saw a grootslang before I died.' Just like everyone else who's ever seen one."

"No," Alianor says. "Pretty sure the last thought of everyone who's ever seen one was, 'Arggh! I'm being swallowed by a—' *Chomp.*"

"Do I even want to know what a grootslang is?" Trysten asks.

"Snake monster," I say.

"*Enormous* snake monster," Alianor says. "Fifty feet long. With poisonous tusks instead of fangs. It has ears like an elephant, and when it rises up, the ears shoot out like a cobra's hood and block the sun, plunging its prey into total darkness."

Trysten looks at me, as he's learned to do whenever Alianor describes a monster.

"Ninety percent true," I say. "Yes, they're up to fifty feet long. Yes, they have *venomous* tusks and hoodlike elephant ears. I doubt their ears would block the sun, but no one's ever survived an encounter to tell us."

"Uh, and you *want* to see this thing?"

"The trick is diversion. You need enough people in your party to fill its belly and give you time to escape. I think we have enough. So if we see one, remember that I'm the royal monster hunter and it is imperative—for the sake of science—that I survive to provide an accurate report for future generations."

"We will *not* see a grootslang," Wilmot says. "Whenever there's a sudden onslaught of monsters, people start claiming they've seen a grootslang. What they actually see are other—much smaller—serpent monsters. In this case, it might even be the dragon herself."

"But there *are* grootslangs?" Trysten says. "Somewhere?"

"Very few," I say. "According to legend, there's only one. Past monster hunters have found evidence of them in the mountains, and while we can joke that no one has survived, there are historical accounts of them being spotted from a distance. They're believed to have lifespans even longer than dragons."

"And they live in the mountains?"

"Under them. Legend says their tunnels run all the way to the ocean, and they swim out there sometimes. Which would mean that when sailors report seeing giant sea serpents, they've really spotted a grootslang. That would be amazing."

Dain grumbles. "If your idea of 'amazing' is a snake big enough to eat you."

"It is. Thank you."

"So people have recently claimed to have seen one?" Trysten says.

I nod. "Hunters out in the grassland and forest nearer the mountains. No firm reports—just something glimpsed in the distance. As Wilmot said, they're almost always another monster."

"What if something *else* is actually a grootslang?" Trysten says. "Like the ramidrejus. People saw one or two ramidrejus, so they think that's what's doing all the damage, but it's really a grootslang."

"No," Wilmot says when I open my mouth. "It is not a grootslang."

"Are you sure?" I say. "Trysten has a point. Imagine a grootslang sneaking around under the earth, slurping down carrots, and everyone thinks it's just ramidrejus. Then one day, it crashes through the ground, rising up and—"

"No," Wilmot says. "Stop."

"We're about to see our first grootslang," I say. "Hope everyone's ready."

CHAPTER SEVEN

I t is not a grootslang. Which I knew and, honestly, if a grootslang burst from the earth, I'd be running for my life alongside the villagers. I just can't resist teasing Dain and Wilmot.

Even as we near the village, I spot signs of ramidrejus at work—holes in fields and damaged buildings where the unstable ground wouldn't support aging stonework. King Estienne has sent one of his guards to ride ahead to each village to tell them we're coming, and we're still making our way down the road when a carriage drawn by matching horses comes to greet us. It stops, and a portly man climbs out.

"I am the village mayor," he says. "We are so pleased you could take time from your expedition to aid our modest village."

The man strides over and bows to Kaylein.

"Princess Rowan," he says. "Royal monster hunter of Tamarel. We are honored to meet you."

Kaylein points my way. The man doesn't even look over, just keeps talking. "I am delighted that you brought your pupils today. I only hope our infestation does not prove too dangerous for the children. The creatures may be small, but they will bite. I'm sure you know what you're doing, though, Princess—"

"Kaylein," she says.

"Princess Kaylein?"

"Just Kaylein. Bodyguard to her royal highness, Princess Rowan of Tamarel."

Again, she points at me, but the mayor looks straight over my head and down the dusty road. "Ah, the princess follows, does she? I have heard she rides a unicorn. That will be a sight to see."

"That was my aunt Jannah," I say. "My brother rides Courtois now. I'm not a fan of unicorns."

The mayor goes still. Then his gaze slowly drops to me.

"*She's* the royal monster hunter." Alianor points to the ebony sword across my back. "The big pointy thing gives it away. And if it doesn't, check out the warg and jackalope." She looks at me. "Maybe Jacko should have been riding on your head. That always looks impressive."

I straighten. "My Lord Mayor, I am pleased to make your acquaintance. I am Rowan of Clan Dacre. Daughter of Queen Mariela and Tamarel's royal monster hunter."

His mouth opens. Shuts. Opens again. "You're—you're a child. A little girl." His gaze sweeps the group. "You're all children. Well, except you." A chin jerk Wilmot's way. "But even your guard here is barely an adult. I heard the royal monster hunter was young, so I presumed it must be her, but . . ." His gaze drops to me again. "How old *are* you?"

"I'll be thirteen in a couple of weeks," I say.

He looks ill. "Oh no. No, no, no. This will not do at all. Children," he whispers as if to himself. "The king sent me children."

"As you've said," Wilmot says, "*I* am not a child. I'm Wilmot of Clan Kendral, and I trained as a monster hunter alongside Princess Jannah. I'm now training Princess Rowan, at the request of her mother, the queen. I've been a monster hunter for fifteen years, most of that spent working independently, which means I have handled problems like yours on my own."

"Independently?"

"Yes, until I was joined by my foster son here, Dain."

"Why were you not a royal monster hunter all that time? Did they kick you out?"

Wilmot's face darkens and Dain opens his mouth, ready to snap something, but Wilmot says coldly, "They did not kick me out, and they welcomed me back. The point is that you have been sent a young—but precociously capable—royal monster hunter as well as an experienced one, in addition to others."

"Maybe you just don't want your problem solved," Alianor says. "We do have other villages who need our help. There's a whole herd of perytons a half-day's walk from here. We can bump them up on the schedule."

As they talk, a green-furred nose rises from a distant hole. I start toward it, and no one seems to notice except Jacko and Malric. They accompany me, and a moment later, I'm crouching by the hole as Dain joins us.

"Letting them fight it out while you get to work?" he says.

"Yep."

"Good plan."

He lowers Dez, who snuffles at the hole. Jacko nudges her aside and sticks his head in. While rabbits live in burrows, jackalopes use dens. Their antlers make tunneling impossible. Jacko is still young, though, and his antlers have only begun to branch. He chirps at me, as if to say, "I'm going in." Then he disappears. A moment later, a shriek sounds deep in the tunnel. A long, green-furred body erupts from another hole and sprints across the field, with Jacko following right behind.

The ramidreju is about the same size as the young jackalope, but it's a herbivore and lacks proper defenses. It's also not nearly as fast as Jacko, whose semi-retractable claws let him dig into the ground for traction. There's a shriek as he catches up, and then a tumble of brown and green, and a moment later, Jacko has the ramidreju hanging from his mouth. A yip sounds, like from the prairie dogs we've seen out along the way. Then another yip, and I look to see two ramidrejus staring in horror at this small beast with their dead pack mate in its jaws. Jacko drops his prey and gnashes his teeth, and they shriek and disappear.

Dez gives an excited yip and breaks into a gallop, which is kind of funny to see. Being arboreal, dropbears spend most of their lives in trees. On the ground, their walk seems awkward and lumbering, but they can break into a full gallop for brief sprints. Admittedly, the first time I saw dropbears run, I hadn't been nearly as amused. If Dain and I hadn't found shelter, Dez's pack would have overtaken and killed us as easily as Jacko killed that ramidreju.

Dez gallops to a hole and pokes her head through, but she's too stout to squeeze inside. Jacko chirps and waggles the dead ramidreju, then tosses it her way before shooting off in pursuit of another.

"The children play so well together, don't they?" I say.

Dain rolls his eyes.

"As a temporary solution, this might work," I say. "Get Jacko's scent in the burrows and Malric and Dez's scents out here. It would scare the ramidrejus off for a while. Then we'd need to come up with a long-term solution."

"It's tricky," Dain says. "Once beasts find easy pickings, they don't go away."

"I wonder how close to harvest the village is. Temporary measures could save the rest of the crops, and then if they secure the storehouses, the ramidrejus would move on. Eventually, the monsters will return to the woods and the mountains. The dragon is calm now that the poachers are gone."

A ramidreju pops up near us, and Malric gets to his feet, only to have the beast shriek and dive into its tunnel.

"You'll need to ask Jacko to get you one," I say. "Ask nicely."

I swear the warg glares at me. Then his gaze shoots upward. Before I can even look, the sky darkens. My heart thuds, and in my mind I imagine a grootslang bursting from the earth, its hood blocking the sun. It's no such thing. I'm not sure what it is. I rise, shading my eyes. Dark shapes dot the horizon, growing closer with each passing heartbeat.

A whinny sounds overhead, and then a streak of white appears as Sunniva swoops in my direction. She skids to the ground and stands at my side, head ducked toward me for reassurance. I pat her as my other hand reaches for my sword. Above, the flock of dark shapes wings toward us.

When one finally comes into view, I grin. "It's the peryton herd."

It is indeed. At least twenty of the winged deer fly overhead. Sunniva stamps and shakes her mane, unnerved by the sight. I rub her neck, and she tucks her head against me, hot breath rippling my hair.

"Wilmot!" I call. They're still locked in their dispute, and I need to shout again before he looks over to follow my finger. "The perytons!"

I put my sword back in its sheath and Dain lowers his bow. Malric pops his jaw, as if thinking he might not miss out on a meal after all.

"Not yet, please," I say. "Let's see where they're headed first."

Dez glances up from her meal but seems unperturbed by the herd of deer flying our way. Has she seen them before, in the mountains? They'd be prey to her, though I suspect dropbears would pay them little mind. A peryton's wings make the hunt enough of a challenge that dropbears would be better off dining on regular deer.

The herd flies clear over us. In the distance, Doscach whinnies—he's been following along in a nearby river. The open savanna doesn't have a lot to offer a water horse, and he's been taking advantage of the break to play in the water. Now he whinnies, but only in curiosity.

"He's saying how pretty they are," I tease Sunniva, but she doesn't hear me. She's too busy following the herd with her eyes and stamping one red hoof. I stroke her mane. "Never seen perytons?"

"She might have," Dain says, "and they could have given her trouble. A herd will chase a pegasus from good grazing ground."

The perytons land in a field behind us and begin to graze.

"No!" the mayor yells, lunging forward as if to stop them himself. "Oh no. Not the ginseng."

Dain and I walk toward him as Wilmot says, "Ginseng?"

"It's our most valuable crop." The mayor stares in horror as the perytons graze. Then he spins on Wilmot. "You must do something."

"Must we?" Alianor says. "Maybe you should start by addressing the correct person: the royal monster hunter. The princess."

The mayor glances my way as we draw near. Then he says to Wilmot, "*Please.*"

Alianor lights into him, demanding that he ask me. When I glance over, Dain murmurs, "He's a jerk. Ignore him."

I want to say I'm fine. That I understand the mayor's confusion. I *am* young. What hurts is that he hasn't given me a chance. He never even noticed when I started working on the ramidrejus. Now he's panicking over the perytons but still can't bring himself to address me directly.

I won't say he's a jerk, but Dain's right about the rest. Ignore him. The perytons are devouring a village's most valuable crop,

— 58 —

and I'm not about to let their mayor's attitude cost his people their livelihood.

I put my fingers in my mouth and whistle. The mayor looks then. Everyone looks, as if I've done it to get their attention. Moments later, the top of a green head emerges from the river.

"They're in the water," the mayor groans. "The ramidrejus are in the water now."

"If you have ramidrejus that big, we can't help you," Alianor says as Doscach emerges from the river. "I might also suggest spectacles."

The mayor stares at the young stallion galloping toward me and then falls back, as if Doscach is going to run him down. That's also when he notices Sunniva. Apparently, he'd been too busy moaning about my age to notice an actual pegasus filly.

Doscach stops beside me and tosses his head. His barnacle-crusted green mane whips about, one strand hitting the mayor, who falls back with a cry. When I motion that I want to ride, Doscach whinnies and lowers his front leg.

"You're very wet," I grumble as I climb onto his back. Jacko comes flying over the grass, leaps and lands in front of me. He positions himself there, nose high, claws digging into the ceffyl-dwr's mane.

"Wh-what is *that?*" the mayor sputters.

"A jackalope," Alianor says. "Don't worry. He's friendly." She pauses for a beat. "Oh, you mean the horse monster? That's a ceffyl-dwr. He's not as friendly. Also carnivorous."

"Carnivorous?"

As if on cue, Doscach snorts, showing his huge teeth.

"They only occasionally eat people," Alianor says. "Mostly annoying old men."

I shoot her a look, but the mayor doesn't even seem to hear. He's staring from Doscach to Sunniva. Wilmot starts to say something. I don't hear it. I'm already steering Doscach toward the peryton herd. Then I lean forward and whisper, "Run."

He charges, flying over the land. He's almost at the crop before the perytons notice him. They are beautiful creatures, and I take a moment to appreciate that. Like pegasi, they're smaller and more slender than their animal counterparts. They're all different shades of brown, with white bellies and tails. Like jackalopes, both sexes have antlers. Their wings are like those of hawks, a mottled mix of browns and white.

I get only a few heartbeats to admire them before one spots the ceffyl-dwr charging toward it. It's the largest peryton, a buck. It hesitates, as if considering rushing to protect the does. That lasts maybe a moment. Then it trumpets a warning, and I let out a roar, waving my ebony sword, Malric snarling at our heels as Doscach charges into the field. The perytons lift off, flapping their wings and flying as fast as they can.

CHAPTER EIGHT

That is not the end of it, of course. The perytons have decided ginseng leaves are delicious, and they're only staying out of that field as long as Malric and Doscach are patrolling it. The downside is that we now need to come up with a strategy for both the ramidrejus and the perytons. The upside is that this is almost certainly the same peryton herd plaguing the next village on our list, meaning we're killing two birds with one stone.

The solution for the ramidrejus ends up being the one I suggested to Dain: Use our beasts' scents to temporarily clear them out. Collapse as many tunnels as possible. Then harvest as quickly as possible. Finally, put all food sources in stone-bottomed storage facilities. A lack of food should convince the ramidrejus to return to their mountain home.

For the perytons, the best solution is firecrackers. String tripwires over the crops. When they're triggered, small firecrackers explode. Perytons are even more sensitive to noise than regular deer. That should keep them away until the ginseng can be harvested.

I also make another suggestion. Being able to fly, perytons are more likely to return next year for the ginseng crop. They are beautiful and gentle creatures, and the land here is good grazing for them. Would the village consider adopting the herd? The perytons seem to enjoy the *leaves* of the ginseng crop, rather than their valuable roots. After harvest, these leaves—and others—could be scattered in a nearby field with good grazing and water. If the perytons elected to stay, it would be a draw for the village—their very own wild peryton herd. The mayor's wife—who thinks such a young monster hunter is *delightful*—loves this idea, as do their three daughters. The mayor agrees, and I ask the girls to be the perytons' guardians, ensuring they are respected and not turned into pets, which would endanger crops.

We spend the rest of the day setting up the firecrackers and collapsing the ramidreju holes. At least as much time is spent educating the villagers—especially the mayor's wife and daughters. We cannot stay to keep collapsing holes and guarding the fields, and Jannah always said education is our greatest tool. Teach people how to live with the monsters so they will not need to keep calling us.

We're back on the road the next morning. Wilmot has discussed our route with local traders, and they've advised us on how to get to our next target quickly, now that we can skip the peryton-infested village.

"What's up next?" Trysten asks as we walk.

"Grootslang," I say. "A nest of them was spotted—"

"Stop," Dain says. "Say that word one more time, and I'm walking up there with Alianor and Kaylein."

"Grootslang," I sing. "Grootslang, grootslang, grootslang."

He throws up his hands and starts jogging.

"Have fun!" I call. "They're talking about who's the prettiest girl in our court. I'm sure you can help with that. My money's on Herleva."

He stops. Then he backs up to rejoin us.

"Uh-uh," I say. "A threat is a threat. You gotta follow through on it, or I will never take you seriously." When he hesitates, I sing, "Grootslang, grootslang, where are you little grootslang? The royal monster hunter calls you forth from your subterranean lair to dance with her under the stars."

That gets him running. He zooms right past Kaylein and Alianor and keeps jogging until he's up with Wilmot.

"So," Trysten says, "Herleva is the prettiest girl in your court? She's the tall one, right? With the light-brown hair?"

"Hair the color of honey," I say. "Eyes as blue as a summer's day."

"You . . . like Herleva?" he asks.

"Not that way," I say. "I'm just repeating a really bad song one of the bards-in-training wrote for her. Objectively speaking, I can recognize that she's very pretty."

"But not the prettiest girl in court."

The look he sneaks my way has my face flaming. It also makes my stomach do this weird flutter that isn't completely awful.

Last winter, one of the court pages said I was pretty and tried to kiss me, and I pushed him so hard he tripped and sprained his wrist. I didn't mean to do that. I just panicked. Now Trysten gives me that same look, and I'm no longer horrified or disgusted. I'm not sure what I feel.

In bards' songs, if a cute prince gave me that look, I'd swoon. I definitely don't feel like *that*. Trysten is cute. Alianor says so, and I guess I can see it, but I don't really look at boys that way. Or maybe I'm starting to, but I don't want to, if that makes any sense. I want to just keep being friends with them and not have anything else interfere. But I'm also flattered, and it's not that I *don't* want Trysten thinking I'm pretty. Which is confusing.

I don't know what to say, and so I deflect with, "Mmm, you could be right. Alianor is very pretty. I've heard a few of the boys say so."

"She is," he says. "Same as Herleva. But there's more to being pretty than just being pleasant to look at."

"That's the actual definition of pretty, Trysten."

"Maybe it's the wrong word, then. Or maybe it's the right one, and what I mean is that we all see beauty differently. Like monsters. You might say Sunniva is the prettiest. I might say Malric is."

I sputter a laugh. "Malric?"

The warg looks over, eyes narrowing as if he doesn't even want to *know* what we're discussing.

"Do you think Malric's ugly?" he asks.

"Of course not. Wargs are just . . . I mean, he looks like a very big black wolf."

"And wolves aren't beautiful?"

"Sure they are. But they're wolves."

"What you consider attractive is something unique, something that fires your imagination. You said you even saw beauty in harpies."

"The babies, at least."

"But you also said that you found them ugly because they have ugly personalities. It's the same for people. *Attractive* is a better word than *pretty*. You might recognize that someone fits the standard definition of beauty, but you can find someone else more attractive because of other traits. You like the way they look and the way they *are*."

I nod. "That makes sense. Herleva isn't very nice. I wouldn't call Alianor *nice*, but I like her personality a hundred times better."

"Right, and I can say—objectively—that Herleva is very pretty, but she's not my kind of pretty, and she's definitely not my kind of person. Alianor is pretty, and I think she could be my kind of person as a friend, but otherwise, we're too different. You say you wouldn't call her nice. She wouldn't want to be called nice. But I like nice. I like *kind*. If it goes along with smart and interesting, then that's the best kind of girl. At least in my opinion."

We walk a few more paces in silence.

"Is it weird for me to tell you that?" he says. "If it is, I'll stop now. I don't want to make things weird."

My mouth opens, but nothing comes out. What if he's not talking about me at all? If he's just asking whether it's weird to discuss the kinds of girls he likes?

If he does mean me, am I okay with that? Do I like *him* saying it, or do I just like *hearing* it? I'm flattered. Beyond that, I don't know.

I would like the idea of a boy finding me attractive, but I think I'd like it better if it wasn't coming from an actual boy I know. Like if I found an anonymous note saying, "I think Princess Rowan is amazing."

When the ground shakes beneath our feet, I almost mistake it for my heart pounding. Then Alianor glances back.

"Did you feel that?" she says.

I look around, but we're on a trail leading through grass as tall as corn, and I can't see over it. Malric has gone still, nostrils flaring. Jacko stiffens on my shoulders and Dez peeks from her pouch. Doscach and Sunniva are nowhere to be seen. They do that—taking off for a day or more sometimes.

I press my hand to the ground. It's vibrating too hard to be Sunniva and Doscach galloping.

"Wilmot?" I call. "Can you see anything?"

He's at eye level with the top of the grass and he's squinting, as if he sees something but can't tell what it is. He takes a few steps off the path. Kaylein follows. She's nearly as tall as he is, and when they disappear, I can just make out the top of her dark hair, and his blond crown melding with the brownish-yellow of the late-summer grass. Dain glances back at us and then goes in with them.

"Here," Trysten says to me. "Let me give you a boost."

He laces his fingers. When I hesitate, he gives a self-deprecating smile. "I won't be able to hold you up for long, but I can manage it for a few moments."

That wasn't why I paused. I just wasn't sure I should be sheathing my sword to hop up for a look. I have no doubt he can hold my weight, and I'm surprised he'd question it. Then

I remember him saying he'd always been bookish. His father hadn't wanted him being schooled or trained in any way, lest he prove a threat when he grew up. Forced to choose whether to sneak him school lessons or martial ones, his mother picked the schooling. Yet nearly two years with the poachers meant lots of time outdoors. He's as tall as Rhydd and nearly as strong, and when I boost myself onto his laced fingers, he hoists me with only a grunt of effort.

With one hand on his head for support, I peer over the grass. I can see what I think Wilmot did—the grass is being flattened by something. A *bunch* of somethings running our way, the distant thunder of hooves, the grass vanishing under them and staying trampled in their wake. With every heartbeat, that rippling grass grows closer and the ground vibrates harder.

"Can you boost me a little more?" I ask.

Alianor strides over, and they lift me another foot in the air until I can see what looks like bulls with backward-curving horns. And they're heading our way. Fast.

CHAPTER NINE

"**B**onnacons!" I say, jumping down. "Stampede!" I push Alianor. "Run! That way!"

She does, and I push Trysten to follow, but he grabs my arm to make sure I go with them.

"Wilmot!" I shout. "Bonnacon stampede! They're heading between us. Go the other way!"

A return shout confirms he's heard. We run back in the direction we'd come from while Wilmot, Dain and Kaylein go the other way, giving the bonnacon herd as much room as possible to run between us. We've barely gotten out of their path when the first beast bursts through to the trail. It looks like a bull, but it has a mane, and its horns curl up and back over its head. It doesn't even see us, just charges onto the trail and then disappears into the long grass.

We back up even more, and I keep Jacko on my shoulders,

well out of trampling range. Malric positions himself between us and the herd as we watch them pass.

"Is it true they can shoot acid dung out of their, um, rear ends?" Alianor asks, shouting to be heard over the thunder of running hooves.

Trysten turns, his confused look saying he thinks he misheard.

"Yes, it's acidic," I say. "No, they don't shoot it out of their rumps in defense."

We don't have bonnacons in Tamarel. They're a creature of the open plains, native to this area. Yet we certainly hear about them, due to this bit of misinformation. The mistake comes, weirdly enough, from their unusual horns. The story goes that because the horns are backward, bonnacons can't gore attackers, rendering them defenseless. So they shoot acid dung as they flee.

Like I said, their dung is caustic, and you can get a nasty burn if you touch it, but really, is there ever any excuse for touching such a thing? As for their horns, to think the backwards shape makes them useless is silly. Some sheep have similar horns, and while the bonnacons' aren't as thick, they still use them for ramming.

As we watch the bonnacons pass, Malric keeps his gaze on the long grass to our left. He's listening for any sign that the herd is changing direction or fanning out. They aren't. We're at least ten paces away. I'd get farther, but I don't want to put too much space between us and Wilmot, on the far side of the stampede.

"What makes the dung acidic?" Trysten asks. "Is it their diet?"

I nod. "Partly. They—"

Malric leaps to attention. He's still staring into the long grass to our left. He takes a step that way, listening and watching. A roar sounds to our right. A bull bonnacon, who'd been running past us. It must see Malric out of the corner of its eye, and it wheels, and before I can do more than half shout a warning, it's charging. Malric doesn't even have time to lunge out of the way before the beast hits him, horns plowing into his side with a sickening crack.

"Malric!" I shout.

The warg goes flying. He lands hard a few feet from me. As I rush over, the bonnacon charges again. I pull my sword. The beast stops before Malric's prone body and rears up, hooves flashing.

It's going to trample Malric. The warg is on the ground, too winded to notice the bull. With those flashing hooves, I can't get close enough for a fatal strike. I'm not sure I'd dare even if I could. I'd absolutely do it to save Malric, but if I kill a bull, I could bring the whole herd stampeding our way. I swing, and my sword tip slashes into the beast's breast. It bellows and turns on me, but seeing all of us there, weapons out, it only paws the ground.

"Back!" I shout. "Get back!"

I underscore each word with a wave of my sword. Monsters are smarter than animals, and this one knows the pointy thing in my hand is what hurt it. The bull backs away, shaking its furry head, mane flying. It keeps looking from me to Malric, who is still on the ground, struggling to rise. The bonnacon sees the warg as the real threat. Malric is down, and the bull wants to make sure he stays that way.

It tosses its head and stamps its hooves. Then, without warning, it rears up, and I fall back just as one sharp hoof sheers past my shoulder.

"Hey!" Alianor shouts.

She's darted around to the side, and she rushes at the bonnacon's rear flank, dagger slashing it. The bull bellows and twists, rearing up her way, but she's already disappeared into the long grass.

"Over here!" Trysten yells.

He leaps onto the path, waving his arms. As soon as the bull turns toward him, he disappears.

The stampede is still passing. The fact that the bonnacons are stampeding means they've been spooked, and I don't even want to think about what would make a herd of big beasts run. Thankfully, their panic means that no others have noticed us taking on this bull.

Unlike in some animal herds, there's more than one bull in the group. This one seems young, but that doesn't mean it's small. It's bigger than any cattle bull I've ever seen. Young, big and powerful, and intent on destroying what it sees as a threat to its herd—the warg now unsteadily on his feet.

The three of us keep distracting the beast. Alianor and Trysten leap in and out of the long grass, and when the bonnacon remembers Malric, it turns to find me standing in its way. Then the others attack from the rear. That works a few times, at least until the beast figures it out, and when Alianor slashes with her dagger, it's ready, kicking back at her as it bucks. A hoof slams into her shoulder, and she sails into the long grass. Then the bull spins on Trysten just as he leaps out.

That leaves the beast's rear open to me, and I hit it hard in the flank with my blade. There's no killing blow to be made from this angle, and as the beast bellows in pain, another bonnacon from the herd stops. A cow, turning to shake her horns at us.

"Go!" I shout. "Both of you! Get out of here!"

The cow keeps watching, her shaggy head down. The bull snorts and wheels on me, and when Trysten tries to distract it, it kicks back and narrowly avoids hitting him in the head.

The bonnacon rears right in front of me, and I can see where I need to strike. I have to, because this young bull isn't going to tire. But when I do, I'll bring the cow running, and she's almost as dangerous.

I'll deal with her when I must. I raise my sword as the bonnacon rears.

A cry sounds behind me. Jacko's alert cry. He's been on the other side of Malric, knowing this was no fight for him—not with those flying hooves. Now he sounds his cry, and I glance as far over my shoulder as I dare to see him running full-out at the bonnacon.

"Jacko! No!"

The bonnacon slams down, earth shuddering. It shakes its head at the running jackalope. Before Jacko is within reach of those horns, he leaps into the air, flying clear over my head and onto the back of the bonnacon. The beast rears, but Jacko clings there, all his claws digging in. The bull starts to buck and twist, and the cow just stares, as if she can't see what's making him do that.

Jacko's head swings back and he chomps down hard. The bonnacon screams and rears and bucks, but Jacko's on tight.

The bull rears up one more time, trying to shake Jacko loose. Then it charges headlong into the grass. Farther down, the cow looks from us to where the bull disappeared. The stampede has passed, and it's just us and this cow. One final look, and she ambles off into the long grass.

"Alianor!" I call. "Can you tend to Malric? I need to go after Jacko. If he jumps off the bull, he'll be trampled."

She nods, and I run. Trysten follows. Behind me, I hear Malric grunt, as if he's trying to come after us. I turn and tell him to stay where he is, that I'll be fine. He still tries to follow, but Alianor throws herself onto his back to stop him. I dive into the long grass and run after my jackalope.

CHAPTER TEN

Ahead, I can hear the bull bellowing. I target that sound as Trysten and I run through the grass. We get maybe a hundred paces before I nearly trip over Jacko as he races back to me. I scoop him up, and his little body trembles with adrenaline and exhilaration. I hold him close and tell him how good he was, how brave. I find the last bit of dried meat in my pocket and feed him that as we jog back to the path where we left Alianor and Malric.

It takes a moment to find them. We can't see either of them, and I'm not sure which way to go. Jacko's nose answers that, and he leads us until we locate them.

Malric is standing, with Alianor running her hands over his sides.

"Can you make him lie down?" she calls as we approach.

He thumps to the ground once he spots me, and she says,

"Finally. I know you want to protect Rowan, but you're no use to her if you're hurt."

"*Is* he hurt?" I ask as I draw up beside them.

"He might have a broken rib or two. He's having a bit of trouble breathing, and he really doesn't like it when I touch here." Her fingertips barely graze his side, and he growls. "He won't let me check his ribs, but I'm not sure it matters. I couldn't fix them anyway."

"Could his breathing indicate lung damage? From a broken rib?"

She shakes her head. "I don't think so. He can inhale deeply. He just doesn't want to, which means it hurts. Best thing for him would be rest, as much as he'll hate it."

"Another day cut short," I say. "Wilmot's going to love this." I lower myself beside Malric, and he lets me stroke his head. "It's not your fault."

Malric makes a noise like a grumble, and I suspect he's thinking that it's *entirely* his fault he didn't see the bull charging. It's not. He'd been focused on something else, maybe a shift in the path of the stampede, and the bull's attack had been unprovoked. All it saw was a giant wolf, and it mistook Malric for a threat. Being young, it attacked without waiting to see whether Malric posed an actual danger to the herd.

"Speaking of Wilmot," Trysten says. "May I run and get him and Dain and Kaylein? The stampede has passed."

I hesitate, but I don't want to leave Malric's side, and Alianor shouldn't, in case his breathing gets worse. "Jacko?"

I motion to Trysten. "Will you accompany Trysten, please? Make sure he can find his way back."

"Oh, I plan to stick to the path," Trysten says. "Even Jacko could get lost in that grass."

I nod, and he jogs off with Jacko at his heels. Alianor and I keep checking Malric, to the point where his grumbles turn to growls that threaten to become snaps.

"You are the *worst* patient," Alianor says.

"He's good practice for treating injured monsters."

"I liked the nian better. At least she seemed to appreciate my efforts. Or maybe nians are smarter than wargs."

She raises a brow at Malric, but he's busy grumbling like an old warrior confined to bed rest.

"Let's see if he can walk," I say.

He knows "walk," and he's on his feet in a flash.

"Fine," I say. "Let's go find Trysten and the others. We'll need to stop for the day so Malric can rest. Then we have to get back on the road and fix the last monster problem for King Estienne." Once we do that, we can get to the capital and help Rhydd. He should be there by now, probably already arguing his case. The sooner we can return with good news, the better.

We only get a few paces before Trysten and Jacko come running around the bend.

"There's no sign of them," Trysten says.

I frown. "That's not possible. We were all on the same path—we just got slightly separated by the stampede."

"Maybe they had to get farther away than we did," Alianor says.

Trysten shakes his head. "I ran a good quarter mile.

Maybe more. When I stopped, I could see a long way ahead, and they weren't there."

I'd been mildly concerned when Wilmot hadn't come to check on us. I'd told myself that only meant he trusted we were safe and would catch up. Still, a little voice whispered that wasn't like him, and it certainly wasn't like Kaylein.

"Malric?" I say. "Are you all right to—"

He doesn't let me finish before he's heading out. He's moving stiffly, but at a decent pace, with only slightly labored breathing. I stay behind him to monitor his progress. When I reach for Jacko, the jackalope hops into my arms, grateful for the break after his excitement with the bonnacon.

"Is there any chance we got turned around?" Alianor says. "Both sides of the path look the same, and we can't see over the grass to spot landmarks. With the sun straight overhead, that doesn't help."

I shake my head. "I remember the direction the stampede was heading, and the bull went the same way. That means Jacko and I returned to the proper side of the path."

It also had to be the same path, because we'd left Malric and Alianor on it. That does trigger a thought, though.

"Wilmot *did* leave the path, which means it's possible they got lost," I say. "Or ended up on what they *thought* was the right path. Or even headed in the wrong direction looking for us. They don't have Malric or Jacko to track scents, and I'm not sure Dez is very good at that."

Trysten nods. "They could have gotten turned around. As I said, I didn't dare even step into the grass. It's like being lost in the dark."

We've gone maybe two hundred paces when Malric stops. He tries snuffling the path, but it obviously hurts to inhale that deeply.

"Here," Alianor says, and I turn to see her pointing at a faint path into the grass where people have clearly passed and the grass hasn't yet sprung back up.

Malric sniffs it and grunts, saying yes, this is the way they went. I take the lead then. The trail won't be easy to follow. The grass is already springing back. But I can see it for now, so I move into the field as quickly as I can, trusting my gut when I think I spot signs of passage.

Trysten is right about the grass. When we'd gone after Jacko, I'd been too worried to notice our surroundings. Earlier, Wilmot had warned that if we needed to leave the path for any reason, we had to tell everyone so they could stop and wait. Now I see why.

Turn in any direction, and all I see is grass. Push up onto my tiptoes, and all I see is grass. Squint into the sky, and all I see is sky and clouds. It really does feel weirdly like being in the dark, except even more disorienting because your eyes are open and there's plenty of light.

"Wilmot!" I shout. "Kaylein!"

"Dain!" Trysten calls, and I suspect he does that so Dain doesn't feel left out. Dain doesn't know what to make of Trysten, and so Trysten seems to go out of his way to be nice.

Alianor joins in, and we keep calling. At first, I'd been almost reluctant to shout. I want to find Wilmot on my own and not scream like a lost child crying for a parent. But the more we call, the louder we get, and panic settles into my gut.

It's as if I'd saved shouting for a last resort, thinking once I did that, surely, they'd answer.

They do not answer.

We've walked maybe fifty paces into the long grass, and my heart thumps, telling me we're too far from the safety of the path. We should go back there and wait for them.

"Can I boost you again?" Trysten asks.

"Why is it always Rowan?" Alianor says. "Wait. I know. Because it's Rowan."

Trysten's cheeks color, and Alianor thumps him on the shoulder. "I'm kidding. It *is* kind of like watching Doscach and Sunniva, though."

My look warns her to cut it out, and she mouths an apology. I know she's amused, but I don't want things getting awkward.

Trysten boosts me up, and Alianor helps support me so I can get higher still. My head reaches all the way over the grass, and I look in every direction to see . . . more grass. Endless fields of it, like being in the middle of the ocean, seeing nothing but water. Even the mountains are only distant shapes.

"Grass, grass, and more grass," I say.

"Would getting higher help?" Trysten asks.

I'm about to answer when the grass rustles. Movement ripples back toward us. I can't see what's there, only that it isn't big enough to make more than a rustle and a crackle.

"Dain?" I call.

He's barely taller than me, so this could be him. As the ripple draws closer, I still don't see anything, and my heart falls. It's just an animal. Some small animal—

Dez gallops out, plowing straight into Malric before yipping what might be an apology and backing up fast. She rises on her hind legs and her gaze travels over us, ignoring a trill of concern from Jacko. Trysten lowers me, and she yips in relief.

Dez hurries over and takes my pant leg in one prehensile fist. She looks up at me and yips as she yanks on my leg.

"Follow that dropbear," Alianor says, and I motion for Dez to lead the way.

Dez has trouble moving as quickly as she'd like. With nothing to climb, she starts to struggle.

"Take your time," I say as I bend to pet her. "I'd carry you, but you can't lead us like that."

She appears to understand, but she seems frustrated by her own slow pace. Then she cuts sharply left, and soon we come out onto what's obviously another road, twice as wide as the trail we'd been on. This one has wagon-tire ruts and must be the road that leads to the village we're skipping. The traders had suggested we follow the narrow footpath instead, both because it went in the correct direction and, being less traveled, we were less likely to draw attention there.

Being on the road makes it easier. Dez points us in the right direction, and then Trysten scoops her up and we make our way as quickly as Malric can, which is not much quicker than Dez could. I long to leave him behind with Alianor, but I know he'd only try to keep up. We do manage a quick walk, and when the path curves, there's a body on the roadside.

With a yelp, I break into a run, Jacko holding on for dear life as we race to where Dain lies motionless on the ground.

I drop beside his still form. Blood drips from a gash in his forehead. My hands fly to his chest. It moves under my fingertips.

"He's breathing," I say as Alianor runs up. "He's been hit on the head." I shake his shoulder. "Dain? Dain. It's Rowan."

He doesn't move. Alianor wets a cloth with water from her waterskin. I take it and press it to the gash on his head. He jerks, eyes snapping open, and stares up at me.

"Rowan?"

"It's me."

"Do you know there's a jackalope on your head?" he croaks. "It looks really ridiculous."

I give a hiccuping laugh and resist the urge to hug him. When he tries to rise, I take his shoulders to push him down as Jacko leans over my head and chitters.

"He's telling you not to move," I say. "He's right. You're hurt. Just stay there until Alianor checks you out." I look around. "Are Kaylein and Wilmot nearby?"

He blinks and frowns, as if he can't remember. Then his eyes widen, and he tries again to scramble up, this time needing me and Alianor to hold him down.

"Let me go," he says. "I'm fine. We have to follow them. They were kidnapped."

"Kidnapped?" Alianor says. "Wilmot and Kaylein?"

"They mistook them for—" He waves a hand as he makes a face. "Can I explain as we go?"

"First, tell me where you were hit," Alianor says.

— 81 —

"On the head. See the blood? I can feel it, and I certainly felt Rowan trying to clean it."

"Yes," I say evenly. "But were you struck anywhere else? On the back? The chest?"

He shakes his head. "Twice on the head. That's it."

"Twice?" My voice rises.

"I'm fine," he says. "Wilmot and Kaylein are not. Can we go now?"

"Do we have any idea *where* to go?"

He points at the cart tracks we've been following. They're deeper here, where the cart must have stopped. Then they continue on in the direction they'd been going.

"Follow that wagon," Alianor says, and we set out again.

CHAPTER ELEVEN

As much as I want to know what happened right away, for Malric's sake I need to tell Dain about the warg's injuries so Dain doesn't insist we run. He curses at that, but then passes an apologetic look to Malric and says, "It wasn't his fault."

"No, it wasn't," I say. "We'll walk as fast as we can, and if we need to run, we'll split up. First, while we walk, tell us what happened."

Wilmot had intended to find us right after the stampede, but even before the bonnacons finished passing, they'd heard someone calling for help. They'd run over to find this road and a trader's cart with a woman who'd been struck by one of the bonnacons. She'd fallen and the beast had stepped on her chest, and now she couldn't catch her breath.

"The old 'Help, I'm an injured traveler' routine," Alianor mutters. Then she shoots a guilty look my way. We'd first met when she'd set up a fake accident to lure me in. I'm still upset about it—not so much at being kidnapped as at the idea of bandits taking advantage of people's kind natures. If you stage fake accidents, then those stories go around, and suddenly no one's willing to stop for the real ones.

Seeing the bloodied woman on the ground, Wilmot sent Dain to get Alianor while they tended to her. Dain took off, but as soon as he was deep in the grass, he heard a cry. He wheeled, and someone leapt from the grass and hit him in the back of the head.

Dain fell, dazed. Dez prodded and licked his face until he regained his senses enough to stumble back toward Wilmot. He could hear the voices of strangers. He staggered out to see Kaylein and Wilmot lying in the back of the cart, as if they'd been overcome and sedated. Before he could even pull out his dagger, the woman who'd allegedly been hurt clubbed him in the forehead, and he lost consciousness.

"They took Kaylein and Wilmot?" Trysten says. "I don't understand. Why them? Why leave you?"

"You said it was a mistake," I say.

Dain nods. "That's what I overheard when I was making my way back. They were calling Kaylein by another name. They mistook her for the wife of a noble, I think? This woman—whoever she is—fled her home and the noble sent them to find her and the guy she was with: a light-skinned man from the west."

Trysten nods. "So this woman—who was Roivan and looked like Kaylein—ran away with a man who looked like Wilmot. Someone must have said they saw a couple like that and sent them our way."

"Well, this is inconvenient," Alianor says. "I suppose we can't just leave them behind and carry out the mission on our own?"

She raises her hands against Dain's murderous look. "Joking."

"We'll get them back," I say. "We just need to catch up. We'll tell them they've made a mistake. Even if Kaylein and Wilmot were the right people, what they're doing is illegal."

"It might not be," Trysten says. "I'm guessing this nobleman isn't local, because Roivans aren't known for treating their women like that. But in Dorwynne, if a woman runs away, her husband has the right to bring her back. A *legal* right."

"What?" I say.

"Dorwynne is a patriarchy," he says. "Queens are married to kings and cannot rule on their own. We trace our lineage through our father's line, and our mother's doesn't matter. My mother hoped when she became queen, she could make changes. That's why my father broke the engagement. He realized they didn't share the same values."

"Thinking you own your wife is a *value*?" Alianor says.

He grimaces. "I worded it wrong. That's the way my mother says it, but she means *ideas*. They had different ideas of how wives should be treated. The point is that if this lord is from someplace like Dorwynne, the captors won't be scared off if we demand Kaylein back, and they won't believe that she isn't their quarry."

"Even without the runaway-wife part," Alianor says, "we can't just expect them to take our word for it."

I'm quiet, my gaze fixed ahead on the empty road, tall grass rising on either side. We're still walking as fast as Malric can manage. Not fast enough—I know that. But we need to work this through first.

"So walking up and telling them they made a mistake isn't wise," I say. "We should approach with care, analyze the situation, and then decide what we'll do next—explain or act." I look at Dain. "Does that work?"

He nods, his mouth set in a grim line.

"Then let's split up. I'll need to stay back with Malric, or he'll try to keep up with me. Alianor, will you stay with us, in case his injuries give him trouble?"

"I will."

"Trysten and Dain? Go on ahead. Just be really careful, okay? If you see them, don't engage. Not until we're all there. Got it?"

"Got it," Trysten says.

I keep hoping we'll meet travelers coming the other way so I can ask if they've seen the cart. We encounter no one, and except for the cart's fresh tracks, all the others are clearly old.

"I don't think this road gets used much," I say.

"Really?" Alianor says. "Who wouldn't want to use a creepy road in the middle of nowhere, surrounded by grass so long that bandits could jump out, slit your throat and be gone before you saw them?"

"I thought throat-slitting was bad bandit manners."

"Bad practice, not bad manners. Still, out here you could be jumped and scream your head off and no one would hear you."

"It's just the time of year," I say. "In winter or spring or even summer, you'd be able to see. It's fall, when the grass is this long, that no one uses it."

Dain said the cart had been a simple one, drawn by two goats. That means they won't exactly be speeding along, not with two unconscious people in the back. We'll catch up. I'm sure of it.

We've been walking less than an hour when Trysten and Dain come running.

"They've pulled off," Trysten pants between breaths. "There's an old trail up ahead. Dain noticed that the tracks went along it, though they tried to cover them up and make tracks heading straight. The grasses end a little past there, and there's a watering hole. That's where they are, watering the goats."

"How far ahead?" I say.

"Maybe two hundred paces."

"Run back and keep watch from the grass. We'll catch up."

The kidnappers aren't watering the goats—they have a broken wheel. A couple of the spokes snapped, probably from the weight, so they'd pulled off on that old side road and covered their tracks in case of pursuit. Now they're arguing about what to do with the wheel. It's a man and a woman, and Dain confirms they're the ones who tricked them.

"They're from Havendale," Trysten whispers.

"Between Roiva and Dorwynne," I say. "That's where Cedany is from."

He nods, and I can tell he's right by both their accents—which sound like Cedany's—and their appearance—light-skinned like her and also like Wilmot. So a Havendale lord married a girl from Roiva, who fell in love with a Havendale man, and they tried running back to Roiva together. Just our luck to be traveling with two people who matched that description.

The woman wants to fix the wheel herself, and the man wants to get it repaired in the next village.

Finally, the man grabs the wheel and marches off. The woman follows, arguing. They keep going as one of the goats idly watches, chewing a mouthful of grass. We're downwind and well hidden, and they don't see us.

The couple keep arguing even after they're out of sight. Their voices fade, the man determined to take the wheel to the next village and the woman trying to stop him but following when he keeps walking.

"We need to act now," Trysten says. "Before they come back."

I hesitate, though I'm not sure why. The couple is out of sight, and we can see Wilmot and Kaylein right there, their boots sticking out from under a blanket in the cart.

Is something bothering me? Or am I just waiting in the hope they get farther away? I'm not sure. I only know that a few months ago, I'd have already been out there, sneaking up to the cart, and now something stops me.

"Rowan?" Dain says.

Alianor shifts and rolls her shoulders. "I don't like it."

"You don't like anything," Dain says. "You're paranoid."

"Yeah?" Alianor says. "Well, I wouldn't have fallen for that fake accident, would I?"

I lift my hands. "I agree with Alianor. I don't like this."

"I think we need more than that," Trysten says gently. "I hate disagreeing with you, but we have a limited window of opportunity here. Can you tell us what about it bothers you? I can still hear those two fighting, and they're almost out of earshot. They can't run back before we can get to Wilmot and Kaylein."

I open my mouth. Objections swirl, but they won't solidify. Something about this really bothers me. I need to put it into words before—

"I'm going," Dain grunts, not meeting my eyes. He holds out Dez. "Take her, please."

He jogs off. Trysten looks from me to Dain, and then says, "I should go with him."

I nod, and when I don't follow, when I stand there holding Dez, I feel like a coward. What about this bothers me?

All of it.

The answer comes in an instant. On the surface, the story about the wife makes sense, but would her pursuers really mistake Kaylein—in a royal guard uniform—for a runaway bride? Maybe they thought it was a disguise. Or maybe they only recognized it as expensive clothing. But who did they think Dain was? A random boy and his dropbear tagging along with the runaway bride and her lover? Wouldn't whoever set them on our trail have mentioned *four* young people with them? And a *warg* and a *jackalope*?

Then I realize the biggest problem with this story: Kaylein could easily take on two people herself. With Wilmot's help, they'd have definitely won. Even if this couple managed to surprise them, who'd followed and knocked out Dain while they were fighting Wilmot and Kaylein?

I leap forward. "Don't!"

Too late. They're already at the cart, and Dain is reaching for Wilmot's leg. He glances back at me just as both figures in the cart leap up. They're strangers. One swings a knife. Trysten falls back, but another figure vaults from the other side of the cart. She grabs Trysten and has a blade at his throat before he can react.

The man in the cart—the one wearing Wilmot's boots—grabs Dain. Dain manages to throw a punch, but he didn't have a weapon in his hand, and the man quickly pins Dain's arms behind his back.

I have my sword out. Alianor has her dagger. Malric is between us, on his feet and snarling.

"Call your dog to heel," says the woman holding Trysten.

"He's not a dog," Alianor says. "He's a warg, and he could take on all three of you."

The couple who'd walked away arguing now step from the long grass. Another two women appear on the other side, one with a sword and one with a bow.

Malric snarls again, but it wavers. He's having a hard time even making the noise with his sore ribs. He's in no shape to fight.

"Control your pets," the woman holding Trysten says. "Or we kill your friend."

"Don't listen to them," Trysten says. "Run. Just run. I'll be fine."

The woman snorts a laugh. "Brave words, but we didn't mean you, Prince Trysten. We meant *him*." She nods at Dain. "Control your pets and lay down your weapons, girls."

"You know who I am," Trysten says. "You're here for me."

"Your father got word that you'd escaped. He has a bounty out for your return to Dorwynne . . . a secret return to his dungeons."

Trysten squares his shoulders. "All right, then. Let my companions leave, and I'll go with you quietly."

"Valiant words, prince," the woman says, "but there's a reason we separated you four from your guards. The bonnacon stampede didn't quite go as smoothly as we'd hoped, but it worked out for the best." She looks at me. "Princess Rowan. Royal monster hunter of Tamarel. I am so pleased to make your acquaintance."

"What do you want from her?" Alianor snaps.

"Alianor of Clan Bellamy. Daughter of the legendary bandit. I am pleased to meet you as well." The woman looks at me again. "Prince Trysten's royal father knew he'd escaped because one of his previous guardians told him what happened. Seems the Tamarelian royal monster hunter showed up while Prince Trysten's guardians were trying to steal a dragon egg for the king. The monster hunter thwarted their plans, and this man saw the girl talking to the dragons. Communicating with them. Taming them."

"That's not—" I begin.

"No need for modesty, child. You have your clan's gift. You wield magic over the beasts."

"We don't—"

"Enough," she says, her voice sharpening. "Play us for fools and this shall not go well. Your friend asked what we want— the same thing Trysten's guardian wanted, though he can't get it now. The poor fool lost a prince, and the price for that was his head."

Trysten pales.

"I wonder what your father would pay for that egg," she says. "At least as much as he's paying for you, I'll wager. So that's the deal, Princess Rowan. The cost of freedom for you and your friends is a dragon egg. Make it two, and I'll throw in the prince himself. We'll tell his king father that he was no longer with you and your companions."

There is no response to this. It's not a negotiation. They have us at knifepoint. I don't agree to their terms. There's no need to. They recognize my silence as surrender, and so the woman—the leader of the group—tells the others to prepare to leave.

CHAPTER TWELVE

We walk for the rest of the day. While I have no intention of getting dragon eggs for them, I need to wait for our chance to escape or figure out a way to change their minds.

Alianor says the troop are mercenaries: fighters who can be hired for jobs, usually illegal ones. She presumes these are bounty hunters. Trysten's father has learned what happened to him, and he doesn't want Trysten returning home to his mother. Sending him away didn't work. The dungeons are next. Trysten has said before that his father doesn't dare have him killed outright, but if he dies through misfortune—in the Dunnian Woods or the castle dungeon—that's not his fault.

There are seven people in the troop. The leader is Madlyn, or that's what we're told to call her. She's maybe my mother's age, with light skin, reddish hair and a scar running across her face. That scar is the easiest way to tell her apart from the other four women. Maybe they're related or maybe it's just because they're all from Havendale, with similar coloring, but they look alike to me. I have to find distinguishing traits, like Madlyn's scar or another one's short hair or another's heavier build. One of the men is also from Havendale. The other looks Roivan. I don't know their names—no one tells us anyone's name except Madlyn's.

We've seen no sign of Doscach or Sunniva all day, and I find myself torn between thinking they might help and being glad they aren't here to get hurt. So far, the bounty hunters have shown little interest in our monsters. Complete indifference, actually. I know Havendale doesn't have many native monsters, and it seems that, to them, our monster companions are just unusual pets. They might know what a warg or dropbear is, but they still keep referring to Malric as my dog, and it doesn't seem to be intended as an insult.

As for Kaylein and Wilmot, they left them—unconscious but unbound—near the watering hole. I'd have liked to see that with my own eyes to be sure, but the offhand way Madlyn says it suggests it's the truth. They were just obstacles in getting "the children."

That's how she sees us. Children. The monsters are pets, and the monster hunter and her companions are children. Madlyn doesn't doubt my abilities, but she seems to think my skills with monsters are some kind of magic. I'm a little girl with magical powers, nothing more.

Part of me wants to set her straight, but it doesn't help our cause. As long as she thinks we're all harmless, we're allowed to walk without any bonds. Oh, she's confiscated our weapons and her troop surrounds us, but we aren't tied up in the back of a cart, and that's to our advantage.

The best plan of action seems to be to act as she expects us to act: as children in need of protection and guidance. And without Kaylein and Wilmot to lead us, we'll just follow along and do as we're told. Once our captors relax their guard, we can escape.

We don't get that chance on the first day. We walk until nightfall, and we don't see another person. We're heading for the mountains on narrow and empty trails, and by the time we stop for the night, I can just make out the mountain range on the horizon.

We're given adequate amounts of food and water, plus sleeping blankets. Madlyn's troop spread out their own blankets in a wide circle around us, which affords us a little privacy but no chance of escape—half the troop stays awake and on guard at all times.

We don't get our own campfire. I'm not sure whether they're afraid we'd use it against them or afraid we'd accidentally fall in. There are two fires near them, and we huddle in our blankets, sitting in a silent circle. Malric is behind me, pushed up against me for warmth. Jacko's on my lap, and I'm petting him, soothing myself that way.

We've barely said a word to one another since we were taken, but I realize we should talk. If we're going to act like normal children, then it was fine to spend today quiet and confused, but tonight we should start chattering. I open my mouth to begin when Trysten says, "I'm sorry, Rowan."

He fidgets with a pebble, not looking my way.

"I didn't listen to you," he says. "You thought the setup felt wrong, and I should have trusted your instinct."

"Don't," Dain says, the word coming out as a growl.

"Don't what? I *am* sorry. Rowan and Alianor both hesitated, and I ignored their judgment, so I'm apologizing. Why is that a problem?"

"You know why."

Trysten flips the stone away. "No, Dain. I don't. Care to explain?"

"Nope."

Trysten glares at him, but Dain just keeps adjusting the lace on his boot.

"Just because I'm apologizing doesn't mean I'm including you in that," Trysten says. "If you don't think you made a mistake—"

Dain yanks the lace so hard it snaps, and he whips it away, startling Dez. "Don't try that."

"Try what?" Trysten throws up his hands. "I honestly don't know what I'm doing wrong here. Is there some Tamarelian custom I'm breaking? A certain way I'm supposed to apologize? If there is, then I guess I also apologize for not knowing it."

"Hey," Alianor says. "How about we play a game?"

Both guys turn such startled looks on her that you'd think she'd suggested we all pull out needles and sew pretty hats.

I bite back a laugh as I say, "What kind of game?"

"Do you know Snowman?" she says. "I think up a word, and you all guess letters. For each one you get wrong, I add a piece to the snowman. If I finish before you guess the word, I win."

"Can I ask what a snowman is?" Trysten says.

"No. Now hand me that stick, Dain."

He passes it over and she writes in the dirt. "First word, four letters."

According to the game, she'd have made four lines, one for each letter. Instead, she's written a four-letter word.

Plan.

She erases it and hands me the stick. "On second thought, Princess Rowan should go first."

I take the stick and write five letters. Then I say, "Play?" and point to the word. Trysten gets it first—I wrote "along."

Play along.

"Yes?" I say. "Reasonable?"

They nod, and I scratch out my plan in the dirt, the simple one: that we play along, act like children and wait for the mercenaries to lower their guard. The others take turns with the stick, making suggestions and asking questions, and in the end, we have a plan. Give it another day. Stay calm. Play along. Wait for our chance.

Two days have passed, and we are still with Madlyn's troop. We've done our part, acting like children with our pets. Even Malric, who is walking much better, seems to understand and just trails along after me. If I wander off, he keeps a subtle watch on me but doesn't insist on sticking to my side.

The four of us talk about monsters and fancy balls and sports and games. We squabble a bit, joke around a bit, go quiet a bit. No one overdoes it, and no one makes even the slightest move to escape. Madlyn's troop seems very happy with our compliance. She tells us multiple times how good we're being and even rewards us by teaching us how to track and hunt. We play along with that, too. Hunting? For our dinner? What a novel idea!

What they do *not* do is lower their guard. If we need to go to the bathroom, only one of us can leave the group, accompanied by two guards. At night, half of them stay awake. We've tried waking up at all hours to check. This morning, Dain asked for his bow back for target practice, and they refused. I faked a stumble on the path to see how they'd react to a sudden movement. Three of them drew their weapons. The other four had already been holding theirs.

We've succeeded in confirming their assessment that we are innocent and harmless children. But all that means is that they don't tighten their security measures. They started off treating us decently, and that was apparently an incentive for us to behave and not cause trouble. We didn't, and so we continue to be treated decently and with exactly the same amount of security.

By day three, my plan has evaporated. The cart is gone, and so are the goats. It's been a day since we were on a path wide enough for them. We're so deep in the forest that I'm not sure I'd run even if they let us. On this side of the mountains, there's heavy rain, and the forest is more of a jungle. We haven't followed a path since we reached the edge of Roiva. The adults are hacking through this jungle with machetes, which should leave a clear trail for us to follow back, but when I turn, I can't even see our path—the jungle swallows it.

I've failed in my mission. I set off to solve King Estienne's monster problems, completed two of the three quickly . . . and then got kidnapped. Rhydd is in the capital right now arguing our case, counting on me to do this and prove we're capable of resolving the dragon problem. Except I'm not capable. I've failed.

We're heading in the direction of Mount Gaetal, which appears occasionally over the treetops. Even if we escaped, where would we go? How would we get back without those machetes? What would we eat without their food supplies? We haven't hunted since yesterday. I can hear monkeys in the trees and I see plenty of bugs, but the usual food sources—rabbits, deer, small birds—are gone.

There are monsters, too. While it's not infested, we catch glimpses of them. I even think I saw a shug monkey, the monkey-faced canine, peering through the leafy fronds before deciding our party was too big to attack.

The troop don't seem to care about the monsters, even the predators. This is where treating them like weird animals is going to get us into trouble. A shug monkey could sneak into camp and carry one of us off in our sleep. As dusk falls, I hear what could be harpies, and that sends a shiver through me, but the troop doesn't even notice.

How do I handle this? Convince Madlyn of the danger? What if she thinks we're safe because I have "magical powers" to subdue the beasts?

Madlyn announces we're stopping for the night, and as tired as I am, I want to urge her to keep going. The jungle closes in on all sides here, and I keep catching glints of eyes reflecting in the falling light. To her credit, Madlyn continues until we find a clearing where rocky soil has kept it from becoming overgrown. There's a spring nearby, too.

"We'll camp here," she says. "It seems quiet. Those dragons are keeping all the critters away."

I open my mouth, but a look from both Alianor and Dain warns me to be quiet. I'm glad I am, because her next words give me a little more hope.

"You kids can run around a bit," she says, as if we're five-year-olds. "We won't make you stay so close here. Explore. Have a bit of fun. Stretch your legs."

That's promising. Can we use it, though? I just finished thinking that I wasn't sure I'd run even if they let us. With those words, though, comes an actual chance. I'll need to talk to the others and see—

"Don't go running off together," she says. "I'm not that stupid. You can take turns. Pairs or whatever. I want eyes on two of you at all times."

My hopes plummet and Alianor glances over, shaking her head, her own disappointment clear.

"Let's get this camp set up," she says. "Then you can play."

CHAPTER THIRTEEN

Dain sits at the edge of the clearing whittling an arrow shaft. They still aren't allowing us our weapons, so he's using a sharp stone. He's facing the jungle, knowing better than to turn his back on it. Alianor catches my eye and jerks her chin toward Dain. She wants me to talk to him and see whether he has any ideas.

Where he's sitting, he and I would have a bit of privacy, as long as Alianor and Trysten stay where they are by the fire. Malric is sleeping beside them—actually sleeping, not faking it. With all the monsters in this unfamiliar place, he spent the day on high alert, and he's exhausted. Earlier, I'd settled in with him at the fire, and he'd fallen asleep quickly and didn't wake when I moved away.

No one's paying any attention to me as I walk over to Dain. I sit beside him, our backs to the others.

"I could use some advice," I whisper.

"Don't have any."

I pause. Then I try again. "My plan isn't working."

He gives a derisive snort that makes my shoulders tense. I force them down and say, as calmly as I can, "If you had a better idea ..."

"Didn't."

"If you have any ideas now ..."

"Don't."

"Look, I know you're upset with me. You've barely said a word in two days, and I keep telling myself not to bug you, but I need help."

"Go ask Trysten."

Something in me snaps. "Really? Really, Dain? We aren't sitting around the castle trying to figure out what to do for the afternoon. We're in trouble, and I'm asking for your help, and you're giving me that?"

Before he can answer, I stalk off into the jungle.

I hear him sigh behind me. Then a grunt as he stands.

"I didn't mean it that way, Rowan. I honestly meant that maybe he has an idea, because I don't."

I keep walking, Jacko hopping along at my side. I'm not angry. Just tired and frustrated, and feeling as if I didn't think things through. I'd been waiting for our chance to escape, and only when we finally get it do I realize it's useless. Escape to what? I should have taken a chance two days ago. Come up with a solution. Now we're right back where we were weeks ago, dealing with people who want the dragon eggs.

"Rowan," Dain says. "Come on. Don't be in the jungle. It's not safe. I saw leopard tracks."

"I'm fine." I circle left, to show that I'm not wandering far from camp.

He jogs up behind me. "If you want to walk, I noticed a kill over on the other side of camp. Could be from a shug monkey. We should check."

I shake my head. "I need to figure this out."

He exhales, a long hiss of breath. His feet tramp closer as I keep walking. "If it seems like I'm being a jerk, I don't mean it. I'm worried about Wilmot. I agreed with your plan, and I don't have a better one or a new one or anything like that. I'm not good at coming up with ideas. Trysten is smarter than me. You really should ask him. That's not me being—"

Dain yelps, and I spin to see nothing behind me but thick jungle.

"Dain?" My heart speeds up as I jog back the way I'd come. "Dain? Where—?"

Jacko grabs the back of my leggings, and I stop short just as my one foot touches down on empty air where there should be solid ground.

"Rowan?"

Dain's voice comes from somewhere below us. I step back fast and drop to all fours. I can't see a hole, but I know one's here, and when I rip aside vines and fronds, it appears: the opening to some kind of underground cave. It's partly covered in crisscrossing vines, and there's so much vegetation here that I could have stepped right into it and never seen the hole. Which is apparently what Dain did.

"Dain?"

"Down here!"

His voice sounds miles away, and when I lower my head, I can hear a distant scrabbling, as if he's trying to climb out.

"Are you hurt?" I call.

"No. I didn't fall far, and then I slid the rest of the way. I'm trying to climb up to where I started sliding." He grunts. "Looks like some kind of cave. Lots of roots."

"Use them to pull yourself."

"That's what I'm doing, princess."

I reach to light a fire stick and then remember that Madlyn confiscated them. After a moment of squinting, I can make out the tan color of Dain's tunic.

Jacko chitters and dances along the edge of the opening.

"Careful," I say. "I'm not rescuing both of you."

"You aren't rescuing me either," Dain says. "This is as far as I can get. You'll have to go and ask them for a rope."

I grab a vine and feed the end down. He tugs on it.

"Satisfactory?" I say.

When he doesn't answer, I call, "You do realize I can't hear your grunt of agreement. Or see your eye roll of dissent."

"Yes, princess. It's satisfactory. Now tie it onto a tree. I don't want to pull you down."

I do that. I consider calling for help, but if I did, Madlyn would come running with knife in hand, expecting a trick. Even if she did help, she could then use it as an excuse to keep us from going back into the jungle. I might not be sure how to use this new freedom, but I want to keep it.

I tie the vine tight and then double-check it. I also push on the tree as hard as I can to be sure it won't topple.

"All right," I say as I crouch by the opening. "Come on up."

Dain grabs hold. I peer into the darkness and focus on his tunic. Jacko perches beside me and chatters encouragement.

"I'm sending Dez up first," he says.

I'd forgotten Dez was even with him. That's easy to do. Whereas Jacko is always hopping around my feet or riding on my head and shoulders, Dez spends most of her day curled up in the pouch on Dain's chest. She's nocturnal and presumably slips off to hunt at night.

It only takes a moment for me to spot her red eyes glowing in the darkness. She climbs easily. Halfway up, she looks down at Dain and chirps.

"I'm right behind you," he says.

Louder, more distressed chirps suggest she doesn't quite believe him. When she starts sliding back down, I say, "Grab the vine. Pull on it, and let her know you're ready to climb."

That works. Once the dropbear feels the vine go taut, she makes a noise of satisfaction and continues climbing. I resist the urge to haul her the last bit. Even her juvenile claws and teeth could carve me up.

She clambers out beside Jacko. Then Dain begins his climb in earnest. He gets just high enough that I can make out the top of his dark head. Then, with a grunt, he falls back again.

"Are you—?" I begin.

"Yes, I'm fine."

He tries again and makes it another foot before falling. I bite my tongue against a comment or a question. After a few moments, he says quietly, "It's harder than I thought."

"It's upper body strength," I say. "You have your entire body hanging from your arms. I'd have a hard time with it, too."

"That's because you're a girl."

I don't take offense at that. Wilmot has said many times that I cannot expect to swing a large sword as easily as my brother or to pull a bowstring as easily as Dain. I need to focus on speed and accuracy while building up my muscles. Girls aren't weaker—they just have different muscle structures.

"You're strong," I say. "I just mean you don't have the same build as, say, Rhydd. You're smaller. Leaner."

"You mean Trysten could do it."

"I said *Rhydd*."

"You were thinking—" He cuts himself short. Then his voice goes softer still. "I don't know why I keep doing that. Yes, I'm not as big as Rhydd or Trysten. It's embarrassing, but it's a fact."

"I don't know why it'd be embarrassing. You're you. Different genetics. Now, are you going to keep talking or should we solve this problem?"

He chuckles under his breath. "That's usually my line."

"Beat you to it. Your issue is arm strength. I'd have the same problem. I'd compensate by using my legs. Lever them against the wall to help you climb. Let them support some of your weight."

"That's a good idea." He pauses. "You have a lot of good ideas. I don't say that enough."

"Because you're you, and I don't expect you to."

"I still should."

I sigh. "I love that you're seeing this, Dain, but maybe come up first? So I know you're safe?"

He pauses.

"Dain?"

"It's easier to say stuff like that down here. Harder to do it face to face."

"Then I'll turn around next time we talk. Now, can you please climb out?"

He braces his legs against the wall and leans back as he begins climbing. He's nearly at the top when his boots scrabble, dirt raining down.

"The side's collapsing," he manages between grunts of exertion. "I can't—"

His body swings down, feet losing their grip, and he drops but manages to hold on. When he looks up, hanging from his hands, sweat sheens his face and his teeth are gritted.

"I can't—" He still inches one hand up, despite his words. "Can't—" He tries to move the other hand, but his whole body sways.

I lie flat on my stomach. When I reach down, my hands graze his.

"You'll fall, princess," he wheezes.

"I'm fine. My feet are hooked under roots. Don't let go of the vine. Just let me help steady you so you can make contact with your feet. Anything will help."

I wriggle forward and wrap my hands around his wrists. Jacko races along the edge, chittering in concern, and Dez peers into the hole.

"You've got this," I say. "My feet are secure, and I'm holding your wrists. Get steady, and find a foothold."

"Got it," he grunts after a moment.

"Good. Now, when you're stable enough to climb—"

Something smacks square into the center of my back, hard enough to knock the wind from me, and my foot snaps free of the vine. I don't even realize it's Dez at first. Before I can release Dain, the dirt edge crumbles into the hole, and I slide.

I let go of Dain, and my arms windmill, but it's too late. I tumble face-first into the hole, hit dirt and keep sliding. Above me, Jacko shrieks, and Dez chirps in alarm. Dain shouts something I don't hear.

"I'm all right," I croak, though I'm not sure how true that is. "Just keep hold of the vine and—"

Dez jumps. All I see are red glowing eyes leaping down into the pit. She lands on Dain's head, the vine snaps, and he plummets. He crashes beside me, flat on his back, vine still clutched in his hands, with Dez on his chest peering into his face as she makes a clicking sound of concern. Jacko lands beside her and starts scolding, and she ducks her head and whimpers.

"You are a menace," Dain says between his teeth.

"She was trying to help. Clearly, you needed company in this hole, and now you have it."

He grumbles and rises, brushing dirt from his tunic and leggings.

"Yes, you told me not to try rescuing you alone," I say. "I should have gone for help."

He mutters something about interfering dropbears and keeps brushing off dirt.

"That isn't coming off without a wash," I say.

More grumbling.

"Up top," I say, "you were trying to distract me with an adventure. Well, guess what we got? Exploring a cave is much better than checking out a possible shug monkey kill."

He looks around and sighs.

"Oooh," I say. "You didn't growl that it's a terrible idea, which means you're considering it." I peer into the darkness. "It'd help if we had a fire stick. Once we're past here, we'll lose the light from above."

Another sigh. Then a scratching noise and a moment later, he's holding two unlit fire sticks in front of my face.

"You are *amazing*."

I reach for one, but he pulls them back and bends out of sight. When he rises, he's holding a length of thick, dead root. He lights the end, and I grin.

"See, you do have great ideas," I say. "When we get back to the castle, I'm having you knighted."

"Tamarel doesn't have knights. That's Roiva."

"Then I'm insisting King Estienne knight you, because Sir Dain sounds awesome."

He shakes his head and hands me the makeshift torch. "If you keep talking, we'll run out of light before you get a chance to explore."

I pause, going serious as I peer into the cave.

"What?" he says. "You're thinking something."

"If we could escape Madlyn, this might be a good place to hide. I'm just not sure there's any point in escaping. I have no idea where we are, and we don't have any weapons or food."

I look over at him. "Should I wait until we're near the mountains? At least then I'd have some idea where we were."

"I don't know," Dain says. "I'm not saying that to be a jerk, Rowan. I honestly do not know. I feel like the answer is obvious: We should escape while we can. But if we're stuck in a jungle full of monsters with no weapons or food, is that better than staying with Madlyn a while longer? I don't know. Since we're down here, though, we should explore. If we could get our weapons, get our packs, then this would be a good place to hide."

I wave the torch around. "Looks like an underground cave system."

"You want to check it out?"

"I do."

CHAPTER FOURTEEN

We've been walking for at least a hundred paces. Making our way upright through a tunnel that stays exactly the same circumference. It stretches about two feet over my head and when I put my arms out, they're still a foot from each wall. That perfect circumference bothers me, and I'm not sure why.

"I think someone made this," Dain says. "That's what it looks like, doesn't it? Some kind of mining tunnel."

"I was just thinking it bugged me because it's too symmetrical. Cave tunnels get smaller and wider and branch out all over the place. This looks man-made."

"Then maybe it goes somewhere," Dain says. "To a village or something."

"What would they be mining out here?"

He shrugs. "I don't know the area. Could be anything."

"That would explain the clearing up top," I say as I touch one cool, damp wall. "Maybe for the miners' camp."

We continue walking. At some point, Madlyn is going to realize we're gone and send someone to find us. Or maybe she'll presume we're off in the jungle doing silly kid stuff like smooching. That makes me laugh, which has Dain asking what's so funny, but I'm certainly not telling him.

"We shouldn't go much farther," I say. "We can see that it goes on and on, so if we did want to hide, this would be a good place. Only we'd need to sneak down into the hole because if Madlyn figured out where we'd gone, we wouldn't be able to get away. It's just one long tunnel."

No sooner do I say that than the tunnel branches. One arm goes straight and the other veers north.

"Do you smell that?" I ask.

"Hard to miss," Dain mutters.

Jacko hops forward, audibly sniffing. When he disappears, I gasp and rush forward, thinking he's fallen, but instead he's hopped into a side cavern.

"Oh!" I say. "There's a room here."

I lift the torch at the entrance to an oddly circular room. I say "oddly" because it's perfectly round. I take a step forward, and my foot sinks into something. As I pull it out, the smell surges, and my free hand flies to my mouth; there is no doubt what I just stepped in.

"Scat," I say.

Dain snorts. "That's the polite way of saying it."

I think I've put my foot into feces, but as I lower the torch,

I realize it was just coincidence that I smelled feces as my foot hit something. The object I stepped on is much too large.

It's dark brown, and my foot definitely sank into it. A ball of dirt. My light picks up more balls like this one, and I frown. Is this what they're mining? Some kind of special dirt for fertilizer?

I crouch in front of the ball, and the smell nearly rocks me back. This *is* what smells like feces. It must be the dirt they're mining. It's a rotting stench, like mud hauled from bogs.

I spot something stuck in the mud ball. It's a round white orb. I'm not keen to reach into this foul-smelling mud, so I use a piece of root to pry it out. That should be easy. It's not. The white ball doesn't pop free, and I keep digging to find a second ball, attached to the first. I know then what I've found, but I keep going and soon the bulbous end of a bone is exposed.

"Uh, Rowan?" Dain says.

I've been so preoccupied digging out this bone that I didn't notice he'd moved away. Jacko is perched on my head, intently watching my work. Dez is with Dain, who's crouched at another ball, poking it with a root. He pries something out and holds up what looks like a white globe nearly as big as my head.

I hold up the torch . . . and a skull grins back at me. I give a start and nearly drop the torch.

"What is that?" I say.

"Monkey, I think. A large monkey or possibly a small ape."

"I mean, what is it doing—why is it—?"

The answer hits me like a fist to my gut.

"This *is* scat," I whisper.

I expect a sarcastic remark. Duh, that's obvious, isn't it? Looks like scat. Smells like scat. There's just one problem.

"How big—?" I swallow. "That skull . . . Whatever it ate was nearly as big as me."

Dain doesn't reply. My brain skids this way and that. One answer keeps screaming in my head, but I stop my ears against it. I'm overreacting. Seizing on that possibility because we'd joked about it.

I hurry out to the tunnel and lift the torch. I look at the walls. *Really* look at them. I thought it had to be a mining tunnel because it was so wide, but there's another answer. I stand in the middle and put my hands out, and then I reach over my head. The same distance. The tunnel is exactly as wide as it is tall, and it's that same size all the way along. Humans wouldn't bother being so perfect for a mining tunnel. They'd also put in braces to be sure it didn't collapse.

I jog back into the room. Perfectly circular. Burrowed out. Like the tunnel. Something burrowed through the ground. Something big enough to eat an ape's head whole. Something as big around as this entire tunnel.

"You can say it, princess," Dain says. "*Now* you can say it."

"Grootslang."

We're barely back in the main tunnel when a distant rustling sounds. Neither of us says a word. We just keep walking fast, not even running, because running would mean acknowledging what we heard, and we're both telling ourselves the other didn't hear a thing. It's just our imaginations. I've realized we're in a grootslang burrow, and so naturally I think I hear a grootslang in the distance.

We're fine. Just fine. Walk quickly and get out. The exit is only a few hundred paces away.

I stop short.

"The exit," I whisper. "We can't get out. We're stuck down here. That's why we went exploring."

Dain takes Dez from her pouch and holds her up in front of him. "We need you to get Alianor. Okay? *Get Alianor*. I know you can climb out."

He sets her down and gives her a nudge, but she only looks back at him and puts a tentative hand on his leg, asking permission to climb back up to her pouch.

"No," he says sharply, pushing her harder. "Get help."

"She doesn't understand. Jacko?"

The jackalope sails off my shoulders, as if he was waiting for this. He bounds a few paces down the tunnel and then looks back.

"Get Alianor," I say. "Bring her to the tunnel. Quickly, please."

He knows "Alianor." He also knows "get." He'll puzzle out the rest. When he hops back, it's only to herd Dez, nudging and nipping her along. She understands that, and the two disappear into the darkness.

"We're okay," I say as my heart thumps. "Right? We're okay?"

"I thought I heard something, but it's quiet now. We're fine. These tunnels probably go all the way to the sea, a hundred miles away. That's what people say, right?"

"It is."

"Then we're fine." He gives a strained chuckle. "So, you got your grootslang."

When I don't answer, he says, "I'm teasing, Rowan. You didn't conjure up this hole by joking about them. There were sightings. Maybe this one burrowed closer to Roiva because of the dragon."

I look at the size of the hole. "I can't imagine a monster this size would be scared of anything, even a dragon."

"Well, the good thing is that you got to see an actual grootslang burrow without seeing an actual grootslang. Best of both worlds."

I have to snort a laugh at that. When Dain's steady foot-falls stop behind me, I glance back to see him peering into the dark tunnel.

"That was me," I say. "I made that noise."

He nods, and he's turning toward me when I catch a papery rustle. Fingers of icy cold tickle down my back.

"That's not the grootslang," Dain says. "Other creatures would use this burrow. It'd be like a giant road, a safe way to travel through the jungle."

The sound comes again. A memory pokes at me. "Jba-fofi. That's what it sounds like. That scratchy noise."

"Never thought you'd be relieved to hear a giant spider, right?"

"We've come a long way, fellow monster hunter." I glance back into the darkness behind him again. "We should move faster, even if it *is* just a jba-fofi."

We break into a jog. When Dain catches my arm, I nearly fall. I grip the torch tighter.

"Wh—?" I begin.

"Shhh."

I hear it then. That papery rustling is louder now. Closer. It sounds like something gliding along rather than skittering.

"That doesn't sound like a spider," I whisper.

"I know." He leans into my ear. "Tell me more about snakes. How do they detect prey?"

"Smell, mostly," I whisper back. "Through their tongues. Some can use infrared detection, picking up heat."

He curses softly. I know what he means—this doesn't help our situation.

So do we run and risk making noise? That's the question. A snake doesn't need noise. A snake would detect us even if we were sitting still and silent in perfect darkness.

I listen, and without a doubt, the sound is getting louder.

"Run," I whisper.

We do that. We run as fast as we can without slipping on the dirt floor. Even before I can see the light at the end, I hear voices.

"Thank you, Jacko," I murmur.

We keep running, and when we reach the cavern where we'd started, I'm hoping to see a dangling rope. There's nothing except Jacko on the edge of the hole and that coiled vine on the ground at our feet.

"Hello!" I call.

A face appears. It's the lighter-skinned man. He scowls down at us.

"There you are," he says.

"We fell," I say. "We need to get out."

"I can see that."

"Quickly!" I say. "Something's coming."

"Oh, something's coming all right, girl. Her name is Madlyn, and she's very unhappy."

"Just hurry, please. Something's down here with us."

The man's face disappears. "They're here," he calls. "Spooked by rats, and in a big hurry to get out."

"Not rats!" I shout. "There's a monster down here!"

Laughter drifts down. The rustling behind us is loud enough that Jacko sounds his alert cry.

"Someone shut that rabbit up," the man snarls.

"Give me the torch," Dain says.

I do, and he darts into the darkness. My heart skips, but then I see what he's doing—lighting afire any roots old enough to burn.

A rope hits me on the head. I grab it.

"Hold on tight," the man says. "We'll haul you up. Don't try to climb."

I want to scream at him to hurry. But the more I talk, the slower they'll move. They heave me up, and I scramble out and toss the rope back in for Dain. That makes them laugh and joke about frightened children.

I ignore them and lean over the edge, watching as Dain comes up. When something brushes my legs, I almost tumble in from the shock. It's Malric. Alianor and Trysten stand behind him.

"There's something down there," I say as Dain clambers onto firm ground. "I think—" I swallow. "I think it's a grootslang."

Madlyn's face screws up. "A what?"

"Giant snake," the Roivan man says.

"A giant *snake?*" Madlyn sputters. "What kind of monster is that?"

"One big enough to devour you in a single bite," Alianor says.

The bounty hunters all laugh.

"You truly are children," Madlyn says as she shakes her head. "What bedtime tales they must tell in Tamarel."

"I'm serious," I say, herding Alianor and Trysten back toward camp. "Something is down there, and we need to get away from that hole."

Madlyn strides into our path. "Or perhaps not so childish after all," she says. "Is this your plan, princess? Scare us with wild stories while you flee?"

"I'm not fleeing. I'm getting away from that hole."

I try to pass, but she stops me with her sword. "You'll go nowhere unless I say so."

"We need to get to camp," Alianor says. "Retrieve our weapons. There's a giant man-eating snake coming, and this is the royal monster hunter. She can protect us."

Alianor doesn't wink at me, but she might as well. With horror, I realize she thinks we're making up a story as an excuse to get our weapons.

I shake my head frantically, but she's already turned away.

"We need to act fast," she says. "Give Rowan her ebony sword. It's magic, and it'll drive off the grootslang."

"I suppose you need your dagger, too," Madlyn says dryly.

"It would help. We should all be armed."

"No!" I say. "This isn't a joke. There's a—"

The earth quakes beneath our feet.

"What's that?" Madlyn says.

"The grootslang! Run!"

Madlyn grabs me by the arm. "What did you do in that tunnel, girl? Set up some kind of landslide? You're a clever child, but not as clever as—"

The ground behind her erupts.

CHAPTER FIFTEEN

Something bursts from the earth so fast that I see only a gray blur. It shoots up right under the Havendale man, and he goes flying through the air. There's another blur and then a snap, and the man is gone. One second he was there, sailing through the air, and now there is only an enormous snake. Its jaws snap shut, and a huge lump juts from its throat before disappearing down its gullet.

A huge lump.

The Havendale man. The one who'd just helped me from the pit.

"Sweet mother," Madlyn gasps. "What is that?"

I wheel and shove her as hard as I can. Malric hits my legs from behind, herding me deeper into the jungle. I grip Jacko on my shoulders as I wave for the others.

"Follow the girl!" one of the women shouts.

We race into the deep jungle. A scream sounds behind us, and I turn to see one of the women in the mouth of the beast. For a moment, we all stare in horror. The snake has her in its mouth, and its head waves, hood flapping. There's something on that hood. A shape, undulating as the beast weaves its head, and I find myself no longer looking at the poor woman but staring, transfixed, at the beast's hood.

That's when Jacko bites me. His teeth sink into my shoulder and I gasp, blinking. I glance to see everyone around me also staring fixedly at the beast's hood, equally transfixed by those hypnotic patterns.

"Don't look at the hood!" I shout as I give Dain a shove, then Alianor. Alianor knocks against Trysten, and I nudge Malric sharply with my foot. He breaks from his trance, shaking his head.

"Run!" I say.

Forget the poor woman held in the beast's mouth. That is a distraction. Her screams are a lure to make us look at the creature's hood.

"Help!" she shouts. "Someone! Please! Madlyn!"

I glance back just as the snake throws the woman in the air. Something darts beneath it: Madlyn, stabbing the creature.

The grootslang doesn't even seem to notice. Madlyn's sword bounces off the gray scales. The woman flies through the air, and the beast rears up to catch her in its mouth. It swallows. Madlyn screams in fury, but when the beast turns her way, she runs.

"Into the jungle!" I shout. "Get in as deep as you can. Find the thickest part."

The four of us—me, Dain, Alianor and Trysten—stick together with Malric right behind us, herding us in. Madlyn is still out there somewhere. The rest of her troop has fled in here with us, but they move away, one of the women shouting to the others in a language I don't know. From her motions, she seems to be saying they should spread out, so if the grootslang attacks, it'll go for us "children," clustered in a group. Two obey. One young woman stays close to us, though.

"You can fight it, yes?" she says, her accent heavier than the others.

We're hunkered in deep jungle, surrounded by trees and vines.

"If I get your sword, you can fight it," she repeats.

"Yes," Alianor begins. "If you get—"

I cut her off. I'm not sending this woman into the open clearing to fetch what she clearly believes is some kind of mystical weapon.

"I don't have magical powers," I say. "Neither does my sword. I'm a hunter who specializes in monsters. That's it."

"But you have special blood," she says. "I know the stories."

"She has skills," Trysten explains. "She understands monsters, and she can calm them, and that might seem like magic, but it's not. She can tame a jackalope. She can't tame something like that." He gestures at the grootslang. "She can't tame it or kill it. No one can."

"If we can safely get our weapons, we should," I say. "But Trysten's right. All of us together couldn't kill that beast. Madlyn's sword bounced right off its scales. Our best bet is to hide, like we're doing right now."

The grootslang is still where we left it. We can just make it out through the thick greenery. It's reared up, but its hood has lowered as it peers into the jungle. It's only partly out of the hole, and I don't even want to think how long it is. The part that's reared up towers fifteen feet in the air. Its tusks are nearly as long as my entire body.

"The tusks are venomous," I whisper. "Remember that. And there's something about the patterns on its hood."

"They're hypnotic," Dain says. "I'd never heard that."

"Probably because no one who's ever seen a grootslang survived to tell the tale," Alianor says. "Isn't that what you said?"

"Well, we'll be the first," I say firmly. "Yes, when it undulates with the hood open, the pattern seems to hypnotize."

"Undulates?" the young Havendale woman says.

"Weaves and sways," Trysten says with a quarter smile. "our princess likes to use exactly the right word. So the grootslang has impenetrable scales, venomous tusks and a hypnotizing hood. Anything else?"

"The fact it can swallow a person whole?" Alianor's voice drops as she shivers. "It's easy to say that, but I figured it was an exaggeration. I never thought . . ." She swallows.

"We're fine here," I say. "If anything happens, stay in the jungle. Watch the others, and if you see someone hypnotized, give them a—"

The ground quakes as the grootslang drops to the earth and begins slithering into the clearing. Its tongue flicks in and out as it samples the air.

"We're downwind," I say. "It can't smell us."

Dain glances over but says nothing. He knows the

grootslang's sense of smell may be acute enough to pick up our scent without any wind. He also knows better than to say so. Keep everyone calm. The worst thing we could do is panic and attract its attention.

I can see Madlyn on the far side of the clearing. She's watching the snake from the jungle, trying to figure out how to kill it. I must give her credit for that—she didn't flee with the rest of her troop. Even alone, she's trying to solve this problem.

The grootslang doesn't seem to notice her. It weaves through the clearing. Then it stops and rises up. It's looking somewhere to our right. Its hood flutters but stays shut as it sways, peering into the jungle, tongue flicking. Then it begins to move forward.

From the jungle comes a yelp and then a crashing, and the grootslang shoots forward. *Shoots* isn't the right word to describe a serpent, and as Trysten said, I always like to use the right word, but I'm not sure how else to describe it. One second, the grootslang is meandering along, and then someone in the jungle runs, and it fires itself in that direction. Like an arrow, a gray blur that mows down trees as if they were twigs.

There's a scream and a thrashing, and the grootslang launches itself into the air, flinging one of the women back into the clearing. She sails clear over the treetops and lands with a sickening crunch.

We all stare, unable to speak, unable to move. I'm sure she's dead. She must be. Then she twitches, trying to lift her broken body. The grootslang whips around and scoops her up on its tusks. Then it throws her in the air again, opens its mouth and catches her, and swallows her whole.

"We aren't safe," Alianor whispers.

I'm about to tell her we're fine here when I follow her gaze to the trail of destruction left by the grootslang. It slammed through the jungle like a plow, uprooting trees as it went.

I look around us. All the trees here are young, no more than a foot in diameter.

"What do we do?" Alianor whispers.

My mind spits out ideas. Climb a tree? The grootslang can knock it down. Get into rocks where it can't follow? There are no rocks here. Find a hole? It can burrow. Grab our weapons? It has impenetrable scales.

"Rowan?" Trysten murmurs. "May I make a suggestion?"

"Please," I say, and hope I don't sound too desperate.

"We can't fight. We can't hide. The only thing left is to get as far away as we can, as fast as we can. It can't knock down miles of jungle without hurting itself."

"That would be inefficient feeding," I whisper. "Expending more energy than it consumes."

"Right. So we run."

I shake my head. "That woman tried to run, and you saw what happened to her. We'll sneak. We'll move as quickly and as quietly as we can. First, though, we need our things."

"There isn't time," Trysten says.

"Then we'd escape a grootslang to be stranded in a monster-filled jungle with no weapons."

"Rowan's right," Dain says. "We need weapons. I'll get them."

"*We'll* get them," I say. "You and me. Alianor and Trysten will sneak away."

Trysten opens his mouth, but I say, "All four of us getting our weapons will attract its attention."

I nod to where the grootslang is resting in the clearing, digesting its meal while looking about for more, tongue sampling the air. Our weapons and packs are on the far side of that clearing. They're near the edge, which helps, but it'll still be dangerous.

Alianor turns to Trysten. "We'll climb a tree so we can watch them. If there's trouble, we'll provide the distraction."

"And my people?" asks the young Havendale woman, who's been quietly listening.

No one speaks. She swallows. "That is a foolish question."

"It's not," I say, my voice low. "But it's going to take everything we have getting *ourselves* out of here. You should go with Trysten and Alianor. If you'd rather stay to help your people, we understand. Just don't try to stop us. Please."

She nods. "I will go with you to get your weapons." She lifts a dagger. "I am armed. It will help."

"Thank you, but I'd like you to lag behind. The more people moving, the more likely the grootslang will notice us."

She agrees, and I bend to Malric.

"Stay close," I whisper. "But be safe."

He grunts, and I lift Jacko onto my shoulders before we set out.

CHAPTER SIXTEEN

The grootslang has slowed down. A snake's body needs to work hard to digest a meal devoured whole. After this, the beast will retreat into the tunnels and probably not eat for weeks. That's cold comfort. It isn't ready to retreat yet. It isn't full yet. It's just circling the clearing slowly, as if picking its next meal from the puny humans hiding in the jungle.

I've noticed that it sticks to the clearing. As Trysten said, it won't plow too far into the jungle. That takes energy and risks injury.

Maybe we *should* just try to all sneak away. Forget our weapons and gear. It's two days' walk to the edge of the jungle. We can do that without food. Yes, without a fire we couldn't dare stop at night, but we could walk all night and sleep with a guard during the day. It's no more dangerous than getting near that clearing for our weapons.

My gut clenches at the thought of abandoning my ebony sword. Leave behind one of our nation's greatest treasures? If I return without that—worse, if I admit that I abandoned it while fleeing a monster—Heward will surely claim that proves I'm not worthy of the royal monster hunter title.

It doesn't matter. It can't matter. My mother will argue my case, and anyone with a lick of sense would see her point. My duty is to my troop. To Dain and Alianor and Trysten. This monster isn't in Tamarel. It's no threat to our people or country.

I pause and turn to Dain. "Maybe we should—"

In the clearing, the grootslang rises, hood billowing. I freeze, certain it's managed to hear or see me, despite the fact that we're carefully circling deep in the jungle. It's not looking our way, though. Then I hear the patter of footsteps. Someone moving through the jungle, trying to slip away. Not Alianor or Trysten. This is one of Madlyn's troop.

The beast shoots out again, plowing through the jungle in pursuit of its prey.

"Run!" Dain whispers, pushing me. "Get the stuff! Now!"

When I hesitate, he shoves me harder. I understand then. Even as a man screams, I know what Dain's getting at. The beast is distracted. Move now.

I tell the Havendale woman to wait, and Dain and I run into the clearing. Our weapons and packs are right there. Ahead, all we see is the torso of the grootslang, its head deep in the jungle as it toys with its prey.

I block out the screams and grab my ebony sword. I throw Dain his bow as he grabs the sack of our daggers. I also snatch up the other sack—it's where Madlyn put our more dangerous supplies, like fire sticks and Alianor's medical kit. I'm glancing around for anything else when Malric growls. *Move faster.*

I race back into the jungle, with Dain just ahead of me, Malric behind, Jacko bounding along at our sides. I get maybe three running strides in when Malric grabs me. I twist to see the grootslang wending its way back into the clearing. When it stops, my heart does, too. It's looking right at us.

No, I realize in a heartbeat. It's not looking at us. We're in the jungle. It's looking at the young woman who'd been with us, the one I'd told to wait out of sight. She's ventured into the clearing, where she's holding a pack and standing frozen, spotted by the beast.

The grootslang rises up, hood flaring. It undulates, and the woman stares at that hypnotic pattern.

"We should go," Dain says, but his voice is barely above a whisper. Quiet and uncertain. We *should* go. Can we, though? Let this young woman's death distract the beast while we flee?

I crouch, looking for something to throw. When my fingers close on a rock, Dain's hand lands on my shoulder. I glance up to see him poised with his bow. Before he can loose an arrow, someone runs out between us and the woman.

"Hey!" Madlyn shouts, waving her arms. "You! Big snake!"

The grootslang ignores her. It's moving closer to the young woman. Madlyn runs and gives her a shove, and the young woman snaps out of her trance just as the beast strikes. It scoops up the young woman and throws her aside.

"We should run," Dain says again.

"Walk," I whisper. "Retreat slowly."

We get two steps before Madlyn shouts again. She's waving her arms, trying to distract the grootslang from the woman on the ground. Except when the grootslang turns her way, it doesn't just see her—it sees us in the jungle, twenty paces behind her.

Its head shoots out, and it impales Madlyn on its tusks before I can blink. Then it throws her aside and plows into the jungle, coming straight for us.

We run. There's nothing else to do. We run with Malric at our heels, and we plow straight into a solid wall of thick jungle, crisscrossing vines blocking our path.

"Climb!" I shout.

I grab the nearest vines wrapped around a thick tree. A tree that *might* be too thick for the grootslang to uproot. I swing myself up and Jacko climbs alongside me.

"Go!" Dain says, and I think he's talking to me, but when I look down, he's pushing Dez up behind me. Then he grabs the tree and we're climbing as fast as we can.

Below, Malric snarls.

"Run!" I shout. "Just run!"

I twist to see Malric leaping at the grootslang. "No!" I shout but he ignores me, and the grootslang ignores him. It's focused on us. On this tree. We're climbing as fast as we can, and then the beast slams into the trunk. Dain yelps in alarm, and I turn and all I see is the open maw of the serpent and Dain falling into it.

I see Dain tumbling into that horrible open mouth . . . and I jump.

CHAPTER SEVENTEEN

I jump into the mouth of the beast. The mouth of a grootslang. I see Dain fall, and I act without thinking. No, that's not right. I do think. I think that if I don't jump, I will never see him again. There is no hope for him once he is in its jaws. No way to stop it from devouring him. Not from the outside, at least.

I leap in, sword in hand. Behind me, Jacko lets out a terrible shriek. Somewhere in the distance, Malric roars.

And the grootslang? It tries to close its mouth, to swallow Dain whole, but I ram my sword into the beast's mouth to steady myself. Then I grab his free hand before the grootslang's gullet opens.

"Stab!" I say.

He blinks up at me, his face blank, as if he can't process what I'm saying. I wrap my hand around his wrist, brace my feet, pull out my sword and slash as best I can, one-handed. It doesn't have to be a good slash. It only needs to cut, because we are inside the beast's mouth and it is not armored. Here my blade slices, and blood sprays, and the grootslang whips its head in shock and fury.

I nearly fly out. There's nothing to hold onto here. I'm trying hard not to think about where I am, to pretend it's some kind of cave. I'm in the jaws of a giant snake, and it's wet and slimy and slippery, and there are two ways out—down its gullet or out its mouth.

When it whips its head, I fly, about to tumble out, my grasp on Dain slipping. Then I see the one thing I can grab, and I manage to hook my sword arm over one tusk. That keeps me from being catapulted through the air. Mostly, though, it keeps my other hand from letting go of Dain's. He's grabbed my wrist now, our hands locked together, and in his free one he has his dagger.

Dain stabs as hard as he can inside the beast's mouth. Blood spurts, and the grootslang gives a gurgling roar of rage and pain. I manage to hook my feet inside its mouth as it tries to dislodge us. Dain slams from one cheek to the other. The gullet opens, a black hole into certain death.

I twist to look down. I could let the grootslang throw us free, but if I do, we'll suffer the same fate as the bounty hunter earlier, left broken on the ground for the grootslang to devour at its leisure. There is one chance here. One hope to be absolutely certain no one else dies. The problem is that I need to let go of this tusk to do it. Unless ...

"Hook the tusk with our arms!" I shout.

I'm sure Dain would stare at me if he wasn't being slammed around the beast's mouth, stabbing whenever he gets the chance. He hears me, though. That's enough.

I tug our entwined arms, and he slides my way, and we manage to get our arms wrapped around one lower tusk, which stabilizes us as the beast continues to thrash. It is in pain, but seems more confused and angry than genuinely afraid for its life. That gives me the advantage I need. With our arms secured, I unhook my sword arm from the other tusk—and the beast chooses that exact moment to throw its head up. The sharp tip of the tusk slices into my arm.

"Rowan!" Dain shouts, and as his eyes widen, I realize why.

Poison. Grootslangs have venomous tusks.

Nothing to be done now. I grip the ebony sword as hard as I can. Then I brace both feet and slam it up into the top of the monster's mouth, driving the razor-sharp blade into its brain.

The beast does not scream. It does not thrash. It stops, and its mouth convulses around us as I push the blade in with all my might. The grootslang's head falls forward, body slumping to the ground.

Dain and I barely have time to brace ourselves before the beast's head hits the earth. The giant mouth closes around us like a clamshell as I fall onto the floor of its mouth, and I have this terrible image of sliding down its throat in its death throes. But there are no violent death throes. Just twitches as I yank out my sword and Dain drags me from the beast's mouth.

He keeps pulling me until I'm clear of it, and then he's on his knees grabbing my arm and shouting for Alianor.

"I'm fine," I say. "My arm's just . . . Oh."

I almost say my arm's "just scratched." Then I remember the venom.

"Wrap my arm," I say. "Quickly. Whatever you have. Cut off the blood flow."

He yanks off his belt and wraps it around my biceps, pulling until I hiss in pain.

"Poison," he blurts to Alianor. "The tusks. She got cut."

Alianor grabs my arm and then shouts for someone to find water. Dain asks what to do, whether they can suck out the venom. And I may be in shock, but it keeps my brain clear, and my mind turns this problem over, examining it calmly from all angles.

"Is it showing any sign of venom?" I say. "I feel fine."

"That's shock," Alianor insists. "Now stay with us. Don't pass out."

"I'm honestly fine," I say. "It just feels like a cut. Malric?"

"She's going into shock," Alianor says to Dain. "Keep her with us."

"Malric?" I call louder. When the warg appears, I say, "Get him to sniff my arm. He can tell if there's venom."

"Of course there's venom," Dain snaps. "It's a grootslang."

"Right, which no one has ever survived an encounter with. That means the tusks might just be tusks, with no venom."

"She's right," a voice rasps, and we all look to see Madlyn dragging herself toward us. She's covered in blood and her face spasms in pain. "No poison. Just really sharp tusks."

"See? I'm fine," I say. "Go look after her."

Madlyn waves a bloody hand as she sinks to the ground. "No point, princess. There's no stitching this up." Her hand moves from her chest, where a wound gapes. "I'm surviving on pure stubbornness right now."

Alianor kneels beside the woman and does a quick check. Then she looks at us.

"You can say it, child," Madlyn says. "There's no hope for me. But there might be hope for my people. Cut into the beast. See if you can save them."

I crouch down beside Alianor, who takes my arm and resumes examining the gash. She says nothing about Madlyn, but her hands shake and she avoids looking at the woman, as if unsure what to do.

I know what to do. I was there when my aunt died. This is the death of a warrior, even if this particular warrior was a mercenary bounty hunter. Madlyn tried to save her people—she's *still* thinking about her people—and so I will grant her the death she deserves. One where I look her in the eye and listen to what she has to say.

"We'll do our best," I say.

"Do you want me to try freeing her people?" Dain asks.

"No," I say. "I can do it."

He straightens. "I'll manage. Trysten? If you have the stomach for it, I could use some help."

They take daggers and head to the dead grootslang. Alianor pauses, her fingers gripping my arm. She half glances at Madlyn. "I have pain medications. They could make you more comfortable."

"Save them for yourselves."

I start to rise. "Let me get—"

Her fingers close on my wrist, surprisingly strong. "No, princess. I mean that. Save them. My people may need them or you may. I wish to speak to you first."

Her eyes meet mine and she struggles to focus. She's obviously in great pain despite her calm acceptance.

"I won't say I underestimated you, Princess Rowan." She glances at the dead grootslang, and her laugh turns into a blood-flecked cough. "That much is obvious, and I'll waste no words on it. Save what people of mine you can, but look after yourselves. Take as many supplies as you can carry. Also this." She reaches for her boot but can't quite get there through the pain. "Fetch my stiletto, please."

I feel around inside her boot and withdraw an ivory-handled knife with a needle-thin blade. The handle is carved, and the blade a material I don't even know, one that shines bluish in the moonlight.

"That is yours," she whispers, grimacing. "My apology to you. May it serve you as well as it served me."

"Thank—"

"Save your thanks. Now take my pendant."

I unhook it from her neck. It's a jade pendant engraved with some kind of glyph.

"That is for my niece. I have no children, but I have a niece I'd hoped to train as my successor. She'd have none of it. Took off for your country and left our ways behind. For the best, though I'd never have said it to her face. If she survived her

— 137 —

journey, you'll find her in Tamarel, working as a forest healer. That was her calling, as much as I tried to fight it."

Alianor's head whips up. "Is her name Cedany?"

"You know her?"

"She's a friend of ours," I say. "Kaylein—the young warrior you kidnapped—is her girlfriend."

"I kidnapped Cedany's girlfriend?" Madlyn chokes on a chuckle. "Then I have made many mistakes, have I not? So many. Apologize for me to both of them. Your Kaylein seems a fine young woman, and I did leave her unharmed, in case you have doubted that. I'm very glad I did. I hurt Cedany enough for one lifetime. Take the necklace to her and—"

She breaks off, wheezing, and I grip her hand. When she finds breath again, it is faint as she says, "You are very kind, princess."

Alianor mutters something under her breath, and Madlyn's gaze slants her way.

"I'm sure you'd rather your friend was less kind, Alianor, daughter of Everard. You worry it will put her in danger, but you will be there to balance it out. I think you and I could have gotten along well under other circumstances. You'd have made a fine mercen—"

She coughs, struggling for breath. Trysten runs over as if hearing her struggles.

"We've freed your people from the belly of the beast, Madlyn," he says. "They'll be fine."

She smiles up at him. "You're a good boy. Stay away from your father. Never go back, if you have the choice. Not until you are old enough to knock him from his throne."

Trysten nods. "I won't."

She opens her mouth to say something more, but all that comes out is a long rasp. I grip her hand tight, and after a moment, her eyes shut and her hold on my hand relaxes. When her breathing stops, I release her hand. I pause, looking down at her.

"She's gone," I say. Then I back onto my haunches and look up at Trysten. "Her people didn't survive, did they?"

He shakes his head. "They suffocated inside the beast. I thought it would be better for her to think . . ." He trails off as he looks at Madlyn's body.

"It was," I say. "Thank you. That was very kind."

He flushes and nods, then looks out over the clearing. "We should check for survivors."

I agree, and we leave Madlyn to try to do what she would have wanted—take care of her people.

CHAPTER EIGHTEEN

We don't find any survivors. That doesn't mean there aren't any, only that the two bounty hunters in the clearing are dead, including the young woman who'd tried to take shelter with us. If only she hadn't run to grab her pack, she'd be alive. Even Madlyn might still be alive. When I say so, Dain corrects me.

"She was wrong to run for her pack," he says. "But if she hadn't, then I wouldn't have nearly been swallowed by a groot-slang, and you wouldn't have jumped in after me and figured out how to kill it. If you hadn't done that, we might all be dead. I'm not sure we could have escaped."

"Wait," Trysten says. "Rowan *jumped* in? We thought she fell."

I shrug. "Dain fell. I had to do something."

Alianor thumps me on the back. "And *something* obviously meant leaping into the jaws of the beast. Or it did if you're

— 140 —

Rowan. This story just got ten times better, and when I tell it, I definitely saw her leap in myself." She heads to the grootslang. "We should take some scales for souvenirs, right?"

"They aren't souvenirs," Dain says. "They're proof. They're also a token that a royal monster hunter can give others with the story, to remind them that she keeps them safe."

"Whatever," Alianor says. "I'm taking scales."

"Get some for me," I say. "I'll be going through the packs."

"Good idea," she says. "Gather what we need from their stuff."

"That, and also I want to leave a few weapons behind, in case the woman who fled comes back."

Her look says it's a waste of time. Yes, one member of the troop is unaccounted for, presumably having fled safely. But even if she survives, she won't dare come back. I don't care. Leaving a few supplies is a simple thing to do when we don't need all of them.

Trysten helps. I go through the packs, and he checks the bodies for weapons. I offered to switch jobs, but he insisted. Malric stays close to me, as he has since the grootslang died. I think he blames himself for being asleep when we fell into the pit, and now he's sticking *too* close. Jacko hops off to help Trysten.

We end up with far more tools and weapons than we need. I make a pile so the others can take what they want. The rest will stay in the clearing, along with the extra waterskins. We'll take all the food—if we left that behind, it'd be scavenged by morning.

When I'm done, I walk over to find Dain holding the grootslang's tusks. Each is nearly as long as my leg, but he seems to be able to hold both easily enough, suggesting they aren't as heavy as an elephant's ivory ones.

"Good idea," I say. "We can see now that they're solid, proving they don't contain venom."

He grunts and looks down at them. "Guess so. I wanted them for you, though. One to show, and the other so I can make you something. I've never carved tusks, but someone can show me how."

I don't say he doesn't need to do that. Mom taught us that when someone gives a gift, they know they didn't *have* to. It's their choice and we don't argue, even if it means lugging tusks through the jungle.

"Thank you," I say. "I think I saw an auger in one of the packs. If we can make a hole or a groove, they'll be easier to carry. I'll take one—"

"I've got them."

He hasn't said anything about me jumping into the groot-slang after him. He won't—that isn't his way. This is how he's saying thank you.

"Do we head out now or wait for dawn?" Alianor asks.

I look at the carcass of the giant snake monster. "Better to go now. The smell of blood is going to bring scavengers."

"Uh, Rowan?" Trysten says.

I follow his finger to see eyes glowing in the darkness beyond the moonlit clearing.

"That's not good," Alianor murmurs.

A shape slinks forward, and there's a heartbeat moment of relief when I see it's only a jaguar. Compared to the grootslang, a jaguar seems as harmless as a kitten, but then it snarls, showing its fangs as its sleek muscles ripple. Something moves out of the corner of my eye, and I spin just in time to yank Alianor as another jaguar leaps at her from a shadowed tree.

"Run?" Alianor says.

"The cave," Dain says, circling with his bow ready. "Get to the cave. They want to scavenge the grootslang. We'll be safe there." He pauses and then rolls his shoulders. "I mean, if you think that sounds okay—"

"It sounds genius," I say. "Everyone stay close. The jaguars might try to pick one of us off. Don't let them. Jacko?" I put out my arms, and he leaps into them. "Malric?" The warg grunts as he scans the clearing.

We make our way toward the cave. As we walk, I grab a dead branch. Alianor gives me a look, but I wave for her to keep going. Around us, more eyes glint in the darkness. Somewhere in the jungle, a creature unleashes an unearthly screech. Another answers. The hairs on my neck prickle, but I force my brain to stay on track and don't even *try* to identify the cries.

We're almost to the mouth of the tunnel when another screech comes, this one human. I grip my dagger and grit my teeth. If that's the last mercenary, we can't go to her aid. She's too far away through a night-black jungle. I block out any other noise from that direction, and then we're at the mouth of the cave.

We take turns lowering each other in. Malric waits for the end and then jumps. I push him past me, which he does not appreciate, and he stays close enough to brush my leg. Eyes peer into the pit. One pair. Then another. I take Dain's second fire stick from my pocket and light the branch I brought. Then I stick it into the dirt at the bottom of the pit.

"Ah," Alianor whispers. "I wondered what that was for."

I break off a lower part of the branch and light it to show our way. Then we slink off, and the jaguars outside the pit growl and pace, but they do not follow us past that flaming torch.

The cave tunnels are indeed a genius idea. With the grootslang dead, it's a big, empty road through the jungle. The trick will be to make sure we're heading in the right direction. We spend some time wandering and boosting one another up through the periodic breaches to check our navigation. Head *away* from the mountains—that's our only real point of reference.

By dawn, we're sure we're going in the right direction. Then we need to sleep. We find another of those circular "rooms," one blessedly free of feces, and we gather dead roots to light a very small fire for light. Then Malric insists— through growls and snarls—that we all sleep while he stands watch. He apparently napped enough earlier that evening, though I'd never be so rude as to say so.

We sleep for as long as we need. Then we eat and get on our way to quickly discover that the tunnel is veering east, toward the mountains. We take a couple of branches that seem to lead west, only to have them curve away.

"It makes sense," I say as we stop for a water break. "West is civilization, and the grootslang wouldn't get too close."

"It was spotted there, though," Alianor says. "Maybe one of these paths goes closer."

"So we spend the rest of the day trying to find it?" Dain says. "We have weapons. It's still daytime. We'll move faster up top."

We debate this longer than I'd like, until I finally have to say, "Enough. I'm with Dain on this. We'll get farther on the surface, where we can see the mountains. We should climb up top and go as far as we can before sundown. It's not as safe, but the longer we're down here, the quicker we'll go through our food and have to sneak to the surface to hunt anyway."

Alianor still grumbles, but then she agrees, and we head out in search of the next breach to the surface.

CHAPTER NINETEEN

I think I made a mistake. Lulled by the safety of the tunnels, I forgot how difficult and treacherous the jungle is. We need to hack our way through with Madlyn's machete, and that is far more exhausting than it seemed when she was doing it. Yes, up here we can keep an eye on the mountains, but they're constantly disappearing behind the treetops, and we can walk a mile before we see them again. By the time the sun starts to fall, I don't even dare guess how far we've come. The answer, I fear, is not very far at all.

I'm not sure which decision was the wrong one, though. To come up from the tunnels? Or to try walking through the tunnels in the first place?

All I know is that this is not the best way to do things, and by the time I realize that, there's no turning back. I don't tell the others I've made a mistake. How can I when they helped come up with the plan, especially Dain? Also, as Jannah always said, when a leader second-guesses a strategy, there's no point telling her troop unless there's an alternate route available. If you're locked into a path of action, you cannot worry those who are relying on your judgment.

So I doubt in silence, and I put on a good face as we hack out a clearing for our camp. While we're doing that, Malric scouts the area and returns with a peccary, which he offers us for dinner. I gratefully accept—it's big enough for all. We cook that up and eat some dried berries and nuts from Madlyn's food stores. Then we come up with a guard schedule and settle in for the night.

I take first shift, and Malric sits up with me. He lies behind my back as a support, and this time, I don't think he's just doing it for my body heat. He's been quiet. Well, being a warg, he's always quiet. He doesn't chirp or chatter like Dez and Jacko. With Malric, though, his mood seems to crackle through the air, impossible to ignore. That's why I struggled so much in our early days together. His discontent felt like anger, as if I'd stolen Jannah from him and insisted that he shift his allegiance to me, a poor substitute for his lifelong companion.

In reality, it'd been grudging acceptance, grief and, yes, concern that I was not a worthy successor. As much as that stung, it was a valid concern that didn't reflect on me as a person or even me as a warrior. It was the fact that I am a child, and they should have awarded the ebony sword to an adult hunter while I trained. But this is our tradition, and to disrupt it would put the crown itself at risk.

Mom's only recourse had been to make me royal monster hunter–elect and then give me years to train before I was expected to carry out my duties. That isn't what happened, obviously. The return of a dragon and the disruption among the monsters meant I had to start far too young, and Malric disapproved.

Now, though, I don't feel that disapproval. I haven't in a while, but I've still been acutely aware of his moods, which range from grudging acceptance to exasperation. This muted version of him concerns me. It's as if he has withdrawn into himself. As if he's doubting himself.

I understand the source, or I think I do. First, the bonnacon attack that injured him and "let" me be captured by Madlyn's troop. Then, while he was resting from that injury, I fall down a grootslang tunnel, and when the beast attacks, he is powerless against it.

I tentatively reach a hand to pet him, and he leans into it, a sigh rippling through him. Jacko curls up against him, giving his ragged purr, and Malric seems to roll his eyes at that, offended that the jackalope might think he needs comfort. He doesn't shove him away, though, or growl for him to leave.

"I think I made a mistake, too," I whisper. "I'm feeling bad about it. Trying to figure out where I went wrong. Killing the grootslang might have made me overconfident. Or it scared me so badly I couldn't make decisions, didn't think things through."

Malric curls himself around me until his head is on my leg. It's such an unfamiliar gesture that it throws me off balance. Then I realize it's not unfamiliar at all. How many times had I seen him do this with Jannah as she sat by a fire? Wrapping himself around her and putting his head on her leg. I carefully touch his head, and when he doesn't pull away, I scratch his ears, and before I know it, I'm crying, huge tears falling.

"I miss her so much," I say.

Then I swallow and say her name, and his eyes roll up to meet mine as he recognizes it, and that only makes me cry more. My hand wraps in the fur at the ruff of his neck, and as I cry, I pull out the necklace from my pocket. It's the one Madlyn gave me, which makes no sense because it has nothing to do with my aunt. It feels like it does, though, and then it hits hard enough to make me sob a gasp.

When I close my eyes, I don't see Madlyn lying on the ground. I see Jannah. That's what hurts so much. That's what has me feeling down and thinking it's because I made bad choices. Watching Madlyn die had been like watching Jannah die again. It brought back a leaden grief I've been unable to shake all day.

I hold the necklace tight and I cry, and I say her name for Malric so he knows why I'm crying, so he knows I'm still grieving, too.

"This isn't how it should have been," I whisper. "I wanted to be the royal monster hunter so badly that sometimes I think . . . I think maybe I did something. That my wish made it happen. That I wanted to be a hunter, and for me to get my dream, she had to die and Rhydd had to be injured, and it's all my fault for not being satisfied with what I had."

Malric presses against my hand, and I rub his neck.

"I know it doesn't work that way," I say, "but I feel that sometimes. I would gladly have taken the throne if this was the cost."

He exhales a deep breath and leans into me.

"Mostly, I just wish she was still here. I wish it so much, Malric."

I wrap my arms around him, and he presses against me, and I cry until I can't cry anymore. When he stiffens, I let go quickly, cheeks burning, certain he's had quite enough of this, but he's staring into the jungle. A low growl rumbles through him.

I pull out my sword and rise. Madlyn's amulet falls from my lap, but I don't dare reach for it, don't even glance down. My gaze stays fixed on the jungle.

Malric growls again, his muzzle rising, and I follow it to see red eyes peering from a tree.

"Dropbear," I whisper.

Malric makes a noise I can't quite interpret. It almost sounds like dissent.

"Dropbear?" I say, turning it into a question.

The same noise. No, not a dropbear. He recognizes the word, and he's telling me that is not what he smells.

Something in a tree. Something with red eyes.

Leaves rustle and a branch crackles as a shape drops from a treetop. It doesn't fall to the ground, though. It hangs from a branch, suspended by long, spindly arms.

It looks like a small person. Not a child, but a human adult shrunk to a third of its size. I can't see more in the dim light, so I bend, gaze fixed on the creature, and take a branch from the fire. I lift it, and the creature makes a *whoo-whoo* noise and bounces from the branch.

It's a small primate. The face doesn't make it look human—it has a fox-like snout. The illusion comes from its coloration. The beast is light brown, with darker-brown fur on its head that looks like hair. Its rear legs are darker, and it has three dark spots on its belly, making it appear to be wearing trousers and a shirt with buttons.

"Kalabandar," I whisper to Malric, and a thrill darts through me. These little monsters aren't nearly as rare as grootslangs, but they are creatures of the jungle, and we don't have them in Tamarel. Monster hunters certainly know all about them, though, from the stories that travel east to our land. They're also known as monkey men, for obvious reasons, and bards tell stories about people spotting them in the jungle, mistaking them for children and chasing them until they're hopelessly lost.

One thing the lore does *not* imply is that they attack without cause. Like monkeys, they can be jerks, but they're mostly curious and mischievous.

"Hello," I say.

The kalabandar swings by its arms and makes that *whoo-whoo* noise. Jacko chatters at it and rushes between us, as if warning the monster that it had better not try anything. I smile and sheathe my sword. Malric growls at that, but I'm only exchanging it for my dagger. Even the most timid of monsters will attack if they feel threatened, and kalabandars aren't known for being timid. I keep the dagger at my side as I move closer.

I want a better look at the creature. While plenty of royal monster hunters have seen them—and documented their findings—pictures in books are never the same as a real sighting. The beast does look very close to a monkey, with long arms and legs, and prehensile hands and feet. It has the prehensile tail, too, which is gripping onto the branch like a third arm. The snout is vulpine, which always made me wonder how anyone could mistake a kalabandar for a human child, but seeing the beast in low lighting, I can understand the error. Also, when it's facing forward, the snout is less obvious.

As I draw closer, Jacko backs up to protect my feet. He's uncertain, and that might be because the beast's size and primate qualities remind him of harpies. The kalabandar continues to swing and its call changes to a cooing. I take another step. Malric growls.

"It's not going to attack me," I say. "The only incidence of that in the accounts is when someone got bitten trying to grab one. I have no intention of getting close enough to touch it."

Malric grumbles, and I swear Jacko does, too. We've spent days avoiding monsters and fighting monsters, capturing them and scaring them off. Just "looking" at one is alien to them, and in this unfamiliar place, it makes them nervous.

"This is close enough," I say in what I hope is a reassuring tone. "Jacko? Would you get Dain, please? He should see this."

Jacko just keeps staring at the kalabandar.

"Jacko?" When he doesn't even look over, I sigh. "Fine. You're pretending you can't understand me. I know Malric won't leave to get Dain, so I guess I will."

As I turn, movement flashes behind me. It's another kalabandar. It sees me watching and freezes. From one tiny hand dangles the chain of Madlyn's pendant.

"Hey!" I say.

The kalabandar bolts for the jungle, and the one hanging

— 152 —

from the tree shrieks, as if cheering it on. I run, heart hammering as I see Madlyn's necklace disappearing into the jungle. I imagine telling Cedany that her dying aunt asked for one thing, and I messed it up. Lost her necklace to a monkey monster.

I give chase. If the kalabandar reaches a tree, I've lost. It'll be gone before I can even shimmy up the trunk.

Malric sprints past me. The kalabandar veers toward the woods. It makes one giant leap, and Malric flies through the air, knocking it down and then snatching it up by the scruff of the neck and giving it a stern shake.

"Thank you, Malric," I say as I walk over.

I reach out for the dangling chain. The kalabandar chatters and squirms, and I need to pry the chain from its hand, but I get it back. Then I shake my head.

"Nice try," I say. "Let's see if I have something shiny that I can give you in exchange."

When Jacko sounds his alert cry, I sigh. "*Now* you realize something's wrong, Jacko? I have the necklace. Situation under—"

Something's moving in the camp. It's a kalabandar. No, it's *multiple* kalabandars, swarming over our packs.

"Hey!" I shout.

I swear the kalabandar hanging from Malric's jaws laughs. It certainly makes a little tittering noise. Malric tosses it aside and runs for camp, with me right behind him. By now there are at least six kalabandars. They've leapt right past the fire, not caring about it one bit. One is perched on Alianor's back. It lifts a lock of her hair with her sapphire hair clip in it.

"Alianor!"

She shifts in sleep. Then she must feel the creature on her back. She jumps up, and the kalabandar shrieks, hanging onto the clip. The beast falls, clip in hand, and it shrieks anew with delight and victory, and lopes toward the jungle, treasure held over its head. Alianor runs and jumps onto the kalabandar, pinning it down as it screams as if being ripped in two.

Another scream sounds. This one comes from Trysten, who's woken to a kalabandar on his chest, brandishing a dagger. It's *his* dagger—the beast plucked it from its sheath— but to Trysten, it must appear he's awakened to a knife-wielding monkey.

This time, it's Dain who intercedes. He grabs the kalabandar and hoists it into the air. Then he plucks the dagger from its grasp as the kalabandar scolds him.

I snatch up the first kalabandar I reach—one opening Alianor's pack. I shove it aside and grab the pack, swinging it onto my back. The next one already has my pack open, and it's digging through, tossing out food and clothing as it roots around for something more interesting. It finds it at the bottom—the stiletto blade Madlyn gave me. It didn't have a sheath, so I'd wrapped it in clothing, and it tumbles out onto the dirt.

Before I can get there, the kalabandar grabs the dagger by the shiny end, fingers wrapping around the razor-sharp blade. It screams and drops the dagger and shrieks at me, as if I bit its hand. When I scoop up the stiletto, it tries again to grab it by the blade.

I yank it back. "Seriously? No. Sharp. Do not grab by the pointy end. Ouch!"

"Princess?" Dain says. "Maybe you want to save the safety lessons and focus on getting our belongings away from these beasts?"

"Safety is always the most important thing," I say. "And I've rescued two packs. You guys can get your own."

He grumbles but shoos off the kalabandar rooting through his pack. Two others are fighting over Trysten's, shrieking loud enough to make my head hurt. Trysten bounces from foot to foot like a fighter waiting for his shot.

Dain grumbles and marches over, grabbing the pack. "They're just kalabandars," he says. "They aren't dangerous." He hefts the bag, one kalabandar still hanging from it. "And you wouldn't know that, so I shouldn't snap at you."

Trysten smiles his thanks and disengages the dangling kalabandar. Then he takes his pack from Dain and fastens it tightly as the kalabandars dance around, shrieking.

"They're kinda cute," Trysten says. "Does anyone else think they look like little humans with hair and buttons and trousers?"

I nod. "Kalabandars are also known as monkey men for that reason."

"They're like children," Trysten says. "Very naughty children."

I fish a hand into a side compartment on my bag. "Do you have small coins for them? They seem to like shiny things."

"You're rewarding the thieves who failed to pick your pocket?" Alianor says.

"No, I'm rewarding their ingenuity. One of them lured me into the jungle by being all cute and innocent, while another snuck behind me to grab Madlyn's necklace. Then while

Malric, Jacko and I were busy chasing that one, the rest were infiltrating the camp."

I hold a copper coin out for the quietest of the kalabandars. It takes it and races off into the jungle, whooping.

"Hey, monkey kids!" Trysten says, and flings silver coins into the jungle. Alianor does the same. Dain eyes the copper coins in his hand.

"We've thrown enough," I say.

He nods and returns them to his pouch. I'd like to say that I'll happily replace any he throws, but that would be awkward. Those copper coins mean more to him than a gold one does to the rest of us.

Of course, the kalabandars don't stay gone. Some of the bolder ones return hoping for more. By then, we've backed in tight around the fire, all shiny objects secured. The others sleep with their packs held tight, and Malric patrols around the camp, growling and lunging at intruding kalabandars. Jacko does the same, though he settles for chattering at them and keeping close to me.

When it's time to change shifts, both Dain and Alianor go on duty. We do that for the rest of the night, doubling the guard long after the kalabandars lose interest and wander off. When morning comes, we eat and head out.

CHAPTER TWENTY

I t has been an endless day. It doesn't help that I barely slept, plagued by dreams of grootslangs and kalabandars. My spirits have improved, though. I understand that Madlyn's death hit me harder than I thought, bringing memories of Jannah, and that's what made me feel so discouraged yesterday.

It's slow going as we move through the jungle, but we're making progress. We have two more encounters, neither monster-related. One is a wild boar herd that doesn't want to share a watering hole, and the other is a jaguar that stalks us until an arrow sends it fleeing.

We make camp, and our night is uneventful. Everyone's quiet, but it's not a bad kind of quiet. We just don't seem to have much to say, so we save all our energy for what will be another exhausting day of trekking through the jungle. I'm on last shift, and I'm roasting meat on the fire for breakfast when the back of my neck prickles. I tense and rise, looking around.

Malric and Jacko are doing the same, as if they also sense something. I don't see anything in the jungle. It's dawn, and there's a preternatural quiet, as if the nocturnal animals have all gone to bed and the diurnal ones haven't yet risen.

I look up to see a shape moving lazily, like a cloud floating past the sun, and that's what I think it is until I remember that the sun is still hidden behind the mountains to the east. That distant black shape swirls through the clouds, as if flying above them. I squint up.

"The dragon," Dain whispers, and I glance over to see he's awake in his sleeping blankets, both he and Dez looking up, too.

He's right. It is indeed the dragon. Hunting, it seems, moving in slow circles far above us. Then she seems to spot her target to the south, and she unleashes a scream that barely reaches our ears at this distance. She dives, only to pull up short. Then she swoops again and flaps back up, her movements jerky now, agitated.

"Something's bothering her," he says.

"People." The hairs on my neck prickle. "Roivan soldiers. They're moving on the mountains, like King Estienne warned."

He shakes his head. "She's just warning someone off. Could be a trading caravan."

"You're right."

He exhales, as if relieved that I agree. Relieved that we aren't too late, that the attack hasn't begun without us.

"Rhydd and Liliath will slow them down," he says. "They'll talk sense into the prime minster and the minister of defense. They have the king on their side. That must count for something."

"If she is attacking traders, that's a problem," Alianor says from her sleeping blankets.

"I don't think she's attacking anyone," I say. "It's a warning display."

"Yeah, that's not going to matter. I'd like to see you tell a terrified caravan not to worry about a swooping dragon."

She has a point. Not a lot of travelers come that way— one of the royal monster hunter's jobs is to escort semiannual caravans of traders, something that's been put on hold while I train. Still, we can't stop trade for years because a dragon declares that road hers.

"I'll have to think more on that," I say.

"Lots of things to think on," Trysten says with a yawn. "As much as I like the idea of dragons in our lands again, it would be best if she left. However, that can't happen while she has young. How long will it take them to grow up?"

"Years," I say. "And she still has unhatched eggs."

He exhales. "That's going to be a problem."

"We need a long-term solution," Alianor says. "We can't just drive her off now that she's had young. Killing them is out of the question."

"Unless absolutely necessary," I say. "We can never rule it out completely. If she started attacking villages, we'd have little choice. I don't see that happening, though—she has plenty of food. Even in the old accounts, they say dragons only attacked border villages if they were under direct threat."

"Which is exactly what could happen here," Alianor says.

I sigh. "Yes. It could, and I'm trying not to think about that. Step one is to get out of this jungle."

"And step two?" she asks.

We can't just resume our tasks for King Estienne as if we'd never been kidnapped. We need to find Wilmot and Kaylein. But should that be our priority? On Madlyn's deathbed, she swore they were fine, and I believe that. Should we take the time to find them? Or trust that they'll find us, while we focus on the dragon?

I look up at the sky, the dragon now gone but her distant shrieks ringing in my ears.

"I hope she's just scaring off traders," I say, "as upsetting as that will be for them. But I think we need to be sure. Wilmot and Kaylein will find us. We'll leave messages where we can, but we should veer south, getting closer to the dragon's lair."

I look at Dain. "Is that all right with you?"

He nods. "You're right that Wilmot will find us. We need to check on the dragons."

We're now on a southwest path, and as the day goes on, it becomes increasingly clear that it was the right choice. Because it becomes increasingly clear that Momma Dragon is upset about more than a few traders passing through.

Something's happening out there, and she's agitated. She keeps making passes. Keeps making threat displays, swooping at something. She isn't convinced that her babies are in danger yet, but she's on edge and angry, and whoever she's angry with is ignoring her warnings to turn back. We need to get to them before she decides it's time to do more than swoop and scream.

If there's one good outcome of the dragon's anger, it's that every creature in the jungle seems to decide this is a good day to lie low and not bother a group of humans and monsters walking through *their* territory. We see no more than distant movement. Better yet, by late in the day the jungle thins, and we don't need the machete.

"We must be getting close," Alianor says.

"Let's hope so," Trysten says. "Is it possible to die from bug bites?"

"If it is, I'm already gone," I say. "A walking corpse."

"*I* feel like a walking corpse," Trysten says.

Alianor pinches her nose. "You kinda smell like one, too."

"Thanks."

"Hey," I say. "Does anyone remember those baths at Sir Terryn's? Deep tubs of perfumed, steaming hot, *clean* water—"

Dain jostles me, cutting me short. I'm about to keep teasing them when a shadow passes overhead. Everyone freezes and then cranes their necks.

The beast returns, winging above us, shadow lengthening in the late-day sun.

"Nice dragon imitation!" I shout up to Sunniva. "Are you trying to give us all heart failure?"

She flies lower and whinnies, white wings barely moving as she drifts on an air current.

"Right here," I say, pointing ahead on the path. "Land there and you can give me a lift back to civilization." I turn to the others. "Sorry, guys. My princess carriage has arrived. I'm sure you'll all be fine."

Sunniva disappears from view.

"That was a joke," I call up.

She returns and then heads off again, obviously steering us.

"Follow that pegasus," I say, and we all set out at a jog.

CHAPTER TWENTY-ONE

Sunniva leads us to the edge of the jungle. Once the trees are sparse enough for Doscach to pass through, he joins us, too. When we see the long grass of the savanna ahead, I ask Sunniva to land and she does.

"Do you know where Wilmot is?" I ask. "Wilmot? Kaylein?"

She glances to the east and then back at me.

"You can find them?" I ask. "Find Wilmot?"

Another glance in that direction, and I exhale. "Excellent."

I open my pack and take out my spare tunic. Wilmot will need some way to know we're safe. I pull out my sketchbook, too, and I write a quick note telling him that we're out of the jungle, away from our kidnappers and heading toward the road into the mountains to see what's wrong with the dragon.

I tuck the note into the tunic pocket. When I try tying the tunic around Sunniva's neck, she balks, tossing her head and snorting. Then she takes the fabric in her mouth and before I can argue, she's in flight.

"It didn't look good on her," Alianor says. "I'd have to agree. Really not her color."

I roll my eyes, and we set out onto the savanna in search of a road.

It's dusk by the time we find a road. We should probably stop, but being out of that jungle, it feels so much safer that we decide to continue on. There's a low moon, full and heavy, brightening the golden fields so we don't even need torches to see.

Another reason why we keep going? The dragon. Every time we think she's settled for the night, she appears, circling from the mountains. She's still far enough away to be only a small shape against the moonlit night, a reminder of how far we still need to go. Also a reminder that whatever is upsetting her, it's not heeding her warnings.

When we hear someone coming, we slip off into the long grass. Doscach "slips" with us, which means we're hiding alongside a horse monster whose head peeks out over the grass. The passersby don't notice him, and they continue on their way. We just make it back to the road when a rider comes galloping at full speed. Before we can duck out of sight, the oncoming horse sees Doscach and rears, neighing, throwing its rider.

I rush over to the fallen rider. Dain shouts for the horse to stop, but it's already turned and is galloping back the way it came.

"No," the man whispers, watching his horse as we help him up. He's shaking, barely able to catch his breath as his mount disappears down the dark road. "Oh no."

"Are you all right?" I ask.

He pushes me off and clambers to his feet. "You! What do you children think you're doing? Hiding in the grass and scaring . . ." He backs up, hands going to his pockets. "Bandits? Are you bandits? I don't have anything. I was taking a message . . ."

He trails off again. That's when he sees the monsters. Jacko first, and he stares at him in confusion. Then Malric, and that makes him back up so fast he plows right into Doscach, who whinnies and tosses his mane, barnacles clacking. The man yelps and scuttles away.

"Wh-what is that?" he says.

"Ceffyl-dwr," I say. "Aquatic carnivorous equine monster. Don't worry. He won't eat you." I pause. "But if you ever see one in the wild, you should run. They *do* eat people."

At a look from Dain, I clear my throat. "And that is hardly critical at the moment. The ceffyl-dwr is what spooked your horse. I'm sorry about that. We'd stepped off the road to avoid startling a group of traders, and it seems we ended up startling your poor horse."

I reach for Doscach's mane. "If you'll wait with my friends, Doscach and I can retrieve your mount."

The man continues to stare.

"Oh, and we're not bandits," I say. "In case you're still concerned."

"She's the Tamarelian royal monster hunter," Trysten says. "That explains the monster companions. We'll stay with you while she fetches your spooked horse."

"Monster hunter," the man says, the words coming on a breath. His eyes widen. "You're the royal monster hunter."

"Yes, and if you'll allow me to retrieve—"

He lunges to catch my arm, but Malric's snarl warns him back.

"Do not touch the monster hunter," Alianor murmurs. "Rule number one."

"Forget my horse," he says quickly. "There are monsters. Cockatrices. They've laid siege to the farm neighboring ours. I've heard soldiers are on the move from the capital, so I was riding to entreat some to come to our aid, but fortune brought you into my path instead."

"We really don't have time—" Dain begins, but a look from me has him stopping short and grumbling instead.

"We are in a hurry," I say. "How far is this farm?"

"Less than a mile the way I came. You can see the cockatrices from here." He points, and I make out what look like birds circling a distant house.

"And how far to the road into the mountains?" Alianor asks.

"Less than a mile the other way. You are very close, but you should stop for the night. Help my neighbors, and they will give you all you need for your journey after a safe and comfortable night's rest."

I doubt I could have abandoned the farmers to fight the cockatrices alone, but this adds the excuse I need to convince Dain and Alianor. We were stopping to camp soon anyway, and it will be safer to stay in a farmhouse. We could also use supplies, if the farmers can part with them.

"I'll ride out and get an advance look," I say.

"We're right behind you," Alianor says.

CHAPTER TWENTY-TWO

I ride on Doscach, clinging to his mane, with Jacko sitting in front of me and Malric running alongside. At first, I'm not sure whether the warg is up to running—his ribs are still tender—but when I pause to check on him, his snarl tells me to stop fussing. So I do.

I hear the cockatrices before I can clearly make them out. They no longer look like birds—more like large bats—and they're swooping around the farmhouse. Their cries tell me the farmer was correct in identifying them as cockatrices. They have a cry like a rooster, if that rooster was being strangled. It's a gurgling crowing sound that makes my skin crawl.

At first, I think it's only three or four cockatrices. They'll be easy to roust. Then I draw close enough to see more on the roof, where they seem to be battering at a hole.

When Doscach heads closer, one cockatrice swoops toward us, making that terrible crowing sound. Despite the awful noise it makes, it's a very pretty beast. The upper half looks like a rooster, with multicolored feathers that shimmer like jewels in the moonlight. The tail is serpentine, with that same coloration in scales. It has two birdlike legs as well as bat-like wings.

This is one of the creatures that people sometimes mistake for a dragon, and it's believed they may be related. They're smaller than a real dragon's head, and just a little bigger than an actual rooster. That makes them seem relatively harmless . . . unless they're in a flock like this one.

We have cockatrices in Tamarel. I've faced them on training exercises with Jannah. Mostly, they're a nuisance. They eat a diet similar to birds', and they're particularly fond of grain and clever enough to break into silos. I spot a grain silo farther back, yet that isn't what they're targeting at the moment. Why the house? I have a few ideas, but for now, the point is that they are trying to break in, and while they may eat mostly grain and bugs, they can maim people.

The lore says that the gaze of a cockatrice can turn people to stone. That's confusing them with another reptilian monster—the basilisk, which also can't turn anyone to stone either but does spray a paralytic toxin. The confusion comes from the association with eyes. The gaze of a cockatrice can't hurt you, but a cockatrice can hurt *your* gaze.

The cockatrice has a particular defense mechanism that, while horrifying, is actually clever—it goes for the eyes. It uses its long, serpentine tail to grab an attacker around the neck and then plucks at the eyes. When monster hunters are called out to deal with cockatrices, they wear special goggles to avoid this. I have some in my regular kit, but when setting out on this journey, we'd taken the bare minimum. I'll just be sure not to let a cockatrice get its tail around my neck. Malric knows the same. I'll need to keep a watch on Jacko and Doscach. Dain can warn Trysten when they catch up.

The eye-pecking is only used in defense. They don't intentionally seek out people to blind them, though there are some particularly gory bards' tales about exactly that, the sort I'm not supposed to have heard. But the truth is that they're not breaking into this farmer's house looking for tasty eyeballs.

"The first step," I say to my monster companions as we ride up, "is to figure out what the cockatrices want. Preferably before they break through that roof."

I peer down the road. The others will follow soon, and I hope to have answers—and a solution—before then. As for the cockatrices circling the house, they pay me little mind, especially when I turn toward the silo instead.

Knowing how much they like grain, I'm hoping to use a bag to lure them off. As I near the silo, I discover another advantage to this plan: There's someone hiding inside the building. The door keeps opening and then shutting again.

I dismount out of sight of that door. Then I leave Doscach in a harvested field full of corn chaff. The scattered leftover corn has brought mice, and the ceffyl-dwr begins snatching them up and gobbling them down, earning envious looks from both Jacko and Malric.

"You two can stay and hunt," I say. "You're far enough from the cockatrices, and I'll be fine."

Malric plasters himself to my one side, Jacko to the other. I sigh. I'm happy having them along, but it would have been easier to sneak up by myself.

I heft Jacko onto my shoulders, and the three of us make our way around the side of the silo. It's an old building, and the closer I get, the more I despair of finding grain inside. While the farm is surrounded by crops, the condition of the silo suggests it hasn't been used in my lifetime. There's a huge chunk missing from the top, and the roof is half caved in.

Could the farmer be storing grain or corn in his house? Perhaps in a basement? Might that be why the cockatrices want in so badly?

As I near the door, it opens a crack. I wait until it shuts again. There's a latch on the outside, a heavy one, but it's swung open and doesn't engage as the door shuts.

I creep over, grab the latch and yank open the door. A boy about my age flies out with a cry of alarm. I bustle him inside and close the door, leaving Malric outside to guard it.

"Are you alone?" I ask in the common tongue.

He gapes at me. That's when I remember Jacko is riding on my shoulders.

I set Jacko on the ground. There's a lantern on a barrel, and I lift it for a look around. As I guessed, the silo is unused. I see only heaps of straw and a few skittering rats. One fewer rat once Jacko gets in there. He begins tearing into his dinner as the boy watches in horror.

"Is that—is that not a rabbit?" he says.

"Jackalope. Carnivorous rabbit monster." I continue peering around. "Where do you store your grain?"

"Wh-what?"

"Right. Formalities first. I'm Princess Rowan of Tamarel, royal monster hunter. We met your neighbor while he was riding for help. Now, the grain. Cockatrices love grain. You don't store it here. Is it in the house?"

"You're a princess?" he says dubiously as he looks me over.

"Skip that part. Stick to 'monster hunter.' You have monsters. I'm here to hunt them. Do you live here?"

"Y-yes, it's my parents' farm and—"

"Excellent. Sorry. I don't mean to be rude, but I'd like to get on with this. Are there people in the house?"

"My family. They're trapped there, and I'm trapped here, and the monsters are ignoring me, but I don't know how to get rid of them."

"That's my job. Your name?"

"Emayn."

"All right, Emayn, back to the grain. Is it in the house?"

"N-no. We have flour in the house, but our crops are mostly corn."

I peer around the silo. I can see why he kept looking out the door. There's no other way to get a peek outside. While there's a hole in the roof, down here it's a solid stone building with one equally solid door. I open that to check on the cockatrices.

"Do you know why they're trying to get in?" I ask.

"Because they're monsters."

I'm about to deliver a very brief lecture on the nature of monsters when I see his face. It's my first real look at him. He's dark-skinned with dark braids and gray-green eyes. Those eyes have a shuttered look about them. In other words, he knows exactly why they're attacking.

"Was it an egg?" I say. "Or a fledgling?"

His gaze narrows more. "I don't know what you're talking about."

"Someone stole a cockatrice. A young one. Yes, they're very pretty monsters. However, being monsters, they are not pets."

"They aren't for—" Emayn snaps his mouth shut. "I don't know what you're talking about."

"Fine." I reach for the door. "Jacko? Time to go. Emayn here has it under control."

I open the door, and Malric lumbers to his feet.

Emayn starts to step out after me and then sees the warg. "Wh-what is that?"

"Warg."

"Is it tame?"

"A monster is never 'tame,'" I say. "As a companion, it can choose to stay with humans, like any other companion. For example, a cockatrice. It could be a companion, if it so chose, but you can't just steal one from its nest, however pretty it might be."

A groan sounds from the darkness outside, and Alianor appears, shaking her head. "I thought you were getting rid of the cockatrices, and instead we find you giving monster lessons. Typical."

Dain appears behind Alianor, and he looks from me to Emayn. "What's going on?"

"Emayn stole a baby cockatrice, and now his family is trapped in that house, where he's presumably keeping it. The monsters are breaking through the roof. They're almost in."

"What?" Emayn says. "No, the house is solid. They can't get in."

"Mmm, beg to differ," Alianor says. "They've torn something from the roof. They're smart little monsters."

"I didn't steal—"

Just then, a cockatrice hears him. It gives a terrible rasping crow, and three others stop circling, all turning our way as one body.

"Inside!" I say. "Everyone inside!"

We tumble in. When Malric tries to stand guard, I yank him by the scruff of his neck. He snorts in outraged indignation, but I get him inside and then count heads.

"Wait!" I say. "Trysten!"

"He's with Doscach in the field," Alianor says. "We thought that was best. Dain warned him about the eye thing."

One of the cockatrices thumps against the door, as if flying into it. My gaze goes up to that ruined roof. The beasts sound as if they are circling and then flying off. Emayn's voice upset them, but their true target isn't in here. It's in the house.

"Tell us again what you *didn't* do?" I say to Emayn.

"I helped my sister take eggs. She found an aerie in an abandoned barn. The family moved out a few years ago, and no one realized the cockatrices had moved in until Quinta saw them coming and going. We investigated and found a half dozen nests, all with eggs."

"And you saw your ticket to fortune?" Alianor says.

Emayn glares at her. "No, we saw our ticket to *survival*. There's been a drought for years. My sister thought this could be our salvation."

"Cockatrice farming," Dain says.

Wilmot has done something similar with basans, another monster species of poultry. While Wilmot's breeding attempts are half science, they're also a commercial enterprise, unfertilized basan eggs being delicious and valuable.

"How many did you take?" Dain asks.

Emayn's hesitation answers the question.

"Too many," I murmur. "All right, then. We need to get those eggs back to the cockatrices. If we can keep two for your family, we will."

CHAPTER TWENTY-THREE

Step one: Come up with a plan. Emayn's parents, grandmother, little brother and ten-year-old Quinta are in the house. Emayn had been out picking fall berries when the cockatrices laid siege to his home. Whenever he leaves the silo, they dive at him, recognizing him as one of the humans who stole their eggs.

"I'm going to make a run for it," I say. "Emayn? Where are all the doors into the house?"

"You'd better not be planning to go alone, princess," Dain says.

"Of course not. I'll have Malric." I size up the jackalope. "I think Jacko could come safely, though I'd prefer he stayed behind."

"I mean me."

"I'd rather you provided cover with your bow, if that's all right."

"Perfect," Alianor says. "Dain provides cover, and I join Rowan." When I look at her, she says, "Someone inside could be injured and in need of medical attention."

"If anyone goes, it should be me," Emayn says.

Alianor looks him over. "Are you hiding a dagger somewhere?"

"Of course not."

"Then no, you aren't coming. Also, who walks around without a hidden dagger or two?"

"I was picking berries."

Alianor rolls her eyes my way.

"Help us plan a route," I say. "That's where you can be of invaluable assistance."

Alianor, Malric, Jacko and I slip from the silo while Dain shoots two arrows in the other direction, hitting a water tower, the sound attracting the circling cockatrices. That's enough to keep the creatures busy investigating until we're all the way to the house.

There's a cellar door that Emayn said would be unlocked, and we ease in there and shut it behind us. This is where we'll find the eggs. They've been placed in an old hearth set alight with a smoldering heat—low but steady warmth, the eggs wrapped in cloth and held a few inches over the coals.

Emayn thinks his family will be upstairs, and he is correct. I can hear running feet and distant orders as they shore up the roof. No one is down here with the eggs, and I'm grateful for that.

We light fire sticks, leave Malric guarding the hatch, and creep to the eggs.

"Oh!" Alianor says when the light falls on them. "Those are pretty."

"No, you cannot have one."

"I'd settle for a shell," she says. "If one happens to break ... Oh, don't look at me like that. I promise not to encourage accidental breakage."

The eggs are gorgeous, their shells as colorful as the monsters themselves, with rings of golden yellow, rust red and emerald green. I bend to shine my light on one. Then I pick it up and test the weight.

"They're close to hatching," I say.

Wilmot had been unable to bring a basan chick to hatching, and I'd made it a science project to try myself. I'd managed it after many failures, and along the way, I'd learned a few things about hatching eggs. These aren't going to burst open on us at any moment, but they're close enough that I can understand the flock's panic. There are eleven eggs, which would represent this flock's entire generation of cockatrices.

"I'm going to see whether they'll accept nine," I say.

"Give them eight," she says. "Then, if they think you're holding out, produce the last one."

I separate out nine eggs and wrap them in cloth. I'm halfway to the hatch when footsteps sound on the stairs. Alianor tugs me into the shadows.

A light appears. A swaying lantern. I peek out to see a boy, no more than five, dressed in a nightshirt. He's heading for the grate. Checking the eggs as his family deals with the cocka-trices overhead.

Jacko runs out and stops short with a squeak of feigned surprise. The boy pauses, his head tilting. Jacko sits on his haunches and tilts his head, mimicking the boy's gesture. The boy laughs, and Jacko makes as close an approximation to the sound as he can manage. The jackalope dashes off in the other direction. The boy follows, and Jacko leads him into another room.

"Go!" Alianor whispers to me.

She darts ahead and opens the hatch. I hand her one egg to hold back. Then I run outside.

As I duck into the darkness alongside the house, I catch the creak of a door. Dain leans out and madly waves for me to retreat. I do, just as a cockatrice wings over the roof. It doesn't see me as it circles the house, watching for threats.

When it's gone, Dain motions for me to come out quickly. I scamper a half dozen paces. Then I lower the cloth bundle into the wheelbarrow Emayn had told me about.

As I run back, I see Alianor with the hatch opened. She's holding the ninth egg in one hand. When she whips her arm back as if to throw it, I nearly yelp. Then I see it's not the egg—it's a rock. She pitches it into the side of the wheelbar-row, where it makes a loud *crack*. I dive into the hatch just as two cockatrices come to investigate.

One of the cockatrices makes a strangled, gurgling crow and zooms down, the other chiming in. The two start picking over the eggs, prodding and nudging them, checking them while calling to the others. Soon the entire flock is there, and while they still make those strangled sounds, I swear I hear joy in the ugly noise. One picks up an egg in its talons and begins winging away. Another follows.

Then Jacko lets out a cry of his own. It's half alert and half alarm, and I scramble back so fast the hatch shuts with a bang. A woman's voice comes from the other room, warning the boy to stay back, that there's something wrong with the rabbit he found.

I round the corner to see Jacko against a wall. An elderly woman is pushing the boy back and lifting a knife. With a cry, I race forward. I reach to grab the knife, but when I touch her, she screams and the blade clatters to the floor. Then she stares wide-eyed at me before shouting, "Thieves! We are beset by thieves!"

"No," I say quickly as I scoop up Jacko. "We're here to—"

"Thieves! Robbers!" She pulls the boy to her skirts. Then she peers down the hall to the fire grate. "The eggs! You've stolen our eggs!"

A clatter on the stairs drowns out my explanation. A middle-aged man and woman, as well as a girl of about ten, appear; the man is holding a cudgel. That's when Malric shows up. He lunges in front of the trio running down the stairs, and he snarls, his fur on end, making him seem even larger.

The woman screams. The girl says, "Is that a warg?" with more awe than fear. The man lifts his cudgel.

"Don't!" I shout as loudly as I can. "He won't attack unless you hurt us. We didn't steal your eggs. Well, not really."

"That doesn't help, Rowan," Alianor says as she steps from the shadows, dagger in hand.

At the sight of Alianor's dagger, the old woman yelps and draws the little boy in closer even as he squirms to get a better look at Malric. The girl—Quinta, I presume—inches toward the warg as she cranes her neck to look at me.

"Do you see that girl's sword?" she says to her parents. "It's black as ebony."

"Obsidian and ebony," I say. "The hilt is ebony, the blade is edged with obsidian."

Alianor rolls her eyes, but I'm not accidentally lecturing—I'm trying to defuse the tension.

"An ebony sword and a warg and . . ." Her gaze rises to my shoulders. "Is that a jackalope? Wait! The other girl called you Rowan. You're—you're—you're the Tamarel monster hunter. The princess."

Alianor steps forward. "Yes, this is Princess Rowan, daughter of Queen Mariela and royal monster—"

"Yes, yes," I say, waving her off. I turn to the couple. "Your neighbor was riding for help and bumped into us. We met Emayn in the silo, and he explained the situation. The cockatrices want their eggs back. I returned eight of them. We're waiting to see whether they'll accept that and leave."

I brace for them to shout at me for stealing the eggs. But the girl turns to her parents and says, "See? I told you the cockatrices wanted the eggs. Obviously." She looks at me. "I know all about monsters. Well, as much as I can. I said they want the eggs back and we should give them some, but my parents didn't believe me. I also told Emayn that we should only take a few, but he insisted they wouldn't find us." She throws up her hands. "They're monsters, not chickens. Of course they're going to find us if we steal *all* their eggs."

"Your daughter is correct," I say. "Now may we check to see whether the cockatrices are all gone?"

"Can I have your bunny?" the boy pipes up.

His sister sighs. "It's a jackalope, not a rabbit, silly. See the antlers? It's clearly with the princess. You don't ask people for their monsters. Would you like her to ask Mother and Father if she can take you?"

The boy considers. "Would I get to carry a sword and live in a castle?"

His grandmother tousles his hair. "Enough of that. We've all had a good scare, but let's see whether the beasts have fetched their eggs and left."

A crash rocks the house. The grandmother grabs the boy, and I grab Jacko as Malric backs up into me, growling.

Everything has gone still. Then I hear the distant sound of shouting. The house creaks and there's another thump, a loud one from the roof.

"That's not the cockatrices," Quinta says.

Another shout. This one is Emayn. I run to the hatch just as it flies open and Dain leaps in, slamming it behind him.

"There's—" he says before a tremendous thud shakes the house, this one sounding like it's come from just outside the hatch.

I race over and inch it open before he can stop me. At first, all I see is darkness. Then something shiny, right in front of me. A big, shiny black orb that reflects my face, peering through the opening. Two membranes appear, one on each side—nictitating membranes closing and opening in a blink.

An eye. I'm looking into the eye of a giant bird. Another blink and the creature pulls back its head and screams, forked tongue darting out.

Beside me, Quinta whispers a word at the same time I do: "Roc."

CHAPTER TWENTY-FOUR

e slam the hatch shut and latch it as Dain and Alianor drag over a discarded table to brace against it.

"That was a roc, wasn't it?" Quinta whispers.

I nod.

"Have you ever seen one?"

I shake my head. Rocs are one of the rare monsters that a hunter might encounter once in their life . . . and really hope they don't. Jannah never saw one, but our great-uncle did, when he was the royal monster hunter. He died shortly after I was born, but I still remember his stories about the roc.

Rocs are giant birds. Bigger than gryphons and much rarer. Like grootslangs, there's said to be only one or two on our entire continent, and they live so far in the mountains that no one sees them—which is good, just like with the grootslangs.

Someday, I will look back and marvel at all the rare creatures the dragon has brought out of hiding. I will have endless stories to tell about all the monsters I encountered before I was even old enough to *be* the royal monster hunter. Right now, though, I'd like to encounter a lot fewer of them so that I can actually survive to tell those stories.

I look at Dain.

He shakes his head as he jams the table into place. "Never saw one. Neither has Wilmot. I don't know much about them."

"Is Emayn in the silo?" the old woman says.

"I had to make a run for it," Dain says.

"You abandoned my grandson to take shelter with us?"

Dain scowls. "No, I left him in a safe place so I could warn you that there's a giant bird perched on your roof." He shakes his head and turns back to me. "What I do know about rocs—"

"Don't turn away from me, boy," the grandmother snaps. "I was talking to you."

"Yeah? Well, you got into this mess because you stole cockatrice eggs. So I don't care how old you are. I don't have any respect for thieves."

I struggle not to stare at Dain. Alianor is usually the one with a sarcastic comeback. Yet there's a note in Dain's voice that dips past sarcasm into real anger. Maybe because she's rebuking him for shirking his duty when he was doing the right thing?

After a moment of shocked silence, I rally with, "Dain made the correct choice coming to warn us. Now if you have nothing to add, ma'am, please go tend to your cockatrice eggs and let us handle this."

"She's right, Grandma," Quinta says. "We took the eggs. That brought the cockatrices, which brought the roc. The princess and her friends are trying to help, and they don't need to. This has nothing to do with them."

"Agreed," her mother says. "Quinta? Stay and help them. Mother? Please take Grigge into the coal room. That's the safest place for him." She turns to me. "I'll be upstairs watching for trouble. If you need anything, send Quinta to fetch it."

"Thank you," I say.

The old woman still huffs as she shoos the little boy off, but the father murmurs, "What can I bring you?"

"Nothing right now. Maybe find things we can use to reinforce the entry points. I need to figure out what the roc wants."

"To eat us, yes?" the man says. "It's hungry, and the cockatrices brought it to our house."

"No, Papa," Quinta says. "A monster isn't going to break into the house for a meal. That'd be too much trouble."

"It's not trying to break in," I say. "I don't know what it wants, but Quinta is right—the answer isn't 'dinner.'"

"I don't suppose you have a roc egg hidden somewhere," Alianor says.

Quinta smiles. "I'd never be *that* foolish."

Her father murmurs that he'll be upstairs and then leaves.

"Is there a place I can peek out?" I ask.

Quinta shows me to a narrow window. It's covered in dust, and I clear it and squint to see the bird monster. Earlier, the beast had seemed all dark colors, but in the moonlight, I see it has the coloring of an eagle, with varying shades of brown. Without the black eyes and the head crest, it could be mistaken for a giant eagle. A *very* giant eagle. I'm surprised the house didn't collapse under it. While it's not quite as big as I feared, it's at least the size of the dragon.

The roc is pacing around the yard, poking at this and that. When it reaches the wheelbarrow, it lowers its giant head to sniff, accidentally topples it, and leaps back with a deafening squawk.

The roc eyes the wheelbarrow with grave suspicion, as if the thing had attacked it. It pecks at it once, backs away quickly at the hollow clang of metal, and then pecks again. This time, the clang doesn't make it jump. It lifts one handle in its beak. When the wheel rolls, the roc gives a start and drops it. More scrutiny and pokes, and then it lifts the wheelbarrow by the handle and pushes it back and forth on the wheel, giving a very different squawk—one of almost childish delight.

"Is it *playing?*" Quinta asks.

"I think it's a juvenile," I say. "The pictures I've seen show a white head and a dark-brown body, and that one is all mottled brown. While that could make it a female, there's not supposed to be sexual dimorphism in rocs."

"Di . . ." Quinta looks at me. Then she grins. "*Di* means 'two.' *Morph* means 'shape.' Sexual dimorphism means the sexes are different. Like sheep, where only the males have horns."

"Right, and sexual dimorphism is much rarer in monsters."

Alianor groans. "Please don't encourage her, kid."

"She's fine," Dain says. "Also, I think Rowan's right. That's a juvenile." He eyes the beast. "As terrifying as that is to think. How much bigger is an adult?"

"In raptors, a juvenile that has left the nest is nearly as big as an adult," I say.

Quinta peers out. "Could the parents be close by?"

"I don't think so. If they're like dragons or grootslangs, which I presume they would be, they'd have an extended juvenile period of semi-independence."

I watch the roc, which has abandoned the wheelbarrow and is now poking at the well, trying to get its giant head inside and then jumping back when its beak hits the bucket.

"It's curious," I say. "I think that's the answer to why it's here."

"It heard the cockatrices," Quinta says. "And wondered what was going on. Like me hearing others playing a game."

"Yep. The cockatrices are gone, so it's not sure what brought them here, and it's trying to figure it out."

I push back from the window. "I'm going outside to talk to it."

When Dain jumps, I say, "Kidding. Well, mostly. I think I should go to the silo, in case it gets curious about that. Emayn is there alone, without a weapon." I raise a hand. "Which is not to say you shouldn't have left him there."

"I know. I did tell him to hide, but I agree. This roc is too curious for its own good. Kind of reminds me of a certain princess. Let's get out there."

This time, we do leave Jacko behind. He isn't thrilled about it, but after a good look at the roc, he decides maybe I'm right, which shows that both of us are growing up. Dain, Malric and I will go, while Alianor and Quinta will stand watch at the hatch. If the roc causes trouble, they're ready with potatoes to throw as a diversion.

"Okay," Dain says as we creep out the hatch and close it behind us. "It's still busy figuring out the well. If we sneak across the lawn—"

"Hello, young roc!" I say as I step out.

Both Malric and Dain let out exasperated growls behind me.

"It was going to notice us," I whisper. "Better that we don't startle it."

The roc peers over at me. I wave a hand above my head, my sword held in the other.

"Hello, young roc," I repeat. "You're trying to figure out why the cockatrices were so interested in the house. It's this." I lift the egg I took from Alianor. Then I bend and roll it toward the roc as carefully as I can. The beast tilts its massive head, black eyes fixed on me. It inhales through its nose holes.

"Yes, I am the girl you saw in the hatch," I say. "Don't worry, I'm not a threat."

I swear Dain chuckles at that. He has a point. I very highly doubt the massive bird monster has, for one heartbeat, wondered whether this puny human is a threat.

The beast makes its way over, and I brace myself, but its gaze is fixed on the egg I offered. It lowers its beak to it and inhales loudly. Then it gives it the tiniest nudge. I tense, certain the egg will break, but it only rolls a bit. The roc considers. It looks from me to the egg.

"That's what the cockatrices wanted," I say. "And they got it. They're gone now." I wave my arms. "No one left but squeaky humans."

It tilts its head one way and then the other. Then it clacks its beak, as if thinking harder.

"There's nothing for you here," I say. "You should go back into the mountains."

A distant scream sounds. The cry of the dragon. The roc's head jerks that way.

"Ah, that's what *really* caught your attention, isn't it?"

The roc looks back at me, as if listening to my voice. As the dragon circles, I catch another sound. A more distant one. Horse hooves beating a staccato rhythm on the road. Multiple horses, if I'm hearing right.

Could it be Wilmot? Sunniva got to him, and he rented horses to get to us faster?

I glance at Dain. "Do you hear that?"

He nods, but his attention is fixed on the roc. He's studying the beast as carefully as it's studying us.

"Well," I say. "I wish I could actually talk to you, young roc, and I'd tell you to stay far from the dragon, but I get the feeling that you can take care of yourself. You're no threat to her, though she might not see it that way."

It clacks its beak.

"Are you mimicking me?" I say with a soft laugh. I glance at Dain. "While it looks like a giant eagle, it behaves more like a corvid—a crow or a raven. It seems mostly curious. Though I wouldn't want to be around when it's hungry."

I look at Malric. The warg has been so quiet I've nearly forgotten he's here. He's just sitting and watching the roc with calm interest.

"Malric isn't concerned," I say. "I take that as a good sign. He doesn't sense threat."

"So how do we convince it to move on?" Dain says.

"I'm not sure we do. I think it needs to decide that for itself. Finish checking out what it wants to check out, and then it'll leave, like a raven. Just don't feed it or give it any reason to stick around. And make sure everyone stays safely inside until it decides to—"

The roc flaps its wings and screams an eagle's cry, loud enough for me to cover my ears.

"What is that?" a woman's voice calls.

"Not a cockatrice," a man replies.

I curse under my breath, making Dain raise his brows.

"The *worst* of timing," I say. "Can you go tell whoever it is that we're fine? It's just a roc."

Dain snorts. "I'm not sure 'just' and 'roc' ever go in the same sentence, princess." He waves for Malric to stay with me, to which the warg gives him a look, as if there is no other option. Then he heads out at a slow run. The roc rustles its wings, as if considering flying after him.

"Uh-uh," I say. "This isn't a game of chase." I step out farther and Malric joins me, and that pulls the roc's attention away from Dain. It looks at Malric as if it hadn't seen the warg until now, Malric's black coat helping him disappear into the shadows.

From out front, I hear, "You there, boy! Get behind us. There is some dangerous creature about."

I roll my eyes. While I'm tempted to go handle the newcomers myself, I don't want the roc following. This is also good experience for Dain. I'm usually the one who does the talking.

"Out of our way, boy!" the woman says.

The thunder of galloping hooves drowns out Dain's shout. The roc shrieks, wings flapping out. I run into the path of a horse charging around the house.

"Stop!" I say, lifting my sword.

The horse is a gray charger in full leather armor, the rider wearing the same. The roc shrieks again and I turn to it, waving my free hand as I lower the sword.

"Enough of that," I say. "You're fine."

The horse snorts, and the woman on it snaps something at me. I ignore her as I watch the roc. It might be young, and it might not have done anything threatening, but one clack of its giant beak could snap that horse in half, armor and all.

Malric steps between me and the roc. He doesn't growl or snarl, though. He just stands there, looking up at it. That gets the roc's attention, its curiosity roused again. It lowers its huge head to sniff Malric. The warg sniffs back, and the roc seems satisfied that it's a friendly encounter. It lifts its head to snap its beak at the snorting horse before returning its attention to Malric.

"I think it's telling your horse to mind its manners and play nice," I say to the rider.

"Princess Rowan, I presume."

The woman opens her helmet visor. It's only then that I realize she isn't alone. There are at least a dozen horses behind her, each with a fully armored rider. Dain stalks out from the front of the house, scowling.

"I tried to tell them," he says. "No one was listening to me."

A man says, "Perhaps you should have specified, boy, that by 'roc' you meant a giant bird and not a giant boulder."

The woman gives a humorless laugh. "No, Watkin, somehow I don't think that would have made us put down our weapons faster." She hefts her sword as she eyes the roc, now nudging at Malric.

"I take it that is Princess Jannah's warg," she says. "I've forgotten his name."

"Malric."

She nods. "He makes a much better monster babysitter than I would have imagined."

"He had practice with a young gryphon we raised."

"I see. You'll notice, princess, that I am speaking very calmly, as if there is not a bird the size of a house fifty feet away."

"You're doing very well."

Her laugh is genuine. "I take that as a compliment. I presume there's no danger from this bird?"

"It's a roc. Very rare. It's young and curious. I think the dragon drew it out. It came to see what she is, and then got sidetracked by the cockatrices." I glance at the woman. "The neighbor said there were soldiers on the road. I'm guessing that was you?"

She nods. "High General Corisande at your service, princess."

High General. I don't know military systems well—Tamarel doesn't really have one—but that sounds like a lofty position. Maybe even the leader of the army. General Corisande is Roivan—I can tell by her accent. These are soldiers being sent to the dragon, and this is one of their top-ranking leaders. In other words, she's just the person I need to speak to.

I incline my head. "I am pleased to meet you, General Corisande. I was just suggesting to my fellow hunter here,

Dain, that we leave the roc to get bored on its own. I don't see that happening with so many people here. Perhaps we can wear out its curiosity instead."

"I am at your command, my lady."

CHAPTER TWENTY-FIVE

The plan goes better than I could have hoped. We let the roc meet the soldiers and the horses—and thankfully it doesn't mistake them for dinner. Doscach and Trysten come out from the field, and the roc is fascinated by the ceffyl-dwr and the differences between him and the horses. Soon, though, it begins to tire. At my suggestion, we head down the road as a group so it doesn't fly off and come back to the farm tomorrow expecting to find its playmates. We want it to think we left.

It follows us for a bit, and then the dragon's screams catch its attention, and the next thing we know, the roc is sleepily winging in that direction.

"Perhaps the roc will give the dragon a scare," Alianor says as we watch it go. "Make her decide this isn't a good place to raise babies."

I shake my head. "It's too late for that. They aren't big enough to take across the ocean yet."

General Corisande clears her throat. "So it's true then. She's hatched young."

I turn to face her. I'm riding Doscach, so we're on eye level, and she stops her charger to look at me.

"I'd like to speak to you," I say. "I can tell you everything you need to know about the dragon, but I'd also ask you to listen to me, too. You are responsible for your people and their safety. I understand that. My job is different, but my people are my priority, over any monster. May we speak?"

"I would like that."

"I think you did it," Alianor whispers as we curl up under our sleeping blankets.

We're in the silo. General Corisande thought that was the best place for us, so we can come out quickly if the roc or the cockatrices return. Quinta and her mother made sure we had sleeping blankets, pillows and a mini-feast to dine on. I'll admit it's probably more comfortable than the basement . . . or the outdoors, where General Corisande and her soldiers have set up camp.

Malric is backed against me, and we're keeping each other warm. Jacko is snuggled in under my blankets. I'm lying here, replaying my conversation with the general and trying to gauge the sincerity of her reaction. She'd paid attention, and she'd treated me like a fellow soldier, which had been a new experience. A glimpse at how it might be someday, when people can no longer see me as a child.

General Corisande had listened intently. She'd asked questions. She'd admitted that she doesn't know much about dragons. I'd admitted that no one does—no one has seen one in over a century. I can only speak to the experience I've had, combined with the journals of my ancestors who did deal with them.

In the end, she didn't agree to leave the dragons alone. I didn't expect that. She did, however, agree that Roiva might be moving too quickly—that if there was a solution other than "kill the dragons," we should consider it.

More talking will be needed. Much more. But I feel as if I made headway here. As if my years of monarch training have paid off, as has my experience in the past year.

If this had happened last fall, I would indeed have been a child, blinded by the wonder of dragons—real dragons!— returned to Tamarel, bubbling with enthusiasm and plowing through the general's concerns.

I'm pleased with how I handled it, silently proud of myself. When Alianor says, "I think you did it," I should preen with satisfaction. Instead, I'm quiet, appreciating her support but feeling something else poking at me.

When I glance over at Trysten, awake and listening, it is as if I see my own concerns reflected back in his expression.

"What do you think?" I ask.

"I agree that you did exceedingly well," he says, choosing each word with care.

"But you think we still have a long way to go. That I didn't change her mind. I just opened the door to other possibilities."

He exhales, as if relieved he doesn't need to be the one to dampen the moment. "Yes. It's too big an issue to be resolved in a single conversation, and she isn't the prime minister or the minister of defense. She can't recall the troops. However, she *is* the head of the Roivan army, and that means something. She listened to you, *and* she heard you."

"Which isn't always the same thing."

He smiles, and we exchange a look. This is what we have in common. I might not be a politician, but I have the training, as does he.

"It's a good start," Alianor says. "That's the important thing. She's willing to consider other options. She's escorting us to the front line tomorrow. You won't need to fight to get a chance to speak. That's huge."

"It is," I agree. "And with any luck, Sunniva will catch up with Wilmot. Having him there will help."

"It's all good," Alianor says. "We'll fix this."

"I hope so," I murmur, and then we all curl up in our blankets to enjoy our first solid sleep in days.

I wake first. Malric's nudging me and growling under his breath. When his gaze shoots to the door, I chuckle.

"That's the one disadvantage to sleeping indoors," I say. "You can't just wander off to do your business. You need someone with opposable thumbs to open the door. You could ask Dez, you know."

I crawl from my blankets, unseating Jacko, who makes a soft noise of alarm as he startles awake.

I go to unlatch the door. When the heavy metal doesn't budge, I try again, and Malric growls.

"Either it's stuck or they locked us in for the night," I say. "Really hoping it's not the latter. I thought I was past being treated like a child."

I try the door one more time. Then I rap. I'm halfway through a second knock when General Corisande speaks, just outside the door.

"Good morning, princess," she says.

"Good morning," I say. "I can't seem to get this door open, and Malric needs to do his business."

"You'll have to make a spot for him inside, I'm afraid. You're going to be in there a while."

"What?" Dain says behind me. I glance over to see him sitting upright, Dez blinking sleepily.

"I hope that's a joke, General Corisande," I say.

"No joke, Princess Rowan. I planned to leave at dawn, but you've proven you deserve an explanation from me directly."

"You weren't listening to Rowan last night, were you?" Dain says as he walks to join me at the door. "You only pretended to listen."

Something inside me sinks, shame rushing in to fill the void. He's right, and that is humiliating beyond belief. I'd fallen for her trick, been so eager to be taken seriously that I never paused to question whether I was just being told what I wanted to hear.

"You let me talk," I say. "You encouraged me to share my knowledge of dragons. You said you wanted my point of view. You didn't. You just wanted me to relax my guard and agree to sleep in here, where you could lock us in."

"You spoke well, Rowan. You gave an impassioned yet reasoned defense, one I wouldn't have expected from someone so young. But you *are* young, and I do not expect you to understand the reality of what we face here. You obviously love monsters. You surround yourself with them. You have an affinity for them—we saw that last night with the roc. The famous Clan Dacre blood at work. It was remarkable."

"Don't flatter me," I snap. "I'm not a child."

"Ah, but you are, and there's nothing wrong with that. When you're older, you'll understand my position. These dragons are a threat to national security, and as head of the Roivan army, it's my job to get rid of them."

"By kidnapping a Tamarelian princess?"

"Your royal family is interfering with Roivan security, and you are on our soil. Queen Mariela will be angry, but politically she cannot argue. You will be treated well and escorted home after the dragon and her young have been dealt with."

"Those dragons are on Tamarelian soil. We are their stewards."

"Your queen has no villages in that part of the forest. Your family long ago abandoned the region to monsters. That forces Roiva to handle the problem of the dragons."

"King Estienne is allowing that?"

"King Estienne is a boy, hardly older than you. He's under house arrest with Prince Rhydd and the rest of your party."

"What?" I rock forward, grabbing the door handle as if I can wrench it open. "You kidnapped my brother?"

"You kidnapped your own king?" Dain sputters.

Trysten appears beside us. "You've taken two members of foreign royalty hostage. Do you understand what that means?"

"They were on our soil. Interfering with our security."

"And your *king*?" I say. "That's treason."

"We disagree," she says. "Like your mother, King Estienne will be angry, but he'll come around."

"And if he doesn't?" Alianor says behind us. "Whoops? Another tragic accident like his father's?"

General Corisande's voice hardens. "*That* would be treason, girl. Be careful what you accuse us of, lest we take it personally. If King Estienne expects to retain his title and his privileges, he'll have to give something up."

"*All* of his power, right?" I say. "Strip him down to nothing but a title?"

"If necessary. Now, I wanted to pay you the honor of a personal explanation, Princess Rowan, but I will not argue politics with you. We will deal with these dragons and someday, you will understand our choice."

"I *do* understand your choice," I say. "I understand why you feel threatened, and I agree that we do not know what danger the dragons may pose. We may very well need to eliminate them, but I'm asking you to wait. To listen. To consider other options."

Silence answers. I pause, presuming she's thinking it through. Then I say, "General?"

"She's gone, child," a voice says through the door.

"I need to speak to her. I need to—"

"No, princess," the man says, not unkindly. "The general has spoken. You'll be treated well, but she is done talking to you. She's already saddling up to ride for the front line."

I slam one fist against the door, making everyone jump. Then I back away and slump to the floor in despair.

CHAPTER TWENTY-SIX

The others immediately start trying to find a way out. There's a moment when I can't join them, when I can only think of Rhydd and worry about Rhydd. But worrying won't help him, and I'm not going to sit wallowing in self-pity while he's held captive in a foreign palace. I'm just angry and frustrated by all this. Angry with myself, too. I've been treated like a child on this journey, and the moment someone treated me like the actual royal monster hunter, I was so happy that I forgot to be wary.

"Even I believed her," Alianor says as we search for an exit.

"We all did," Trysten says. "She played her role perfectly. She heard you out, but made no promises."

"Just reached out a helping hand that I happily grabbed," I mutter.

"Her problem," Dain says. "Not yours."

"I can't believe she took Rhydd—" I cut myself short and shake my head. "He'll be fine. He's a prince, and they won't hurt him. He won't give them any reason to." I lower my voice. "I'm guessing there are guards right outside the door?"

"Presumably," Trysten whispers back.

I wave him closer. Dain tenses at that, but I say to Trysten, "Can you and Alianor talk near the door? Drown me out?"

He nods and motions for Alianor to join him. They begin griping. *Kidnapped again. Can you believe it? Grumble, grumble.*

"Do you see a way out?" I whisper to Dain.

He squints up at the broken roof. There seems to be a loft up there—a wooden platform below the hole. If we could get to it, we could climb out of the hole. He runs his hands along the smooth wall and puts one foot against it experimentally, only to shake his head. That hole is the obvious answer for an escape, but it's thirty feet overhead, with no way up.

"Ask Alianor," he says. "And Trysten."

I do, each of them switching spots with Dain, while the remaining two talk at the door. No one has an answer. It's a solid concrete floor, so we can't dig out. A thick door, so we can't hack our way out with our weapons, and even if we could, we'd then need to fight whatever soldiers General Corisande left behind to guard us. I keep looking at the roof, but there's no way up.

I sit and ponder the problem. I'm torn between focusing on the roof as the obvious escape point and worrying that I'm fixating on it to the exclusion of other options. When I look over, Dain has a length of rope from his pack. He's unspooling it slowly, as if measuring the length.

"That would work," Trysten says. "We just need to get it up there."

Dain fingers his bow and squints up.

"Maybe?" Alianor says. "But you need to get it up there *and* secure it."

As Dain moves, Dez lifts her head from the sleeping blankets and yawns.

"What about Dez?" I say.

I take a piece of dried meat from my bag, and we encourage Dez to climb the wall for it. She finds toeholds too small for us and gets up about ten feet before climbing down to eat her reward and snuggle with Dain.

"Okay," I say. "Step one is to give her a reason to climb up to the loft. Step two is figuring out how she can secure a line."

"Maybe if we had a longer rope?" Trysten says. "It'd be easier to get her to loop it over something."

"We could *make* a longer rope," Alianor says, looking around.

At a noise overhead, we all go still. We look up, but there's nothing to see.

"Birds?" Trysten says.

"Hopefully not the cockatrices," Alianor mutters.

Another sound, like a creature moving around on the loft platform. Then something appears over the side. It dangles and then starts lowering.

A rope. Someone is lowering a rope.

Quinta's face appears over the edge as she puts a finger to her lips. Then she motions for us to wait.

"Is there enough food here for lunch?" Alianor says loudly, for the guards' sake. "Should we be rationing?"

"I think they'll give us more," Trysten says. "The general promised we'd be looked after."

Alianor bangs on the door to ask about the terribly critical food situation, covering up any noise made by Quinta. She proceeds to demand detailed answers about the food, including the fact that our carnivore monster companions need fresh meat and, oh, has anyone checked on Doscach? I'd sent him off for the night, but when he comes back, he'll be hungry, and we don't want him nibbling on the guards.

While Alianor is doing that, Quinta finishes lowering and securing the rope. Trysten whispers, "You should go first, Rowan. You're the smallest."

I'm about to protest when I look around and realize, sadly, I am indeed the smallest. With the weight of my sword, I'm probably not the lightest, but what Trysten doesn't realize is that the first one out also takes the biggest risk. That means it should be me.

I secure my sword. Then I put Jacko on the rope to see whether he can climb it. He can. I wait for him to get as high as he'll go before pausing to look back for me. Then I follow.

My experience in the tunnel helps here. I know to brace my feet against the wall to take some of the pressure off my upper body as I climb. I've gone only a few feet off the ground before Malric growls. I glance down, thinking he's not happy with my leaving, but he's staring at the door. Alianor is still arguing with the guard—something about needing fresh milk, and this is a farm, isn't it, so why can't she get milk?

Outside the door, there's a sudden commotion, and then

a guard barks, "Stop right there. What are you doing with that horse monster?"

"It's a ceffyl-dwr," says a familiar voice. Kaylein. "He's the Tamarelian royal monster hunter's companion, and he led us here."

I wince. We'd been hoping Wilmot and Kaylein would show up, and now they do at the worst possible moment. I send up a hope that the guards will shoo them off and they'll retreat.

"Take the monster and go," the guard says, as if receiving my whispered hope.

"We're looking for the royal monster—" Kaylein begins.

"Take the beast and leave."

"As soon as you open that door behind you."

"This is private property. We're asking you to leave."

"Are you the owner?" That's Wilmot now, and I wince harder as he continues. "We want to speak to the owner. We had a report that this house was besieged by a flock of cockatrices, and Princess Rowan and her companions came to the rescue. If the homeowners tell us otherwise, we'll go."

"You'll go when we tell you to go."

I'm so intent on listening that I don't move until Dain smacks my butt with his bow. Outside, Kaylein and Wilmot keep arguing. It's a distraction, which is good, except that they don't know we're in the midst of an escape. If they manage to convince the guards to open that door, our plan is ruined.

Alianor is madly gesturing, and it takes a moment for me to notice. She motions for me to get out onto the roof and climb down so I can find a way to subtly warn Wilmot.

I climb faster. When I reach the top, Quinta wordlessly nods to a door we hadn't been able to spot above the loft. I peer out to see metal rungs embedded in the exterior stone of the building: a ladder for climbing up to the loft.

I settle Jacko on my shoulders and begin the descent. I'm a third of the way down when Doscach gives a joyful neigh. I freeze, clinging to the ladder as he gallops around behind the silo. I frantically motion for silence. He doesn't understand. I climb down as fast as I can, but I'm only halfway when one of the guards says, "Where did that monster go?"

Wilmot tries to distract the man, as if he's realized what's happening. But Wilmot's skill is hunting, not deception, and Kaylein is no better. They come up with excuses while I gesture for Dain—now looking out the loft door—to hurry down. I reach the bottom just as a second whinny comes, this one from the air.

Sunniva circles overhead, whinnying as if to say, "I found her!" My wild waves for silence go unnoticed.

"Is that a pegasus?" someone says.

Just then, Sunniva spots me on the ground. She flutters down, completely ignoring my go-away gestures. Dain reaches the bottom now, as one of the guards says, "Isn't there a ladder back there?"

I think fast and wheel on Dain. "Ride Doscach."

"What?"

I tap the ceffyl-dwr's shoulder, a request for him to bow so I can climb on. When I gesture that it'll be Dain instead, Doscach doesn't even blink. I help Dain on. Then I turn to Sunniva. I inhale, suddenly unsure of how to do this, whether it's fair to do it, whether I'm imposing. Before I can ask, she bends her knees, wings fluttering.

"Thank you," I whisper as I ease onto her back. "I'll keep this as short as I can."

Two of the guards appear around the silo. They're walking in no hurry, just curious, their gazes turned skyward, looking for the pegasus.

"Go!" I shout, and Doscach charges straight for them, Dain hanging on for dear life.

Sunniva runs, too, and that's all I want from her. Run and startle the guards. But it's not a run—it's a takeoff, and before I know it, we're in the air.

Doscach plows down one of the guards. I shout for Dain, telling him to attack, as if he's in control of the ceffyl-dwr. Really, I just want him to fake it, to shout and yell and make the guards think Doscach is doing his bidding.

He's too shocked to hear me at first. He isn't an experienced rider, not having grown up in a castle with daily riding lessons. But after a moment, he catches on and death-grips Doscach's mane as he shouts for attack. Then something moves on his shoulders. It's Dez, who must have been in her pouch when he climbed. She's on his shoulders now and screeching. Jacko hears that and joins in from his spot in front of me. Sunniva flies above the guards, and I'm not sure whether her swoops are intentional or she's having trouble holding me aloft, but then we level out and she executes a dive that sends a guard running for the house.

By then, Kaylein is facing off with another guard. Malric comes running—Wilmot must have opened the silo in the chaos. Trysten and Alianor follow, Alianor whooping and waving her dagger over her head as if it's a long sword.

It seems like, including Kaylein's and mine, five guards remain. More than I expected, and these aren't villagers who've barely wielded a cudgel. They're the general's handpicked soldiers. The attack of the horse monsters startled them, but they're getting their bearings.

Doscach is driving one guard away from the silo. Dain and the ceffyl-dwr have that under control. Even with her sword, the soldier is having trouble figuring out how to fight a twelve-hundred-pound stallion. Doscach keeps running and dodging, never close enough for her to get a swing at him.

Sunniva and I manage to scare our guard into the house, but the others have more sense, and they realize my pegasus isn't very big. When one takes out a bow, I urge Sunniva to flee, and she does. I get her into the field, where I dismount and send her off.

I race back into the fray. Kaylein and Trysten are taking on one of the guards. Malric has another, and that's where I head. Before I even get there, he has the young man on the ground, his jaws around the soldier's throat.

I spin. Kaylein and Trysten have their guard under control. Same with Doscach and Dain. That leaves one. Or so I think, until I realize the guard who fled has returned. Wilmot's facing off with him. So where's—

"Rowan!"

It's Alianor. I run around the silo to see a guard has her pinned to the wall, his sword at her throat. Alianor is a good fighter but no match for a soldier. At a noise, I look to see Quinta scrabbling down the ladder.

I lift my hand, telling the young girl to stay back.

"What are you doing?" I say to the guard. My voice is low, the words slow. "You have a sword to the throat of a thirteen-year-old subject of Tamarel. A member of a diplomatic mission."

"My orders—"

"Your orders were to guard us. General Corisande promised we would not be harmed."

"You escaped."

"So that gives you the right to put a sword to her throat? If you were held captive by us in Tamarel, would you accept your fate? Expect to be murdered if you tried to escape?"

I'm hoping to shame him, to see him flush and pull back as he realizes what he's doing. But his jaw only tightens, and I realize he isn't hearing me. Not really.

"Remove the sword from her throat," I say. "We can discuss this once you've done that."

"I am a soldier of Roiva," he says. "I don't take orders from Tamarelian children." He presses the tip into her neck, blood welling. "If you want your friend here to live, I'd suggest you gather your other friends and get back into that silo."

My fingers tighten on my sword. I'm measuring the distance between us. When I ease forward, he presses the tip harder, making Alianor give a small whimper.

"All right," I say. "I will retreat to the silo—"

"Everyone. All of you."

The soldier has his gaze fixed on Alianor. He hasn't noticed Quinta. I meet the girl's eyes and jerk my head, silently telling her to warn the others. What I need here is Dain or Wilmot—our archers.

I can't convey that to Quinta. I just have to trust that the others will see a way to resolve this without us all getting back into that silo. I just need—

The soldier bellows in surprise and pain, falling back, Jacko attached to . . . Well, attached to his buttocks. The jackalope must have snuck over while everyone's gaze was on Alianor.

Alianor doesn't miss a beat. She dodges out of the way, dagger slashing. The soldier recovers and grabs for her. I'm already charging as he raises his sword. Then a roar cuts through the morning air. A bellow of rage. A brown form flies around the farmhouse, running straight at us, a streak of tawny fur. The soldier turns and gapes for two heartbeats before the beast is on him.

The creature knocks him down and pins him before I can see what it is. A lion with tusks and a flat face. A nian. Not just any nian, but the one we left recuperating with Sir Terryn.

The beast pins the man and roars again, the pitch making my head pound. I run forward and disarm him. The nian seems to ignore me, but once I have my own sword to the soldier's throat, she steps off him and bounds to Alianor, nearly knocking her down in enthusiastic greeting.

Footsteps thud and Trysten appears, only to be yanked back behind the silo, presumably by Dain.

"It's all right," I call. "We have it under control."

Dain and Trysten come out. Trysten turns and shouts, "Alianor is fine!" and they come over to help with the guard.

"What about the other four?" I ask.

"They surrendered. Wilmot's herding them into the silo."

I prod the soldier on the ground. "On your feet. You're about to learn what it feels like to be taken captive."

CHAPTER TWENTY-SEVEN

As satisfying as it is to put our former guards into our former prison, they won't stay there for long. Quinta's family will release them, and we can't ask them to do anything different.

We don't speak to her family. They've remained in the house, and while Alianor and Dain both fume at that, I understand the difficult position they were in. Yes, as Dain says, we saved them from cockatrices and a roc while—as Alianor points out—helping them keep a few eggs. This is their country, though, and the guards were acting on General Corisande's orders.

According to Quinta, General Corisande told her parents to stay inside and cook food for us, which the guards would deliver. Otherwise, they were forbidden from interfering in this matter of "national security."

"Do they know you snuck out?" I ask Quinta as we talk away from the others.

She shakes her head.

"Are you going to be in trouble?"

She shrugs. "The guards didn't see me, so there's no way for them to prove I helped. I was careful about that." She bends to give Jacko a scratch behind his antlers. Then she rises and straightens. "I would like to be a monster hunter. In Tamarel. My parents say it's impossible—that hunters must be from Tamarel—but I would like to apply anyway."

I glance at Wilmot, who's making his way to us and who has overheard. He says nothing, just comes to stand with me.

"Tamarel is a long way away," I say. "You can't easily travel back and forth."

"I know."

I glance at Wilmot. He isn't jumping in to help, but he's not jumping in to say no either. I realize why. Because I'm the royal monster hunter. This is my decision.

"How old are you?" I ask.

"Almost eleven."

"Our monster hunters are usually a little older when they start. Dain and I are exceptions. But twelve would be old enough. If your parents agreed and if you still wanted to, you could come and try it for a summer."

"Do you have a sword?" a voice calls.

We turn as Kaylein strides over.

Quinta shakes her head. "I have a bow, and I use that."

"I will ask my cousin to make you a sword. He made one for me when I was younger than you, so that I might practice to be a guard. He is the best blacksmith in Tamarel, when he is not guarding the queen herself."

Quinta's eyes round. "Berinon of Clan Montag."

Kaylein smiles. "We will have him make you a sword, in thanks for your help here."

I nod. "It will be delivered along with an official invitation to come to Tamarel when you are twelve."

"Thank you," she says, her face glowing. "I'll be waiting."

"I have a monster pet!" Alianor crows as we make our way toward the main road. She catches my expression and pats the head of the nian, which is following along at her side. "A pet. A monster pet."

"Monster comp—"

"Pet," she says. "An adorable and deadly monster, who shall do my bidding and slay my enemies." She fakes a tearful sniff. "I never thought this day would come. A monster of my own."

She takes a deep breath and raises her voice, as if giving a speech. "First, I'd like to thank Princess Rowan, for letting me kidnap her and starting me on this journey into her monster world. And then to Dain, who showed me that even the crankiest of hunters can win the heart of a monster. Also to my parents, for—"

"Huh," Dain says. "Your nian keeps looking out at the savanna. I think she's wondering whether she's made a terrible mistake."

Alianor rolls her eyes. "You're just jealous because I get a deadly beast, and you have a baby dropbear. My pet could eat your pet for breakfast."

"Like to see her try."

I lift my hands. "Yes, it seems you have a monster companion, Alianor, for as long as she cares to be with you. I'm thrilled on your behalf. However?"

I point to the sky. A few moments ago, the dragon passed close enough for us to see her.

"We need to talk about that," I say.

"We do," Wilmot agrees, and we begin.

My gut instinct is to skip the dragon situation for now and get to the Roivan capital, where my brother is a prisoner in an attempted coup. The general might have said they still hope to work with King Estienne, but anyone with royal blood recognizes a coup when they see it.

King Estienne disagrees with the prime minister's plan for the dragons, and instead of debating it, the prime minster put him under "house arrest." That's a nice way of saying he's a prisoner.

I haven't forgotten Alianor's jab about whether the king will suffer an accident like his father did. In other words, Alianor suspects the last king was murdered and his son put on the throne in hopes that Estienne was young enough to be manipulated. When he wasn't, they locked him up. It's a warning. *Do as we say. Or else.*

That is chilling to me in a way I don't think the others can understand. My family doesn't rule Tamarel because we're such amazing warriors that we can fight any threat to our throne. We have guards to fend off direct attack. Yet what if our guards were the ones attacking? Or what if they agreed with our attackers and stepped aside?

If we were corrupt, then this would be understandable. But what if someone else decides they want power for themselves and the guards—or army—decide they'd like some too? Then we are at their mercy. It's not something any ruler likes to think about. We can do our best to be fair and good monarchs, but I only need to look at Heward to know there is always danger from those who envy our power.

What matters here is that my brother is caught up in a coup, and I want to free him before anything happens. Except, as I know logically, nothing is going to happen to him right now. Same with King Estienne—they are pieces on a game board that have been put aside temporarily.

The prime minister has sent his general to deal with the dragon. He might honestly believe this is best. Yet having been trained to be queen, I see ulterior motives here. Convince the people that their king faltered and put them at risk but the prime minister saved the day. At the same time, stir up tensions with Tamarel, proving that King Estienne is too young to handle delicate diplomatic relations. For now, though, the prime minister has what he wants—the army intends to take care of the dragons—and so the king is safe and so is my brother.

Wilmot agrees, which settles my fears. I consider sending someone—maybe Kaylein—to the capital, but that would only endanger her and might also endanger my brother. As we saw at the farm, the Roivan guards were inclined to treat us well while we behaved. Once we escaped, that changed.

What, then, is our plan? To stop the army from attacking the dragons, of course. The question is how we'll do that. It had seemed obvious. Talk to them. Explain the situation. Show them that there are options and convince them that Tamarel will take responsibility for the dragons, and if the beasts become dangerous, we'll do whatever is needed to protect our neighbors.

I'd thought General Corisande had been listening to me. I realize now that she'd only been pretending, and at first, I want to think I just need to try harder. I just need to find the right words. But I realize I don't honestly believe the right words exist, because this isn't about a threat to "national security." It's an excuse for seizing power, and that has nothing to do with me.

Or does it? Can I argue from that side? I know what they're up to. What if I confront them? I'm the daughter of the Tamarelian queen. What if I threaten to accuse them of an attempted coup unless they give us time to handle the dragons?

Sure, that'll work. I'll threaten the general . . . and she'll find a way for me to suffer one of those tragic "accidents." My entire party wiped out by the dragons. See what terrible danger they saved Roiva from? Such a tragedy.

Rhydd went to the capital on a diplomatic mission. Not to confront or threaten. Just to talk. And he still got locked up. I'd have no such protections in the forest.

I ask for advice. Wilmot and Kaylein are out of their depth here. This is a political quandary, and they aren't politicians. Trysten helps and Alianor does, too, from their very different perspectives. In the end, we have a plan. It's just not a very good one.

I need to get home and tell my mother what's happening. I think I know a way to do that quickly, using my two equine companions. I'll rely mostly on Doscach. If I can get to a waterway, he can swim faster than he can walk. If we hit a section of woods where it's too thick for him to pass easily, I can ride Sunniva for a short while, if she'll allow it.

Get home. Tell my mother there is an army on her soil. She'll take it from there.

The real problem with that plan? It's going to take time. The others will need to stall the army until my mother can take action. Keep the army from killing the dragon and her young . . . while the very fact they're in the forest with her will only make her more angry, and make them more likely to try bringing her down.

It's a terrible plan, but it's the only one I have.

I'm alone in a clearing. Well, not completely alone, of course. I have Jacko and Malric, but they are always with me, thankfully. And right now, when I say I am alone, there is no discomfort or distress in that. I am happy to be alone, with only my closest monster companions.

I'm tired and frustrated. By the time we'd escaped the farm, it was midday. We didn't reach the forest until near nightfall. We've slept twice since. Or the others have. I'm not sleeping. All I can think about is Rhydd being locked up while I travel in the other direction. That and the fact that my plan is terrible, and every time I drift off, the dragon screams and

I bolt awake. Sometimes she's really screaming, and sometimes it's just in my head. Either way, I don't sleep.

Wilmot is certain we're less than a day's walk from her lair, where we'll find waterways that'll make it easier for Doscach to get me home quickly. We stopped to hunt because our food is running out. I asked to stay behind and let Malric rest. He's been faltering, and I wonder whether he was kicked during the fight with the guards.

He needs a break, and so do I. Kaylein didn't want to leave me alone, but I think Wilmot understood that I need a break from being Princess Rowan, the royal monster hunter who doesn't have a real plan for dealing with this particular monster problem.

We rest, Malric lying against my back, Jacko on my lap. Our fire will keep most creatures at bay, but I'm still alert. It's a miracle I can even rest, considering that the dragon is circling overhead, her screeches shattering the air every time she gets close.

Something has set her off today. The other times, she's seemed to be patrolling her territory and screaming to let someone know she's there. That "someone" was presumably the soldiers.

Today, it's different. Something has her agitated. Not furious. I know what that sounds like. But she's in a worse mood today, and she's letting everyone know it.

When I hear something crashing through the forest, I'm on my feet in a blink, and so is Malric. I draw my sword. Then the shadows erupt as two black forms shoot out like they've been fired from a bow. I fall back, sword ready. They stop and squeal and shimmy like excited children.

It's the juvenile dragons. Both of them. They're about Malric's size, with long reptilian bodies and four powerful legs, plus leathery wings. Small horns curve backward on their heads and a ridge extends down to their tails. Their black scales gleam iridescent when the sun hits just right.

They're on all fours, wings pulled in tight so they can run through the dense forest. One rears up, and there's blood on its muzzle. The other gallops over to sniff Jacko, who sniffs back.

"Well, now we know why Momma Dragon isn't happy today," I say. "You two snuck out, didn't you? She wanted you to stay inside the den while there are strangers in the forest, and after a few days, you'd had enough of that. You snuck out, and you've been running around on the forest floor, where she can't see you."

The one with the bloodied mouth chirps and races over to me, nudging my shoulder.

I sheathe my sword. "You two really need to go home. You know that, right?" I glance at Jacko, who's darting through the clearing, playing with the other young dragon. "Don't encourage them, Jacko. This isn't playtime."

The first dragon nudges my shoulder again. I reach out and stroke its head, which isn't quite what it wants, but it decides this will do and leans into my hand.

I sigh. Overhead, the mother dragon screams and both juveniles run to the edge of the forest. They duck in and wait for her to pass and then come out again.

"You two are *such* trouble," I say. "Don't try to hide with me. You need to go home."

They both race over to nudge at me again. Then one rears up, hissing, its wings shooting open. I hear something in the forest and turn as Kaylein stops at the clearing edge. She stares, and her hand eases toward the sword on her back, but I reach out and stroke the juvenile's neck.

"They're fine," I say. "They must have smelled me and come to play. That's why their mother is so annoyed. They snuck out."

"Sounds like a certain prince and princess I know," Wilmot says as he appears behind Kaylein. "If Berinon's stories are true."

I sigh. "Right? I have never realized how much grief we must have caused Mom until I met these two." I reach down and grab a stick. I throw it and both juveniles chase after it.

"So Alianor just got her monster companion," Kaylein says. "It's my turn, and I know exactly what I want. A baby dragon. They are adorable. Well, terrifying and adorable at the same time."

"Ah, right," I say. "You didn't meet them in the cave. I think this one's female and the other's male, but I'm refraining from giving them names." I throw another stick for them. "We should get them back to their mother. I don't want General Corisande to think the dragon is getting ready to strike when she's only looking for her babies." I squint up into the sky. "I wonder if we can get her attention."

"Could we use the babies?" Kaylein asks. "Not as hostages, of course. But as a way to prove to the soldiers that dragons don't need to be dangerous? They'd probably follow you on their own."

I shake my head. "I'd be afraid I'd get them to General Corisande and then their mother would appear and prove just how dangerous dragons can be."

"True."

"Well, look who came to say hello," Alianor calls as she walks out with Dain and Trysten.

One of the juveniles—the presumed female—squawks in greeting and charges over, only to have the nian—now named Brise, after a ballad heroine—roar and jump between Alianor and the dragon. The dragon rears up, claws and teeth flashing, wings spreading. Her brother races over to rear beside her, and Brise's roar dies mid-note as she creeps back toward Alianor.

"Really?" Alianor says. "You're a scaredy-cat?" She walks around the nian and pats the head of one of the dragons. Brise grumbles and looks to Malric for advice. The warg is lying down, picking something from his paw, unconcerned.

When the female juvenile cranes to see something on Alianor's back, Alianor laughs. "Oh, that's what you really want, isn't it?" She pulls a brace of game birds over her shoulder. When the dragon snaps at one, she pulls it back. "It looks like you two have already been hunting."

"They have," I say. "But I might need those birds to get them to do what I want. Namely, to stick close until I can bring their mother to fetch them."

Alianor's brows shoot up. "Seriously?"

"Seriously."

CHAPTER TWENTY-EIGHT

Obviously, there are many dangers involved in trying to reunite Momma with her troublesome twins. Which is why I insist on doing it alone. Again, as when I asked to be left behind on the hunting excursion, Kaylein balks. This time, it's Trysten who comes to my rescue.

"The dragon knows Rowan," he says. "She's not exactly going to run over to play like these two, but Rowan proved herself the last time. She fought off the poachers and made sure they never came back. I think we need to trust that the dragon understands Rowan is an ally."

"I agree," Dain says. "Though I'm going to be nearby with my bow."

"We all should be nearby and ready to help," Trysten says. "I think Alianor can get closer—the dragon knows her, too. But if we insist on getting *too* close, that endangers Rowan."

Is it still dangerous? Yes, but I do trust that the dragon

understands I'm not a threat. The alternative is to hope the juveniles wander off on their own, which risks the soldiers finding them. It also means Momma Dragon will keep circling and getting increasingly upset as she can't find her babies. And if we continue on our way and the young dragons follow us, their mother could think we've stolen them.

No, I must return her babies and maybe, if I'm lucky, I can use this act to prove that the dragon is a reasonable creature. That if you don't pose a threat to her, she doesn't pose one to you.

Next comes the question of how to get her attention.

"Where's Sunniva when you need her?" Alianor says. "You could have ridden her and gotten these two to follow."

"I doubt they would have," I say. "If Mom sees them, they're grounded again. I think my best bet is . . ." I squint toward the mountains. "Get them to higher ground."

There's a foothill to the north of us, maybe a half mile away. That's where we head. The juvenile dragons follow, and we don't need to use the game birds to tempt them. They've reunited with friends—this interesting collection of people and monsters—and they very happily join our walk through the forest.

When their mother circles anywhere near us, they dive into the woods, but only until she passes. They really do remind me of my brother and me when we'd sneak off someplace we weren't supposed to be, hiding just until the guards passed and then carrying on, oblivious to the fact that our poor parents were freaking out over our disappearance.

At the foothill, we pause to survey the landscape. We find spots for everyone to hide in pairs and keep a watch over me. Then I proceed up through a patch of forest. Before I leave the tree cover, I cut up a game bird. The juveniles get some, Malric gets some and Jacko gets some. We're just stopping for a snack. Not distracting the young dragons with food while we wait for their mother to circle past. No, not at all.

Finally, Alianor whistles from her treetop perch, which means she's spotted Momma Dragon. I jog out, with Jacko romping alongside me, as if he knows we need to convince the juveniles that everything's fine and we're just playing on this hilltop.

I brought one of the grootslang's tusks with me. The juveniles had been interested in them as we walked—nudging poor Dain's back where they hung—and I took one as a distraction tool. Now I toss it into the clearing. It's Malric who goes after it first, making the two juveniles squeal in indignation. The warg runs around the clearing with the tusk in his mouth, and they give chase.

Thank you, Malric. I know this is beneath your dignity, but you are getting the biggest and best piece of meat from my next hunt.

Once they're distracted, I squint up at the shape flying toward us. I'm looking straight into the midafternoon sun, and all I can see is the large dark outline of the dragon winging quickly in our direction.

Then I pause. The dragon looks . . . wrong. It's definitely big, but with a broad body shaped more like a gryphon's.

The beast above lets out a squawk. A very un-dragon-like squawk. It sounds like a bird. Or a certain bird monster I encountered just a few days ago.

The young roc circles overhead, squawking with the joy of discovery.

"No," I whisper. "Oh no." I wave my arms. "Shoo! Go! Scram!"

The roc gives another joyful screech. I am communicating with it! I am happy to see it, too! How wonderful!

Both juvenile dragons stop chasing Malric and stare up. Their eyes bulge in shock at this creature overhead. A beast who is as big as their mother and yet not their mother. The female juvenile hisses. The male rises on his hind legs. Malric sighs. He drops the tusk and bounds to me, and the roc screeches in fresh delight at spotting this old playmate.

The roc lands. Really, there's nothing I can do to stop it. The creature is the size of a house. That's when it sees the juvenile dragons, and it gets even more excited, fluttering its massive wings and bobbing its head in greeting.

I suppose when you're as big as a roc, you could see every other creature as dinner, like the grootslang did. Or you could see it as fresh data for your curious brain. What is this new thing? Could it be a friend? A new playmate?

What you *don't* see, at that size, is a threat. The roc comes from deep in the mountains, where every living creature must flee when it appears overhead. It's alone and friendless, which would be a terrible thing for a youngster. With the dragon's appearance, it's been drawn across the mountains to satisfy its curiosity. Imagine its delight in discovering creatures that do *not* run away from it.

"These are baby dragons," I say as I walk over to pat one of the juveniles. "They have wings, like you. They will be huge one day, like you."

Of course, the roc doesn't know what I'm saying. Nor do the juveniles. But my tone is calm and encouraging, and when the roc lowers its massive head, the female dragon rears up and leans out to sniff. Her brother coughs—trying to manufacture the special breath that will put his enemies to sleep. Except he doesn't have it yet.

The roc only tilts its head in curiosity and then coughs back, mimicking the dragon. The female extends her wings. The roc does the same, the swirl of wind created by this movement nearly knocking the little dragon over. She flutters her wings. The roc copies her, and she chirps in delight. Her brother seems less certain, but he does lean forward to sniff at the roc.

When the sky darkens, I don't notice at first. It's a bright autumn day, with clouds that drift in and out of the sun's path. Then comes the scream of a dragon's fury. I look up to see the mother dragon diving straight at me. Somewhere under *her* scream, I make out the screams and shouts of my companions as they try to warn me.

I start to run. Then I see she's not diving for me at all. She's going for the roc. Before she can hit it, I run between the roc and the juveniles and shove the roc back with all my might, which is probably like Jacko headbutting me.

The force of my push may be tiny, but the surprise of it is huge. The roc has had nothing but kindness from me, so when I push it away, it staggers back with a squawk. Then Malric is in there, pushing. He doesn't growl or snarl. He does nothing that could be interpreted as a threat, and neither do I. We just drive the roc back as the dragon lands with enough of a thud to topple me against the roc's chest.

The dragon whips around faster than one would think possible for a creature of her size. She's longer than the roc, with lean muscles, her black scales glimmering iridescent in the sunlight. Golden eyes fix on us.

"It's okay!" I shout. "No one's bothering your babies. See? They're fine."

They *are* fine . . . and sneaking around Momma to get back to their new friends. Her tail slaps between us and them, knocking the female over. Both juveniles hiss at their mother.

"Uh-uh," I say. "None of that back talk. You two are in *trouble.*"

I turn to the dragon. "They're fine. Check them out. No one's hurt here. Everything is fine. We didn't steal your babies."

The male climbs over his mother's tail, still determined to get to us. I hurry over and block his path. He rears up and coughs at me.

"Yeah, nice try," I say.

The dragon lifts her head to peer at the roc. The bird monster has gone still, all its exuberance evaporated as it stares at the dragon. It makes a tiny sound, almost like a nervous chirp, as ridiculous as that sounds from a creature of its size.

The dragon inhales, drinking in the roc's scent. It stays perfectly still, even as her head moves toward it. She keeps sniffing. She looks from her babies to the young roc, and I'm not sure whether she's ever seen one of its kind before, but she seems to be mentally processing as fast as she can. A very large bird. One big enough to fight her. One big enough to eat her babies, and yet it hasn't harmed them, and her babies want to get back to join it.

"Everything okay up there?" a voice yells. It's Alianor, and the dragon bristles, her head snapping up, but when Alianor asks again, the dragon only grunts, as if she recognizes the voice and knows it isn't a dangerous stranger.

"We're fine," I call back. "Just negotiating inter-species peace."

Alianor's head pops up over a boulder twenty feet away. "Sorry, I mistook the roc for the dragon. I saw something big in the sky and figured it had to be her."

The dragon doesn't move her body, but her head swivels, neck stretching. She's spotted the grootslang tusk abandoned on the rocky ground. I pick it up, and she moves closer. I hold it out and stay as still as the roc did, letting that massive head lower. She sniffs the tusk. Sniffs me. Sniffs the tusk again. Then she noses me so suddenly I jump and stumble. She nudges again, turning me around, and she sniffs the sword on my back.

I tense. Is she working something out here? She seems to be, and that worries me. I have a grootslang tusk. That means a grootslang is dead. My scent is all over the tusk. The grootslang's scent will still be on my sword, despite my washing off the blood.

Is she figuring out that I'm not as weak as I seem? Not as defenseless? Not as innocent?

She pulls back and eyes me.

"Uh, that doesn't look good," Alianor says. "I think she's realized you killed a reptile even bigger than her."

I breathe deeply, hoping to calm my racing heart. The dragon lowers her head to peer at Malric. When she gets closer to Jacko, he scrambles up my leg to perch on my shoulders. She sniffs at him. Looks over at the roc. From me to the roc and then down at the grootslang tusk.

"Rowan?" Alianor says.

"I don't know," I say, trying to keep my voice steady. "Maybe she's understanding that I *can* be dangerous? But that I also have monster companions who *aren't* afraid of me?"

"Working it out," Alianor says. "Okay. Let's hope she comes to the right conclusion."

The dragon turns suddenly, and Malric and I both stagger back to get out of her way. She smacks her snout into the female juvenile, who's leaning over the boulder near Alianor, peering at the nian below.

At the smack, the young dragon squawks, but her mother only smacks her again. Not hurting her. *Herding* her. Herding both of them onto the rocky expanse and then nudging under their hindquarters.

"I think that's goodbye," Alianor says. "She wants them in the air. Now."

That's exactly what Momma Dragon wants. When the female juvenile tries to flee back to me, her mother fairly flips her in the air with her snout.

"Go on," I say. "Time to leave. Momma's nervous."

Did I make her nervous? I can't blame her, I guess, as disappointing as that is. At least she reacted to the "threat" by bustling her babies off rather than killing me.

That's what she does: herds them into the air, and they're off without a backward glance as she sticks right behind them, keeping them on the path home.

"Rowan?" a voice calls from below. It's Trysten. "I think you'd better get down here. We've, uh, got company."

"Right," Alianor says. "Sorry, that's what I was going to tell you. I could see troops from up in the tree, and they saw the dragon landing. They're on their way."

I turn to the roc. "You need to get out of here. You can't be flying around when there are archers looking for a large beast in the sky." I wave my hands. "Go! Shoo!"

I don't expect it to be that easy, but it is, just like the first time we met the roc. It's still young, and this all has to be a lot of excitement for it. Reuniting with "old" playmates. Finding new ones. Finally figuring out what that big monster in the sky was and deciding it's kind of scary.

The roc is sleepy and maybe a little overwhelmed, and when I shoo it away, it nudges me and clicks its beak, and then it lifts off, thankfully heading away from the direction the dragon went in.

"Whew," Alianor says. "All right, then. Time to go argue with the army."

We meet up with the others at the base of the foothill. The soldiers are coming, and we stand our ground to wait for them. It takes a while for them to reach us. Long enough that most of our party sits to rest as the sun begins to drop.

Then General Corisande's armored steed appears, thundering along the road, and she rides so close that I'm ready to dive into the bushes before she finally pulls her horse up short. I scowl at that. It was an unnecessary show of power, one I do not appreciate. It doesn't bode well for this meeting.

The general has stopped about ten feet from me. At a gesture, her army also halts, staying about fifty feet down the road.

"Princess Rowan," she says. "Running after the dragons, I see. You've missed them. They spotted our army and fled back to their den."

Alianor snorts. "Uh, no, we didn't 'miss' them. The babies came to *see* Rowan, who returned them to their mother, who took them home. We were all there." She waves at our party. "And not a single scratch. Not even a threat display. She appreciated Rowan looking after her runaway babies and getting them back to her."

I wouldn't go that far, but I certainly don't argue.

"You heard the dragon screaming today," I say. "It may have sounded aggressive. It was not. Her two young ones snuck out, and she was worried about them, especially with strange humans in the forest."

"It was Momma telling her babies to get on home," Alianor says. "Not the big, bad dragon threatening the humans in her forest."

"*Her* forest?" General Corisande raises her brows.

"Her *territory*," I say. "Her hunting territory, which is on Tamarelian soil. Tell me, General, has she hurt any of your soldiers?"

"We haven't given her the chance."

"If she wanted to, she'd hurt them, and *you* wouldn't have a chance," Alianor says.

"She is on Tamarelian soil," I repeat. "As are you and your troops. We have already dispatched messengers to inform my mother of what has happened—the kidnapping and the invasion."

The general's jaw sets in a way that tells me she doesn't question my lie.

I continue, "If anything happens to us, you won't be able to blame it on the dragons. My mother knows the truth."

"If anything *happens* to you?" The general laughs. "We aren't murderers, child. We're an army defending our—"

"National security," I say. "We got that."

Her eyes narrow, not appreciating the interruption or my tone. I look her in the eye. "What assurances do you want from Tamarel that these dragons will not harm your people? What 'security' provisions do you require?"

"You are in no position to make those promises, princess, as I am in no position to accept them."

"Then why is this being decided here? You are invading my land. You have given us no opportunity to make our case—"

"Dragon!" someone shouts. "The dragon! She's coming!"

I almost snap that this is a poor attempt at diversion. The dragon left. She took her babies home, and we haven't heard anything from her since. Then her dark shape appears against the sunset sky, winging fast as she heads for the foothill where I'd met her earlier.

She sees us. Or she hears the shouts. She hovers for a moment as she searches. Then she spots me. Her gaze seems to fix right on mine. Then it sweeps over the army. She wheels in midair . . . and flies back the way she came.

"Did you see that?" Alianor says. "She saw your army and retreated. She didn't even scream a warning."

"She's only dangerous if you make the first move," I say. "If you attack her or her babies or her eggs. Dain here had one of her eggs. He'd taken it from thieves, and when she grabbed him, I thought she'd mistaken him for a thief. She hadn't. She took him back to her den. All she wanted was her egg."

Dain's tone is uncertain when he speaks. He hates talking in front of others, especially a group, but he finds his voice and says, "Rowan's right. The dragon understood that I wasn't the thief. She didn't harm me."

We're not sure how true that is—at least the part about how much the dragon understood. The point here is that Dain escaped unscathed, and we can use that, along with the fact that she has retreated—

A shadow glides from over the treetops, so silently that the hairs on my neck rise and a memory sparks. The memory of a dream that was not a dream, of a shadow gliding over our camp one night. I know then what she's about to do.

I turn to my companions behind me. "Cover your mouths! Don't inhale!"

I warn them, but it isn't necessary. The dragon doesn't come our way. She glides over the army, breathing her sleeping gas onto them. They don't just stand there gaping. Well, some do, but others reach for weapons. A few arrows fire even as I shout for them to stop. Then the dragon is gone, disappearing over the treetops again.

I open my mouth to warn the soldiers. Warn them not to inhale the mist settling over them. But a hand grabs me. I turn, expecting to see Alianor.

It's Dain. He shakes his head and whispers, "Will it help?"

Will it help to warn them? To panic them? To give them more ammunition against the dragon? See, she *is* dangerous.

I turn to the soldiers. Some foot soldiers are sitting, as if they've slumped onto the ground in exhaustion. One of the cavalry is already sliding off his horse.

"Hey!" Alianor shouts. "What are you doing? You're all in shock. Get up!"

"Right," Kaylein calls. "You're in shock from seeing the dragon so close! What kind of soldiers are these, General?"

General Corisande shouts orders. Being close to us, she didn't see the mist and she seems genuinely confused, maybe from the little bit she *did* inhale.

The dragon appears again. She's going to keep dosing the soldiers until they're all asleep. Or that's what I think until I see her looking at me.

Watching me. Seeing what I'll do.

"Stay here!" I shout to the others. Then I run toward the foothill. Malric races along at my side. Jacko catches up in a flash and runs at my other side.

Get her away from the soldiers. Distract her. Show her that I am not a threat. That I will not attack.

Is that my plan? I don't know. I just know the first part. Get her away from the army before they wake up and attack her.

Overhead, the dragon turns. I glance back to see she's

following me. I exhale and keep running. I start climbing up the foothill on the open side, where she can see me.

"Rowan!" Dain's shout comes at the top of his lungs. A shout of fear and panic. Alianor joins in, screaming at me to turn around.

I glance over my shoulder to see the dragon there. She's silently dropped right behind me, her front talons extended.

I don't have time to grab my sword. Malric doesn't have time for a single snarl. Only Jacko has time to react—leaping onto my leggings just as the dragon's talons close around me.

CHAPTER TWENTY-NINE

ix months ago, a gryphon broke through a barn roof and grabbed me, and I thought I was going to die. I'd been snatched from the earth and wrenched into the sky, and I'd never felt more helpless in my life. But that was then. Before Jannah died. Before I became the royal monster hunter–elect. Before I captured that gryphon and raised her baby. Before I won the respect of Malric and Wilmot and even, maybe, Dain. Before I proved that I deserved to carry the ebony sword.

I have learned so much. Come so far. I barely recognize that girl in my memory, the one who'd thoughtlessly escaped her castle lockdown to take on a gryphon. That girl was brave, but she didn't think things through, didn't consider the consequences her actions could have for others.

I am not that girl. Yet in one swoop, the dragon slams me back into being that girl, snatched from the earth and wrenched into the sky, and all I can do is clutch Jacko and hold onto him for dear life.

I am terrified, and I am ashamed. Ashamed of so much. Of being captured so easily. Of being blinded by pride, certain I could reason with the dragon. Of clinging to my jackalope when I should be fighting for our lives.

And yet . . .

When the gryphon took me, I did fight, after I recovered my wits. I fought, and she dropped me, and I nearly died in that fall, saved only by hitting a haystack. Then she went for my aunt and killed her.

I wished I'd thought it through more. No matter how many people tell me I couldn't have saved Jannah, I cannot help but think that if I hadn't fought for my own freedom—if I'd waited to fight in the gryphon's lair instead—my aunt might have lived.

I'm not holding onto Jacko for comfort. Or because I'm afraid to fight. I'm holding him so he won't fall to his death. Holding him while I struggle to silence the gibbering panic that screams, "We're going to die!" Holding him until I can catch my breath enough to look around.

When the dragon first grabbed me, she rocketed into the air so fast I couldn't even open my eyes. Now the air rushes past in a vacuum that steals my breath. My stomach lurches and my vision goes red. Talons dig into my sides, making it even harder to breathe. Jacko burrows against me, his heart racing so fast I fear it will give out.

I hear shouts below. Screams below. Something hits me in the leg, and pain slams through me. That's all I can register. The world shoots past in a blur.

Finally, the dragon slows, and I can keep my eyes open and catch my breath, and the first thing I notice is something beside me, a wriggling and snarling black mass. It's Malric, seized in the dragon's other foreleg.

I shout for him not to fight, but if he hears me, he ignores me. Or my words don't penetrate his own panic. I try shouting to the dragon. I'm not sure what good that will do, but beneath my terror runs a steel thread of anger, of betrayal. I did nothing to deserve this.

Is that anger? Or humiliation?

She's only dangerous if you make the first move. If you attack her or her babies or her eggs.

I said those words only moments ago. In my heart, I was so certain of them. I told General Corisande that the dragon is no threat . . . and the words were still hanging in the air as the creature grabbed me and flew off with me.

I should have known better. I saw the way she looked at the grootslang tusk. I saw the way she appraised me. Her clever monster brain evaluating the evidence and understanding what it meant. That I killed monsters. That I was capable of killing something as big as her.

I take deep breaths as my heart races. And here I find something I could not find when the gryphon snatched me. I find a measure of calm, and I find resolve. I cannot fight the dragon now. Even if I got her to open her talons, I'd die on the drop and take Jacko with me. I must hold myself still and wait, as excruciating as that is. She is taking me to her den, and there I will have the chance to fight or to flee.

Flee. I will be honest with myself. I might have killed that grootslang, but it isn't as if I'd pondered the situation and realized the solution was to attack the beast from the inside. I had, in that moment, been my old impulsive self—a part of me that will never quite go away.

If I do not have to fight the dragon, I will not. No more than I intended to kill the grootslang.

Let her get me to her den and then ...

We are not heading to her den. I catch a flash of the mountains to my left as the dragon veers right. That's when I begin to squirm, to wriggle in panic, as if I can somehow convince her to turn back.

She isn't taking me to the den. Why would she? Her babies are there.

We're losing altitude. I realize that as I see the tops of trees growing closer. She's coming in for a landing. This is my chance. Fight while we're over the thick forest.

"Malric!" I shout.

I look over to see him limp in her talons. Panic slams through me. Did the dragon squeeze her talons and kill him?

"Malric! Malric!"

He turns his head my way, and my breath rushes out.

"Fight!" I say. "We're going to fight!"

Still holding Jacko in one arm, I pull my leg up. I have Madlyn's stiletto blade in my boot, where I'd fashioned a sheath for it.

I need to get my boot up—

The dragon veers, and the forest opens. It's a clearing. A huge expanse of open land. Rock juts from the earth, as if the crust itself broke open here. If I fall onto this, I'll die.

I fumble for the dagger, and my fingers make contact with my boot. Then the world jolts hard enough that I nearly drop Jacko. My arms squeeze him tight, and the dragon's whole body rocks as she lands on her hind legs. Then she drops us from her front talons. Just lets us fall five feet to the rock, and I smack into it, pain reverberating through me.

With Jacko under my arm, I scrabble to my feet just as Malric hits me. My leg twists, and I gasp in pain. I dimly remember that pain from earlier. It's been throbbing since something struck it, and now it screams. Malric has slammed into me and knocked me down, and he's standing over me, snarling at the dragon.

I lift my head. The first thing I see is a wall of black fur. The second? Forest. Thick forest. It's no more than twenty feet away.

I grab a handful of Malric's fur to get his attention. I point, and his snarl hitches just enough for me to know he got the message. Now I can only hope he understood it. I adjust Jacko under my arm. Then I slide the stiletto from my boot. I count to three, leap up and—

Pain rips through my leg. I look down and see an arrow piercing it.

Someone shot at the dragon and hit me. It's a small and slender arrow, and not a design I recognize. That means it doesn't belong to Wilmot or Dain, who'd never take that risk. One of the soldiers. The arrow went right into the flesh of my calf, and when I put any weight on it, my leg gives way.

Even as I tumble, a plan forms. I'll crawl. Crawl as fast as I can.

The dragon grabs me. Just casually scoops me up in her talons, as if I'm one of her babies trying to escape. This time, I have the blade. I twist to stab her as Malric roars and leaps. My dagger draws back, on target with the flesh over her talons. Then she swings me, and the world goes black with the blur of motion. Before I can recover, she drops me again.

I hit the rock, this time landing on Jacko, who yips and wriggles from my grip. He rears up, hissing and waving his antlers at the dragon. I blink and lift my head to see darkness.

The darkness of a hole. There's a hole in the rock, close enough for me to reach out and touch the edge. A hole big enough for me to jump into. Big enough for Malric. *Not* big enough for the dragon.

"Malric!" I shout.

I shove the dagger back into my boot, grab Jacko and dive in an awkward half lunge, half roll that sends me tumbling through space as I realize I didn't pause long enough to look *into* the hole. To be certain I wasn't plunging to my doom as surely as if I'd fought free of the dragon's talons in midair.

I hit dirt and roll, and as my grip tightens on Jacko, I'm only thankful I at least had the foresight to sheathe my dagger or I'd likely have killed us both. As it is, I still scream in pain when the arrow through my leg hits the ground. That scream is muffled mid-note by two hundred pounds of warg landing on top of me.

Malric tries to scrabble off, but we're sliding, and all I can do is brace for the inevitable stop. When it comes, we all lie there, panting.

"I need to fix my leg," I say, my voice echoing.

I start to sit upright. As I do, I reach out, and my hand comes down on empty air. I blink hard. The only light comes from the mouth of the hole, ten feet above. When my eyes adjust, I'm looking over my shoulder into blackness. We aren't on firm ground. We're on a ledge.

"Malric?" I whisper, as if my voice will bring us tumbling down. "I need to get out from under you. Please stay still."

He does, and I set Jacko on him with the same plea for him to stay where he is. I suspect they don't need the warning. Both have better night vision than I do, and they'll see our predicament. When I do begin to shift, Jacko chirps in alarm.

I pat the rock under me, loud enough for him to hear it. "I'm feeling my way, Jacko. I'm fine."

I wriggle out enough to get to my hip pouch and light a fire stick. The ledge extends maybe five feet behind me. I ease out that way. Then I pull my leg up. The arrow did indeed pierce my calf. Luckily, it didn't tear right through it when we fell.

I touch the shaft and hiss in pain. I'm not sure it's safe to pull it out. I do need to break it off, though. I'm taking out my bigger dagger when I have a better idea.

"Jacko? Can you bite through this?" I point at the shaft just above where the arrow went in and mimic gnawing gestures and noises until he understands. He hops over and cleaves it with one bite. Then I get him to do the same on the other side. That leaves part of the arrow in my leg, but I don't want to pull it out and start bleeding. This will have to do.

Once that's done, I lift the fire stick and peer around. It turns out the situation isn't as dire as it first appeared. Yes, we're on a ledge, but shortly below it, the hole levels out into a tunnel.

Seeing that tunnel, my first thought is "grootslang." This isn't the same, though. That was a burrow dug by the monster. This seems a natural structure, a crack in the rock above that becomes a tunnel, part rock and part dirt. When I lean over the ledge, I catch the smell of decomposition. I squint but can't see what it is. Either something fell in here and died or a creature dragged a kill down here.

From what I can see, the tunnel goes on at least a little farther. If we're lucky, it'll lead to another hole where we can exit. If not, we can stay down here until the dragon leaves.

Speaking of the dragon, I'd expect her to be trying to get to us. Thumping over the ground in a fury, screeching and beating her wings in frustration at our escape. Yet she's silent and has been since we dove into the hole.

It's almost as if she wanted us to do that. As if she picked me up and put me down next to the hole so I'd go inside.

That's silly, of course. Why would she *want* us to escape?

I check my leg. It hurts even to move it, and blood soaks my leggings, but the bleeding has stopped and I think I can stand on it. I push my heel into the rock to test it. Yep, that definitely hurts. It'll work, though. It has to.

"Okay," I say. "We're climbing down and seeing where this leads."

They don't like it, and they register their disapproval with chirps and growls as I ease to the edge and lower myself. They don't stop me, though. I touch ground with my good leg, brace myself on it and then let go. I manage to get my bad leg down before I fall. Jacko follows, leaping into my open arms. Malric paces the ledge once or twice. Then he jumps, lands easily and shakes himself off.

"Time to explore our options," I say, and we set out down the tunnel.

CHAPTER THIRTY

We make our way through the natural underground tunnel, which is fascinating. Alianor's sister, Sarika, specializes in geology and earth sciences, and I'd love to bring her here to both study this and explain what I'm seeing.

Last month, when I'd stumbled on the dragon's lair, I'd been following another kind of tunnel, one in a mountain that had been worn through by running water. This is very different. It's rough, with rocks jutting out, some of them sparkling with minerals. At some points, I can walk upright, while at others, I'm stooped over. This tunnel branches constantly, and a few times I end up in a section too tight to squeeze through. When I retreat and try the other option, I can make it.

Unlike the dragon mountain tunnel, this one is slow going. Every time I need to climb down, I also have to assess how easily we could climb back up, if need be—and whether

I could make it with my wounded leg. This kind of tunnel doesn't seem to be linking two places, like the dragon or the grootslang ones, so it could end at any moment. A few times there's a crack letting in air and light, but none are wide enough for us to climb out of.

The worst of it is the smell. While the tunnel is naturally formed, that doesn't mean it's empty. Animals must have made dens down here. A lot of them, judging by the stink. A few times Jacko or Malric find a nest, but they all seem abandoned, and not the source of the stench.

As that smell grows stronger, I realize it's the decomposition I smelled earlier. It's something dead. Something big? It smells like it. But nothing bigger than Malric could get down here.

The warg is in the lead now. We're on a flat patch of tunnel, easily traveled, but he keeps stopping and holding me back as he sniffs. Jacko tries to get past him, also sniffing, but Malric knocks him back, less gently than I'd like.

When Malric glances the way we came, I know he's considering turning back.

"I just want to see what's making that smell," I say. "Whatever it is, it's dead and not a danger."

He growls, the sound reverberating through the corridor. Then he resumes walking with his head down. Every few paces he stops to sniff and then exhales sharply.

"I don't know how you can smell anything over that stench," I say.

Then I realize that's the problem. It's not that he smells danger. It's that he can't smell anything except that dead creature, and that makes him anxious. The tunnel is dark—save for my bit of flickering light—and it's silent except for our footsteps. He needs to rely on scent, and he can't with that stench.

The tunnel curves, and Malric inches around it, snarling at us when we bump into him. The smell smacks into us like a wave of rotting flesh, and I slap a hand to my nose and mouth as my stomach heaves. When Malric stops abruptly, I crash into him and topple, my injured calf screaming and my fire going out. I quickly relight the stick and lift it to see we're at the mouth of a cavern. A massive cavern filled with—

Bodies. Fur and feather and bone fills the cavern, and my stomach lurches not so much at the smell now as at the sight. My brain boggles, and I stare as if I must be seeing things, because there is no way so many dead creatures could be here underground.

Even as I wonder how such a thing could happen, I remember the colocolo stampede, when they'd gone over a cliffside. It'd been a terrible thing to see, and this reminds me of that pile of broken bodies. Then that memory sparks another, of the mountain caves where we found the dragon, where the water had dried up suddenly, leaving dead aquatic creatures. Neither of those explains what I'm seeing, but they bring yet another memory, this one from the journal of a former royal monster hunter who'd found a pit of dead animals in an underground cave and discovered they'd been falling into it for years. A sinkhole had opened in the forest. The animals didn't notice it until they stumbled in and couldn't climb out.

That's the most likely explanation, and if there's a hole, there's an exit. We just have to get through this sea of bodies.

I shudder at the thought.

"I need to take a look," I say. "I need to be sure there isn't an easy way out of here before we go back and wait for the dragon to leave."

I lift my fire stick. It barely gives off enough light for me to see what's right in front of me. I need more. There's a stick a little past the body of a deer to my left. I inch by the body and lift the stick, which is dry and brittle. It's only when I light the end—and smell burning hair—that I realize it's a leg. I shudder, but it's dried out and lit and there's no point putting out the fire just because my torch is a little gross.

I turn, torch in hand, and the first thing I see is that the dead deer has wings. A peryton.

How would a winged monster "fall" into a pit and get trapped?

I shine the light at the next animal, which is also a monster. A young warg with its teeth still bared. I turn to find myself staring at an almost-human skull. I shine my light along it and see wings and a primate face. A young manticore.

I step forward, keeping my feet on rock and trying not to step on bodies. When bones crunch underfoot, I startle back and look down. At first, I see nothing. Then I catch sight of a double cat tail, long and thick. A full-grown nekomata, the feline monster's fur blending with the color of the rock below.

I stop and rub my eyes. Something's wrong. I cannot be seeing this. It's as if I've fallen asleep and begun a nightmare where all of the monsters I've encountered on my adventures are dead, my subconscious warning me that I must do better or it's not just the dragons that'll pay the price.

Could I be sleeping? I'd been so tired and frustrated when the others left me earlier to go hunting. But I didn't even close my eyes. Everything after that makes sense with none of the weirdness of dreams. Did I hit my head when the dragon dropped me? Am I lying unconscious on the rock?

No, none of it felt dreamlike until now, and even this isn't truly the stuff of nightmares. Horrifying, yes. Illogical, yes. But something deep in my brain prods that I'm seeing an answer here.

An answer to what? It's like being given the solution without knowing the question.

As I pick my way into the cavern, Malric and Jacko both follow, neither seeming happy about it. Malric looks at the dead warg. Jacko nudges two dead jackalopes.

The dead creatures are all monsters. Even when I think I see a regular animal, like the deer, it turns out to be a peryton. Or a wolf turns out to be a warg. A rabbit turns out to be a jackalope.

They aren't just monsters either. While there are a few prey monsters, like the peryton, most are predators, including juveniles of the large ones like wargs and manticores.

What don't I see? A hole in the cavern ceiling. By this time, I no longer expect that. There's no hidden pit that would only kill monsters. Something has done this.

The dragon? That's where my mind goes, but of course it's impossible. She wouldn't fit in here.

A grootslang? No, whatever did this is slaughtering without eating, and the grootslang killed *by* eating. No wasted food there. This is all waste.

Or is it? I look at the torch in my hand. It's the desiccated front leg of a peryton. That's gross, but it also means something. The leg didn't just fall off. I turn to the nearest beast. It's a warakin. There are two of them, side by side. Like the warg, they died with their faces fixed in a snarl. Died fighting. There's still dried blood on one warakin's tusks.

When I examine the bodies, I find the throats are ripped out. Classic killing move, particularly for canines. The bite marks are smaller than I'd expect, though.

I'm trying to figure out what would be big enough to kill two warakins or young wargs or young manticores, and my mind keeps scaling up. Gryphon. Roc. Dragon. Grootslang. None of them fit down here, and that's why the larger predators are juveniles; even the manticore is slightly smaller than Malric. Whatever's killing them isn't one of the giant monsters. It isn't human either—not from these torn throats.

I flip over one warakin. Lying on its stomach, it'd seemed intact except for the throat. Now that it's on its back, I see clear signs of feeding. Or tasting. It reminds me of when I was a child, and we had a midsummer dance at the palace, and food had been spread out for a buffet dinner. There'd been currant cakes, and I'd filled my plate with them. My mother had a talk with me about that—did I not think others might also want currant cakes? When I'd filled my plate, I hadn't been thinking about that, only that if there was a buffet of food, why not just eat the best parts?

That's exactly what this predator did. It ate the best parts and left the rest to rot. I nudge the nearby corpse of a rompo and see the same thing. Killed by a torn throat, but only the choicest parts have been consumed.

This isn't killing for food. It's wanton destruction, with a little feeding because, well, the beast is already dead. Like humans killing for fun and taking only antlers or horns.

I look around. Dead monsters. Only dead monsters. Mostly predators.

Territorial skirmishes? Killing other predators on its turf?

A new monster moves in and clears out the existing ones by killing some and scaring the rest. I feel that nudge again that says this is an answer, and this time, I think I know the question, but I push past it. Don't jump to conclusions. Keep gathering data.

When Jacko sounds his alert cry, I spin, hand going for my sword. There's nothing there, though. Nothing alive, at least. He's standing on a body and calling for me. Telling me he found something I'll want to see.

Whatever he's on, I can't make it out from here, as its hidden behind the body of another young warg. I step around it.

"Oh!" I say, and I hurry to where Jacko stands atop a small black body. It's about the size of a warakin, but slender, with a long torso, four legs and a tail. Black scales cover its body and when my light falls on them, they gleam iridescent.

It's a baby dragon. Half the size of the two juveniles who'd run away from their mother. Half their age. This poor baby has been dead for months. With the prolonged juvenile period of dragons, I think that where there are now the troublesome twins, there'd once been triplets. Three baby dragons, all of an age. A brood of three.

This one looks just old enough to be flying under Momma's watchful eye. Taking its first flights into the forest, maybe landing to explore a bit, as curious as its siblings. Momma Dragon had allowed that. After all, she was the apex predator. Nothing could harm her babies. Nothing would dare. But then this little one scampered a bit too far, maybe into a stand of trees, following its curiosity while its mother was preoccupied with the other two.

It wandered off, just a bit, and something snatched it up. Something even its mother wasn't able to stop.

Malric growls. Unlike Jacko's alert cry, this one doesn't make me reach for my sword as I spin. It's not a growl of warning. Just getting my attention. The warg has picked his way farther right through the bodies. He's nudging something. I need to step on a dead harpy to get to him. What I find makes me gasp in dismay.

It's another baby dragon, this one older and not as decomposed. Somewhere between the size of the dead one and the two living ones.

Not two young dragons. Not even three. The dragon had *four* babies, and she lost two to the same predator. One had been snatched, and I'm certain, as with any parent, she'd become even more careful after that. Like when Rhydd or I got hurt doing a certain activity, and Mom would clamp down on it. Fall out of a tree? No more climbing until you're older. Get lost in the forest beyond our walls? Stick to the forest *inside* our walls from now on.

The mother dragon became increasingly careful, and yet she still lost one of her young, because her babies weren't babies anymore. It's one thing to stop letting them land and explore the ground on training flights. But what happens when they're old enough to fly out on their own?

"No wonder she was in such a panic today," I murmur. "She's already lost two, and the others are tired of obeying her rules, tired of being cooped up in the den."

She is afraid. A creature who should be above fear feels it at the worst possible time—when she has babies to protect. First, something kills two of her hatchlings. Then humans come and steal her eggs. She's not just angry—she's scared.

Yet there's more here. More than just two dragon babies lost to an unknown predator. This creature is killing *all* the predators. Killing juveniles if the adults are too big to take on. Making the adults decide this place isn't safe for raising their young.

This is why the monsters are migrating. It's not the dragon. Or it's not entirely the dragon. We kept presuming that she was freaking out all the other monsters. Momma Dragon starts a family, and her overprotective ways make others decide to move on.

Does that explain the panic we saw? Is it even logical that one apex predator could clear so large an area? Some might decide to relocate, but on the scale we saw, there had to be more to it.

We've seen no sign that the dragon goes after creatures who don't threaten her first. She doesn't need to. Even the roc quailed before her, yet she only analyzed the threat and left it alone.

She's not an indiscriminate killer. She's not slaughtering predators. But something is.

This pit is the solution to the question of migrating monsters. Something moves in and starts systematically killing smaller predators and the young of large ones. It kills two young dragons, which whips their mother into a frenzy. But she can't leave. She still has eggs. Between some creature slaughtering predators and an increasingly agitated dragon, monsters migrated, some slowly relocating and others fleeing in panic.

The dragon showed this to me. Not in the sense that she knew I had a problem and gave me the explanation. Her motivation was purely personal.

This creature killed my babies, and I want you to stop it.

I almost laugh at the thought. That's going too far, attributing a human motive to a monster. But hadn't a gryphon asked us to heal a juvenile? It watched me wrap my own wound and led me to an injured young one. It had the ability to think that through.

Tool use is said to be the highest mark of animal and monster intelligence. That's what the gryphon did. Used me as a tool. Is it impossible for a dragon to do the same, at an even higher mental level?

She'd sniffed the grootslang tusk. Sniffed my sword. I thought she'd realized I'd killed a grootslang and decided that made me dangerous. No, she'd realized I'd killed a grootslang and decided that made me useful.

I am a puny human who can crawl into this tunnel where she can't go. I could kill her enemy for her. That's why she'd deposited me right at the entrance to the caverns. That's why she hadn't been the least bit upset when I "escaped" down here. I was doing what she wanted.

To the dragon, I'm a terrier dropped into a rat hole.

I could grumble at that. But in a funny way, she's just exercising her rights. Haven't I been insisting the dragon is on our soil? She's a citizen of Tamarel. As such, she's entitled to the services of the royal monster hunter.

I laugh under my breath, making both Malric and Jacko look over sharply.

"She wants us to stop this monster," I say. "I agree that we should. I have no idea what it is, but it's slaughtering other monsters and scaring them and upsetting the balance."

I bend to examine the bigger of the two young dragons. It's less decomposed than the other one, and I can make out bite marks on both the back and front of its neck.

"Attacked from behind," I muse. "Dragged into the forest where its mother couldn't follow. Then killed with a throat rip. That's an unusual combination. Ambush predator, I'm guessing. The bite to the back is more feline, but the throat rip is more canine."

I keep talking out loud. It helps me focus and seems to calm the nerves of the two monsters. "Clear bite marks here." I finger the piercings. "Smaller than yours, Malric. Bigger than Jacko's. It's not big, as monsters go. Just very good at killing."

I shudder and rise. "Whatever its size, I'm not hanging around waiting to kill it on my own."

The problem is that the dragon might be sitting outside, waiting for me to do her bidding. That's one of the most common gripes of monster hunters. Whenever someone called Jannah to evict a monster, she'd ask them to go stay with a neighbor while the hunters worked. Some argued. Others pretended to leave only to sneak back and watch.

Jannah used to grumble that she should supplement her income selling tickets. Maybe hire a pie-seller for refreshments. While I'm sure people had watched for entertainment, it had felt like scrutiny. As if they were judging her performance, the way one might watch over a builder to be sure they did the job right. Few things are more annoying to professionals.

Is the dragon waiting at the other end of the tunnel? Making sure we do the job? I hope not. I *will* do this for her. I'm just not the girl I was six months ago, who'd never have considered getting help for one relatively small monster.

I will get help. First, I poke at a couple of the more recent corpses, trying to glean more information on this unknown monster. But I can't. Just more teeth marks of the same size. More monsters killed the same way. Some look as if they were attacked head-on and had time to fight. Others were ambushed. I find no scat or footprints. It obviously relieves itself elsewhere, and the rock floor doesn't reveal any secrets.

We're heading out when we hear the first noise. A rhythmic *skritch-skritch*, like nails on rock? That's valid information. Sharp claws retract. Dull nails do not. Even Jacko's semi-retractable claws make no noise as he walks. This doesn't quite sound like nails, though. It's scratchier.

The point is that the beast is coming. Perhaps the fact that I don't panic at that means there's still a bit of that other girl inside me. The new version won't intentionally tackle an unknown monster but doesn't mind the chance to get a look at it and add data, especially if there's only one exit and the monster is currently in it, blocking her escape.

I look around quickly. The smell of this place will cover our scents. That lets us try a little ambush of our own.

CHAPTER THIRTY-ONE

The first step is to get rid of my torch. Extinguishing it would leave me in darkness, so I find a spot on the opposite side of the cavern and stick in into a ribcage. That'll get the monster's attention.

The tunnel opens into the cavern about twenty feet away. I hurry over to hide behind the corpse of that young manticore. It's large enough to hide us from sight, and in the right state of decomposition to hide us from smell.

I push the manticore corpse onto its side as a shield. Yes, that's as disgusting as it sounds. Malric helps, though, and then we position ourselves behind it, my leg complaining as I bend. I ask Jacko to stay hidden and not be tempted to peek out. I'm the one who does the peeking. The manticore's mane remains intact, and I part that to peer through it as I watch the entrance.

That *skritch-skritch* continues, and as I try to puzzle it out, I hear something else—the dull swish of a corpse being dragged. The monster has brought another kill to add to its store. That means it's distracted. Excellent.

I consider my weapon options. I have my regular dagger in hand. It's small enough to hold while hiding, but not as sharp as the stiletto, which I've accidentally nicked myself with more than once. The weapon I choose depends on the beast that comes through that door. The ebony sword does the most damage, but it's heavy and best used to deliver one or two strong blows. The dagger is good for fast and quick motions. Same as the stiletto, and its added sharpness is perfect for piercing monster armor.

I'm mulling over scenarios when I recognize what kind of nails make that sound. It's the stiletto that helps with the connection. I'm thinking about which weapon is best in which situation, which makes me think that Madlyn would have been better off attacking the grootslang with her stiletto, with the hope that the sharp blade would pierce its scales.

Scales. Snake. Reptile.

That's what I'm hearing. Not the click of nails but the scratch of talons. My mind skates past the possibility of a bird. We're in the wrong environment for that.

This is the lair of a reptilian monster. What if the dragon wasn't the only of her kind to relocate? She comes here in search of a safe place to raise her babies, and another reptilian beast arrives, too. Maybe it even followed her, fleeing a catastrophe in their homeland.

I know a handful of reptilian monsters, but none are this wantonly destructive. This is something new, and I cannot help but be a little excited to see what sort of creature will appear from that doorway. My fingers tap the stiletto in my boot. That's probably the right choice. Just be patient. It's getting closer.

Finally, something appears. At first, it's a dark shape. Then I see color, as it moves into the light. Orange and yellow, a blaze as bright as fire itself. A memory flashes, that of a firebird with the same coloration of feathers.

I blink. These are also feathers. A bird? I'd dismissed that, which was a mistake. Not all birds fly, and some do use burrows.

It's definitely not a firebird, but it *is* feathered and seems to have wings. It's walking with a smooth gait, like a terrestrial animal rather than a bird. Equally at home on land? Or a flightless bird?

When it drops whatever it has dragged in and straightens, it's as tall as me. A flightless bird, I think, given the powerful back legs. Back legs that end in large talons. When I squint, I can make out an unusual talon that doesn't touch the ground as the beast walks. It's curved, and I shiver seeing it. Definitely not like the dewclaw of a canine. This is a killing tool. I remember the torn bellies. Not ripped open but torn as if with a knife. Torn with this claw?

When the beast drops its prey and straightens, I see its head and frown. It's a thick head and not particularly birdlike. The beak must be short and powerful, like a parrot's.

It continues walking with that even, powerful gait. Then the light falls on it, and I stifle a gasp. I blink and look again.

It's not a bird. It's exactly what I originally thought: a reptilian monster. Instead of scales, it has feathers. The "wings" are front legs with a fringe of feathers. There's no beak but a thick head with a snout like a lizard and a crown of feathers that shimmer as it moves.

I fight against the urge to lean closer, to get a better look. I've never seen anything like this. I remember, as a child, Jannah told me that birds and reptiles have common ancestors. I didn't believe her until she showed me a plucked bird beside a lizard and pointed out the similarities. Their internal organs are similar. Both lay eggs. Both can have talons and orbital eye sockets. Birds have scales, too, on their legs, and their feathers are produced by skin similar to scale-producing skin.

The beast is moving toward the torch. It must have noticed it right away, but it seems more curious than concerned. Halfway there, it stops. It goes completely, unnaturally still. Then something on its neck flutters. Gills? I squint. They look like gills.

Is that how it got to our land? It swam?

The gills stop fluttering. The beast goes so still that a chill runs down my spine, and I tighten my grip on the dagger, wishing I'd drawn my sword instead. I'd been so caught up in studying the creature that I forgot I was studying it to figure out which blade to use. My sword is the obvious choice. The beast is too big and muscled for the dagger. I need—

The monster charges. It happens so fast I don't have time to raise my dagger. One moment it's standing still, looking toward the torch, and then it's coming straight at us without even seeming to turn our way.

Malric lunges, but even his move is a fraction of a moment too slow, as if he, too, is caught off guard. Yet the monster is also not expecting to see a full-grown warg in its den.

Malric hits the beast full-on. As it flies back, it snaps at him, mouth opening to show jagged teeth, like dozens of stiletto dagger tips.

Ignoring the pain in my leg, I rush out as I pull my sword from its sheath. The beast sees me coming, and it dives to the side, with shocking grace for such a muscular body. Malric lunges again, and the monster jumps into the air. The move startles us both. It flies up like a big cat, twisting to come down on Malric. As it does, those rear hooked claws extend, and I understand what it plans. Land on Malric's back and tear into him with those claws.

"No!" I shout and I race forward, swinging my sword. The blade sinks into the beast's haunch, and it screams a birdlike shriek of rage.

The sword cleaves deep. Blood sprays. Malric twists and drags the beast down. Its hind legs pull in, ready to rake him with those terrible claws. I hit it again, this time in the ribs. Another scream. Then Malric has it by the throat. He rips in, and the beast screams as if it cannot believe this is happening. This should *not* happen. It is an apex predator. It kills *dragons*.

"Baby dragons," I snarl as the life fades from its eyes. "You kill baby dragons and young wargs and jackalopes and warakins."

When the beast lies still, I prod it with my sword to be sure it's dead. Then I exhale. I would not have wanted to face that on my own, but it clearly hadn't been prepared for a full-grown warg and a human with a sword. It had probably never *seen* a sword.

"We got lucky," I say as I shift my weight off my injured leg.

Jacko chitters.

"All right," I say. "Some skill, too."

He chitters again, and it's an unusual sound, as if he's trying to do it quietly. Then Malric drops the monster. He goes still, staring.

Another sound comes. Almost like Jacko's chittering. A *click-click*. Then another. I grip my sword and slowly turn to see two more of the beasts just inside the entrance. A third one stands in the doorway, watching. All of them are perfectly still. They're making that sound. Clicking as if communicating with each other.

Before I can react, one leaps into the air, propelled by those powerful hind legs. It's not coming at us—it's going for Jacko, still over by the manticore, where he'd wisely stayed out of the fight.

"Jacko! Run!" I shout as I race toward him.

He's already doing just that. Racing across the bodies, a blur of brown fur. Another of the monsters charges, and somehow it moves even faster.

Malric leaps between me and the monsters. I'm running as fast as my injured leg will allow, but I feel as if I'm moving in slow motion. Jacko is the fastest of us all, yet this beast is somehow faster.

They're halfway across the cavern, and I'm still ten feet away when the beast snatches him up. Jacko screams as those needle-teeth chomp down on him. I scream, too. The sound rips from my throat, and then I am there, swinging with all my might. My sword hits the beast in the neck with such force that it nearly decapitates the creature.

Any other time I'd have been shocked and maybe a little elated, too—it's a masterful strike, a feat of strength that I didn't know I had. Later I will marvel at it. For now, all that matters is my jackalope.

When my sword slices into the beast's neck, it should drop Jacko. It doesn't. Even now, head barely attached to its body, its jaws stay clamped around him. I want to free him without a second thought. But I must take that second thought.

"Malric!" I say.

He knows what I need and backs into the space between me and the other two monsters. He snarls and snaps, and maybe that holds them off. Or maybe what gives them pause is what I just did to their comrade. Either way, I have the time I need to pry open the beast's jaws and extricate Jacko. He's bleeding from a dozen tiny stab wounds, and he's shaking as if in shock, but his heart beats strong and his breathing is deep.

As I adjust him in my arms, a movement at the entrance turns into another of the creatures. It hisses at me, and then the other two make those clicking noises, and it stops and eyes me.

Two dead. Three still alive. Are there more? I shiver just thinking that. I'm not sure we can even deal with three, certainly not with Jacko in my arms. If I put him down, though, they'll go for him. I know they will. Those cold reptilian eyes move from me to him, assessing and considering.

I don't know what to do. I honestly do not. We might be able to fight three, if they came one at a time. Not if they launched a concerted attack, and from the way they're communicating, I suspect that's what's coming.

They've noticed we can fight one of them. Therefore, they are not going to let us keep doing that. They will strike as a group, and even if I put down my injured jackalope, Malric and I cannot handle three at once.

When a fourth appears, my gut sinks. We absolutely cannot fight four. But as I see it climb out of the tunnel, something glimmers deep in my brain.

They're coming through the tunnel one at a time. They have to. They're as big as me, as big as Malric. They can't walk two abreast in there.

One at a time.

"Malric?" I say. "We need to get in that tunnel." I gesture, hoping he'll understand, but I don't think he does. He growls, as if to say yes, he knows others could come out.

I bite off more words. I need to act and hope he understands then. First, we must get the creatures away from that tunnel entrance.

I back up. They follow, looking like birds now, gazes fixed on us as they move together, step by step, watching us. Malric moves in beside me, and they click at each other, as if they don't like that. They'd rather there was more space between us. Easier to separate us that way.

I back up until I can reach the torch. Then I cradle Jacko in one arm and grab the torch in the other. When I swing it, they fall back, clicking.

Move fast, my brain shouts. They're smart. Too smart. Give them time to think this through and they will. I shout at the top of my lungs, a wordless scream as I charge, waving the torch. I hit one with it, and the beast shrieks. I slam the torch into another, and it falls back. Then one snaps at me. It snaps at the arm holding the torch.

Smart. *Too* smart.

I slam the torch into its open mouth. Ram it in with everything I have. Its scream of pain sends them all staggering back, and then I let go of the torch and run for the tunnel. My injured leg gives way, and I stumble. Malric pushes from behind, and I grit my teeth and get my footing.

I run the last few steps and dive through, scrambling on my knees and one hand as I cradle Jacko.

I glance back only long enough to be sure Malric has followed. Of course he has. He's in the tunnel. Then he bellows in pain.

I twist. One of the monsters has Malric by the leg. I shove Jacko ahead of me and turn to help the warg, but he's already spun on the beast. It has his leg, but these tight quarters let Malric twist and clamp down hard on the beast's neck.

These tight quarters, though, also mean I can't get back there to help. For a moment, it seems the monster is going to drag Malric into the cavern. But Malric must bite harder, because it lets go and retreats with hisses and angry chatter.

"Are you okay?" I ask.

Malric's answer is a hard nudge telling me to keep going. I try to scoop up Jacko but he hops out of my reach. It's a slow hop—he's hurting badly—but he clearly wants to proceed on his own power.

Behind us, monsters click and chatter, talking among themselves. Planning? Can they do that?

Pack animals can coordinate a strike, but it's instinct plus body language, meaning they can't plan in advance. I know monsters like Malric can think things through and strategize an attack. But the ability to coordinate a plan with others suggests an intelligence that both excites and terrifies me. Mostly "terrifies" right now, and so I tell myself they're just communicating, not planning. That's too scary to contemplate.

They don't come after us. Maybe that's what they were discussing. Whether they should bother giving chase. Good. Jacko is injured. So am I and now, so is Malric. We must get out. Get help. Come back and deal with these creatures.

We move as fast as we can. When the tunnel opens enough, I grab Jacko over his protests and break into a halting jog, my injured leg shaking. I glance back to be sure Malric's own leg isn't too hurt for him to keep up. It's not.

The clomp of my boots swallows all other sound, and when I hear a click, I only slow, thinking I'm imagining it. Then another one comes, and I freeze in place.

CHAPTER THIRTY-TWO

ilence.

Did I imagine the sound? I peer past Malric. The warg is already looking back. We'd just rounded a corner, so we can't see far. Everything is silent and still, and I know I didn't hear the *skritch* of talons against the stone. We resume walking. When another click comes, I pause. Look back. See nothing. Squint forward. Also nothing.

Malric sniffs the air only to shake his head with a growl that says he hears nothing either. Still, to be sure, I hoist Jacko onto my shoulders. That means I have to stoop so his antlers don't scrape the ceiling, but he hunkers down and we continue on.

With my stiletto blade gripped in one hand, I pick up speed. I'm focused on what's ahead, while letting Malric focus on what's behind. When Jacko gives a deafening shriek, I somehow register movement out of the corner of my eye, and I spin just as one of the monsters vaults from a side passage.

I hit it with the dagger. I don't have time to aim. I see those jaws opening, those razor teeth flashing, and I strike.

The dagger makes contact just as the beast grabs my arm. I scream. I knew what those teeth looked like—all those tiny dagger tips—but when they sink in, the pain is excruciating. I'm wearing my hardened leather jacket, and those teeth pierce through as if it's a simple wool tunic.

It's the smallest of the four beasts—able to get through that narrow side passage—but it's still as big as me. I switch the dagger into my other hand. I don't even mentally process the fact that I should do that—I just do. That puts it in my weaker hand, but at least it's not the arm currently being held in a razor vise-grip.

When I pull back to strike, a connection clicks. Something about the color of the feathers reminding me of cockatrices, which reminds me of their signature attack move.

I aim for the beast's eye. As my blade hits, it screams and that frees my arm. I rip away and dance backward. Only then do I realize Jacko has leapt off my shoulders. He's on the floor behind me. I bash into him, but I don't trip, only stagger back into the wall. The monster slashes with its front leg. I haven't paid attention to its forelegs until now. I only noticed the long feathers that made me mistake them for wings. Now I see what those feathers hide. Three curved talons, each as big as my forearm.

I meet the strike with my dagger, but it's the wrong move. The stiletto is too long and thin to block a blow. Talons rake my arm, already raw and bloody from the beast's teeth. I need my sword, but this passage is too low for me to pull it out. I slash. Wildly slash, even as my brain screams that I must do better, must be more precise.

I need help. I need Malric, and it's only as I think this that I realize he hasn't come to my aid. I look over to see him fighting another of the monsters. One must have raced down the tunnel as this one appeared from the side passage.

Coordinated attack.

The monster swipes at me with its front talons. I dodge, and it grabs me with its other talons—as if that first swipe was meant to make me fall right into its grip. The trio of talons wraps around my arm, as if it's a hand, holding me tight while it slashes with the other foot.

I lift my good leg, my bad one screaming at the extra weight. Then I kick. I expect to hit the mass of the beast's torso, and I do, but what I don't expect is for my kick to have much impact. With such solid muscles, it must be a heavy creature. To my shock, my foot slams the beast backward.

I slash upward with the dagger and hit the bottom of that feathered forearm. The blade slices deep and the creature screams. I throw myself to the side hoping to break the beast's grip. Again, I am surprised. The creature flies up into the air. It should be too heavy. But it's light. Maybe even lighter than me. That's how it's so dexterous and graceful. Heavily muscled, but lightweight like a bird.

I switch tactics and drop down while lifting my arm, the one the beast still holds, as I throw it over me. It goes flying . . . and then I see the rear claws. Those terrible rear claws.

I'm throwing the beast down, and it launches itself into a leap, and those two hooked claws extend, coming straight for my chest.

But then the beast's head whips back, and its jaws snap.

That distraction is just enough to allow me to roll out of the way. Then I see what distracted it—Jacko, latched onto the back of its neck, biting and digging in all his claws.

I thrust my stiletto into the beast's throat, but at the last second, it throws its head back again, trying to dislodge Jacko, and I stab through the bottom of its jaw instead. It thrashes, and I have to release the stiletto before I'm slammed into the wall. I reach for my sturdier dagger—

Jacko shrieks. This time, I don't hesitate. I know what he's saying, and I see where he's looking, and I spin just as another monster leaps at me from the back. It jumps with its front and rear talons extended. I twist aside, but it still hits me.

Talons scrape my injured arm and one of those deadly back claws slices through my leather leggings and catches on the arrow still impaled in my leg.

That arrow is the only thing that's saving my leg from being ripped open. The talon catches it, and I go flying. Pain slams through me, so fierce I black out. I hit the floor and startle awake to see one monster on either side of me.

Jacko stays on the back of the first one, ripping into it, but it doesn't seem to care. Growls and shrieks from down the corridor tell me Malric is still locked in his battle.

The two monsters watch me with those unblinking bird-like gazes. As they do, they click to each other. I continue trying to tell myself they aren't planning. Yet I've already seen it happen. Seen three of them split up to confront us through different routes. And the fourth? Where is the fourth? My heart sinks as I look to where Malric fights. He's battling two of them. He must be.

We killed the first two creatures by sheer luck of catching them off guard and separated. They hadn't known what to expect with a full-grown warg fighting alongside a human. Now they do. Split us up. Two of them for each of us.

I don't know how to do this. It's just me and one young jackalope against two beasts the likes of which I've never seen. Predators like I've never seen. I have no idea—

I shake off that crushing fear. I know how to fight them. The answer is right in front of me—or beside me.

"Jacko!" I shout, and I put out my arms.

He hesitates for only a heartbeat. Then he leaps into them, and I dive into that narrow side passage, the one the smaller beast had come through.

As I dive, I do two things. Three, actually. One, shove Jacko into the passage. Two, twist around to face my enemies. Three, pull out my sword.

The passage is barely wide enough for me. That's why I'd ignored it earlier. Malric would never get through. I can, though, and I can wedge myself in so my back is protected and Jacko is behind me.

Make them fight me one at a time. That's the answer.

I hold my sword up and out, both hands wrapped around the hilt. I can't swing it, but it's still big and it's sharp, and when the first monster leaps into the opening, I thrust the sword like a battering ram. It skewers the beast, which fights free and disappears into the other passage, screaming.

I pull back and wait for the other to try the same thing. They're too smart for that, though.

From where I stand, half hunched, sword ready to thrust again, I can't see them. I can hear them, though. One clicks at the other. The other does not answer.

The silent beast is the one I hit. A fatal blow? When I focus, I hear it gasping. Then another sound. The roar of an enraged warg. A thump. A wet ripping sound.

I fly from my safe spot then. I can't hide, not when I can't see what's happening. I get out just in time to see Malric climbing over a dying monster with its chest torn open. Another one lies dead behind it.

My second target stands past the side passage. It's the one I half blinded, the stiletto still in its jaw. As Malric advances on it, talons scratch rock, the fast scratch of something coming at top speed. The fourth monster. It must have retreated from its fight with Malric, and now it's back.

"Malric!"

He twists to meet the oncoming beast as I rush at the injured one, my sword out. It turns, scrabbling at the floor. Then it runs. I give chase, my leg screaming, and I've gone no more than a dozen steps before the beast in front of me screams, too. It falls back, gasping, and I think my stiletto somehow worked its way to its windpipe. Then I see the arrow sticking from its throat.

A familiar arrow with familiar firebird fletching.

"Dain!" I shout.

A light fills the tunnel, and Dain's face appears behind it. He reaches the beast before I do and yanks out both the arrow and the stiletto.

"Yours, princess?"

I don't answer. I'm already running back down the tunnel to Malric. When I get there, he has the other beast pinned. I switch to my dagger and fall on it, and deliver the killing blow as he holds it down.

As the fourth beast twitches in death, I sag against the wall, catching my breath. Then Dain's there, and I fall onto him before I can think twice. I realize my mistake, but his arms only close around me, and I let myself lean against him, shaking in relief and exhilaration.

CHAPTER THIRTY-THREE

We're out of the tunnel. Out into the clearing and staring at the bodies of six more of those monsters. A half dozen of the terrible creatures, all dead. One soldier, his face covered, also lies dead. Several injured are being treated by Alianor and an army doctor. My brother is there, too, and when I see him, I gasp and try to run, only to have my injured leg finally give way. Dain catches me, and I fall into him as Trysten rushes over to help me sit on the ground, and Alianor comes running with, "What happened to *you?*"

"They killed six of them," Dain says, and there's something like pride in his voice, as if he's the one who did it. "*Six* between the two of them."

"The three of us," I say. "Jacko helped. And you killed that last one."

"Yeah, because it was so panicked running from *you* that it never saw me coming."

Rhydd crouches beside me, pointing out all my injuries until Alianor swats him away with, "I have eyes, your highness."

"Jacko's hurt, too," I say. "And Malric. You should check them first."

"I'll check everyone," she says. "You really killed six?"

"Dain killed one."

She rolls her eyes. "Stop that. It was six. You, Malric and Jacko killed six, while *these* six required all of us plus soldiers."

"It's the den down there," I say, raising my voice as Wilmot and Kaylein come over. "They've been slaughtering monsters, including two of the dragon's young."

Dain nods. "I saw it. Rowan insisted I take a look before we came out. It's full of monsters. Dozens of them. All dead. Hardly eaten."

"Because it wasn't about eating. It was about clearing the territory." I look up to see General Corisande standing there and continue, "*This* is what made the monsters migrate. I think wherever the dragon is from, these things followed and started killing competitors, including her babies. She brought me here to kill them."

Alianor snorts. "Sure, one monster hunter to kill a *dozen* of those things. No problem."

I look around the bloody field and shudder as I imagine what would have happened if the other six had come back into the nest. We wouldn't have stood a chance.

Inside, Dain had explained that they'd followed the dragon. The general had insisted on coming after them with a handful of soldiers. They'd arrived just as the monsters were returning to the nest, the dragon long gone.

The monsters attacked, and they'd fought. Rhydd and a few others had arrived just in time to help, having escaped house arrest with the aid of those loyal to the king. King Estienne is back with the rest of the troops. He'd stayed there to take advantage of the opportunity to explain what happened before General Corisande returned.

I look at the general. "These monsters are what caused the disturbances we've been seeing. I don't care if you don't believe me. Or maybe you do believe me, and *you* just don't care. It wasn't about the dragon. I understand that."

I lock gazes with her, and she straightens. "Of course it was about the dragon, princess. Whatever else you are implying—"

"I don't care," I say. "Really don't. Rhydd is the politician. I'm the royal monster hunter. I hunted these monsters, and your soldiers helped." I push to my feet to stand before her. "I take responsibility for the dragons. I believe I have resolved the issue that was upsetting the matriarch. If I have not, then I will fix that. Tamarel will fix it. Our dragons. Our responsibility."

Rhydd steps beside me. "Rowan is right. *Our* dragons. *Our* responsibility. We appreciate what you did here today, helping us end this threat. We will happily send a few of these corpses to your universities for study. Otherwise?"

"Get off our land."

I expect that to come from Alianor. Instead, it's Dain, who moves up on my other side.

The general looks between us. Then she dips her head. "All right."

I arch my brows, and that makes her laugh.

"I'm agreeing with you, princess," she says. "Conceding that the danger posed by the dragon seems to have been exaggerated. She attacked none of my soldiers, despite having multiple opportunities to do so, especially after knocking them unconscious. These other creatures posed a far greater threat, and we seem to have exterminated them."

"We'll make sure of that," I say.

"I have no doubt that you will, and so I agree. Your dragons. Your responsibility. We will return to our king, resolve our issues with him and leave you to your land."

We're back at the camp the Roivan army erected. King Estienne has spoken to the army, and I don't know what he said, but when General Corisande returns, her soldiers don't run out to take her prisoner. They don't even give her sidelong looks, as if suspecting she'd been part of a coup to overthrow the king.

Whatever King Estienne said to them, it gave her an opening, a chance to continue as his general, while they both know what she attempted. Is that the best way to handle it? I have no idea. Which proves I was never cut out to be a monarch.

Liliath has arrived with the guards who'd stayed behind to accompany her at her slower pace. While the others settle in to our camp, away from the army, Liliath, Rhydd and I go to speak to the king about Trysten. We don't bring Trysten. This is a private conversation to explore options. We tell the king about Madlyn and the bounty and what Trysten's father planned. He seems sickened but not particularly surprised, given what he knows of Dorwynne's king.

We talk options. Then I speak to Rhydd on the way back to camp. When we reach it, it's not Trysten I ask to come for a walk. It's Dain.

"You shouldn't *be* walking," he grumbles as soon as we're out of earshot of the others.

"Are you offering to carry me?"

"No, but I think Malric is." He turns to the warg. "You'd be fine with that, right? Get a cart to pull your princess."

I laugh. "I might actually go for that, but I don't think *he* would. Right now, he'd probably like a cart for himself."

Malric's limping slightly. Earlier, Dain brought me a makeshift cane, and that helps with my leg. Malric has ignored all my invitations to stay behind. Same as Jacko, who won't even ride on my shoulders. He knows I'm injured. He is, too, with a score of piercings and bruises. Still, we're all on our feet and moving, at least until Dain insists we sit.

He takes Dez from her pouch, and she snuggles in with Jacko as they rest.

"I'm guessing you want to talk to me," Dain says.

I nod. "It's about Trysten."

He stiffens and then hides it by fussing with his boot. "All right."

"He can't go home, and King Estienne is happy to foster him, but we're thinking of inviting him to make good on his father's lie to his mother. To come to our castle for fostering."

"All right."

"But living with King Estienne would be good, too. Maybe even more what Trysten would want, being closer to his mother."

"What he wants is to be closer to—" Dain cuts his words short and adjusts his other boot. "All right."

"I haven't spoken to Trysten because I wanted to talk to you first."

"Me? I don't have anything to do with it."

"Yes, you do. You're my friend. You live at the castle, and you're training to be a hunter. I don't want to do anything to change any of that. Which means if you don't want Trysten there, then he won't be there."

Dain sighs, a deep sigh that ripples through his entire body. "I don't *not* like Trysten, Rowan. That's impossible. He's *very* likable." There's a note almost like bitterness in his voice, but he swallows it before squaring his shoulders. "I'm fine with him."

"No, you're not."

He goes quiet and keeps fussing, as if longing for an arrow to whittle, something to do with his hands. Then he blurts, "He likes you. He's made it very obvious that he likes you as more than a friend, and that makes me feel . . ." He rolls his shoulders. "Uncomfortable? Awkward? Weird? I don't know the word. It just bugs me."

"Because if I liked him back, as more than a friend, then he might have a problem with me having other boys as friends."

"*Yes.*" The word comes almost on a sigh of relief. "That must be why it bugs me." He nods. "That must be what I'm worried about. That he'll see me as competition. Which I'm not. But it could make things uncomfortable, if you liked him back." His gaze lifts to mine. "Do you like him?"

"Trysten is very likable, as you said. He's smart, and he's kind."

"And a prince."

I shrug. "I don't think that makes anyone more likable. It just makes people want to like them more and be liked by them more. Which doesn't apply with me, already being a princess."

"But he'd be a good match."

"Are you trying to marry me off, Dain? I'm *twelve*."

He blushes. "Of course not. I'm just saying, if you like him and he's a handsome prince, then . . ."

"I do like him. As a friend. That's it."

"That could change."

"Maybe? I don't think so, though. I know he likes me, and that's flattering, but it also feels awkward. I'd rather he liked me as a friend, because I can't imagine thinking of him any other way. I just can't."

He looks at me. Just looks, his expression unreadable. Then he nods and rises. "I'll go get him. Wait here."

He lopes off. Dez gives a chirp and leaps into the trees to follow aerially. A few moments later, Dain returns with Trysten.

"You want to talk to me?" Trysten says to me.

"We do," Dain says. "It's about where you go after this. Obviously, you can't return to Dorwynne. Not yet. King Estienne offered you a place there, but Rowan and Rhydd thought you might prefer to go home with them and be fostered, like your mother already thinks is the case."

Trysten looks from me to Dain and back. He's wondering why Dain is the one telling him this. Dain never speaks for me, and he hardly speaks to Trysten at all. Then he seems to understand. Dain is saying it to be clear he's okay with it. That the invitation comes from *all* of us.

"You might want to check with your mother first," Trysten says to me. "It's not exactly like inviting a friend over for the night."

"She'll be fine with it," I say. "It's up to us, and we'd like to extend the invitation."

"I'd still rather get the queen's approval," he says. "But I'll happily go back with you to ask her."

"Then that's what we'll do."

Today is the day I officially become the royal monster hunter of Tamarel. I'd been given Jannah's sword at her funeral, which made me the royal monster hunter—elect. Then, after my adventures, I'd been unofficially promoted. I still needed to do my trials, though, and the council had agreed that if I solved the dragon issue, that would count. I've done that. Now I'm home, in my chambers, preparing for the ceremony.

Alianor is with me. It's just us. We've been bathed and primped and pampered by maids, but Alianor insisted on doing my hair, and that means we get some time alone. Well, alone with our beasts.

Brise prowls my chambers, checking everything out. She's settling in, though the staff isn't quite sure about having a nian living *inside* the palace. Malric is another matter—they've known him since puppyhood and he plays an official role. For now, Brise is allowed to stay in Alianor's quarters and venture out only when Alianor accompanies her.

When Brise gets too close to Malric's spot by the fire, the warg growls. He's warming his injured leg by the flames. It's healing better now that we're home and he can stay in one place. Same with my leg. My arm is bandaged and will probably scar, but Alianor keeps telling me scars are a mark of honor, like beauty spots from battle.

Jacko's healed and doing well. He's curled up next to Malric, and when no one's looking, Malric lets the jackalope lean against him.

Chikako is there, too, though the chickcharney has taken refuge on my bed, where she can watch the prowling nian. Her big eyes follow Brise, who has learned to pay her no mind after being scolded by Alianor.

"How big do nians get?" Alianor asks as she twists my hair up.

"As big as Malric, maybe bigger. You're going to need to do some training with her. Socialization and manners."

"Manners?" She wrinkles her nose as I watch her in the mirror. "Hardly befitting a wild beast. What about tricks? Can I teach her tricks?"

"Hardly befitting a wild beast."

She laughs and twists another piece of my hair. Neither of us is wearing a ball gown, which Alianor has already complained about. We aren't going to the ceremony as a princess and her friend. We're going as a hunter and a future doctor. Professionals with careers. I'm dressed in a new ceremonial hunter outfit, leather tanned and dyed black and green. She wears an adventuring outfit, so everyone will know she was part of our expedition.

"So what are we going to do about Sarika?" she asks as she fusses with my hair.

I frown at her in the mirror.

"Sarika and the king?" she says with exasperation. "The royal romance? We have to do *something*. We can't just let the young lovers pine in their separate lands, never to be reunited. That's a fine bard's tale, but not nearly as satisfying in real life."

"What do you suggest?"

"We need to invite him to the castle. And then make an excuse to invite Sarika."

"He's a king dealing with the aftermath of a coup. He can't go on social visits."

"Then we'll need to take her to him," she says quickly, as if this had been her hope all along. "You insist you need Sarika fully trained in geology, so she can check out the dragon's cave and what stopped up the river. We'll escort her. We need to check on the dragons, after all. Plus, you should visit King Estienne to be sure everything's fine there with their new relationship to the dragons. Oh, and we can stop in to visit the gryphons, see how Tiera is doing. Then we'll take my sister to the kingdom and . . ."

Alianor launches into an elaborate plan to reunite her sister and the king, and I just settle into the chair, smiling and listening to her chatter.

CHAPTER THIRTY-FOUR

We are in the courtyard. I'm with Dain and Alianor, standing on a small platform and feeling like an animal on display. The real "display" is down below us: tables set up with specimens from our latest adventure. The grootslang tusks on one, along with the sketches I made of the beast, complete with humans for scale. Dain still promises he's making me something from one tusk, though he won't tell me what it is. Another table holds feathers we'd taken as souvenirs—from the cockatrices and the unknown monsters, plus one huge one Alianor scooped up from the roc and presented me with on the way home ... mostly so I'd offer to carry it.

Another table holds the preserved remains of two of the unknown reptilian monsters, which Alianor insists we call "rowansaurs"—and Sarika is writing up a petition to the Roivan university to do just that, which is embarrassing but exciting, too. We brought home two of the rowansaurs—yes, I'm going to start calling them that—one for display and one for the hunters to study, in case we ever encounter more, though I'm really hoping we don't.

A third table holds dragon scales and the preserved body of one of the dead juveniles. We'd brought the dead young dragons up into the clearing, and I'd stayed there until their mother came. She'd sniffed both. Then she sniffed the dead rowansaurs. Then she left. We took that to mean it was okay to do what we wanted with the juveniles, so one came with us and one went to the Roivan university for study.

As we stand on our platform, an endless queue of people pass by the tables. They marvel at the creatures and glance surreptitiously at us, standing ten feet away. I long to be at the tables instead, talking to everyone and explaining what they're seeing, but my sketches and notes will need to do. If we were at those tables, the line wouldn't move. Most people don't want my facts and science anyway. They want the stories, and we can write those up later for the bards.

Trysten is on the other side of the tables, standing with Wilmot and Kaylein; they are positioned so everyone understands they were part of my excursion. I wanted Trysten with us, but he bowed out.

He *will* be fostering at the castle. As expected, Mom has no concerns with that, and she's been nothing but welcoming. We've already dispatched a letter to Trysten's mother.

Mom herself stands closer to the castle, with Berinon and Rhydd. Every time I glance over, I see Mom and Berinon watching us with a pride that settles my racing heart a little.

Cedany is off to the side waiting for Kaylein. She wears Madlyn's necklace. She didn't have a good relationship with her aunt, who'd wanted Cedany to join her troop of mercenaries, but it helps that, in the end, Madlyn saw her mistake and supported Cedany's choice.

Malric is with me, lying at my feet. Jacko sits calmly beside him. They're the only monsters around. Sunniva and Doscach had joined our journey home, somehow managing to slip in *after* the rowansaurs were all dead, as we've teased. They're in the pasture resting. Dez and Brise are in Dain's and Alianor's quarters, neither yet accustomed to large crowds.

When Heward and the other council members file into the courtyard, it shatters any calm I've managed. They need to recognize me as royal monster hunter, and I'm terrified that Heward will find yet another reason to refuse. While most things are decided by a majority vote, in this they must be unanimous.

When Alianor sees me watching them, she takes my hand. Then she leans across me to whisper, "Take Rowan's hand."

Dain blinks at her.

She rolls her eyes and lifts our linked hands. "This is the big moment, and she's nervous. She needs her friends."

Before I can tell Dain that he doesn't need to, he clasps my hand in his and squeezes. I look at him and then at Alianor, and then down at Malric and Jacko, and I smile. As much as I appreciate everyone else here, we were the first. The five of us, on that initial adventure together as monster hunters. It is fitting that we are here together now.

A trumpet blares three notes, telling people to hurry into the courtyard for the ceremony. The specimens will remain afterward for those who didn't get a chance to see them.

When the passage between us clears, Mom comes over to escort me to the dais. Malric rises, but she puts out a hand to stop him.

"No, Malric," she says. "Just Rowan."

Dain scoops up Jacko, who chirps in surprise but doesn't fight. We proceed into the courtyard and up the steps to a small platform. The council members stand below.

The trumpet sounds again, and everyone goes quiet. Mom moves to the front of the dais and addresses the crowd.

"We have a tradition in Tamarel," she says. "The monarch's firstborn child inherits the ivory throne. But an equally important job goes to the second-born. Perhaps, in some ways, an even more important job. We are a country of monsters, surrounded by them on all sides, cut off from other nations by them. My clan—Clan Dacre—developed a talent for fighting monsters. Call it a gift or a skill, we understand and respect beasts, while never putting their needs above the needs of our people. We united our great country under the promise that we would keep you safe from the monsters. To do that, a monarch's second-born is tasked with overseeing that duty. With being the royal monster hunter."

She pauses. This is nothing new to anyone, but everyone listens as if they've never heard it before.

Mom continues, "My sister devoted her life to this task. She gave her life to it, at far too young an age. And so my daughter took up the ebony sword at a *ridiculously* young age."

Mom's smile for me is half fond, half sad. Then she turns back to the crowd. "Princess Rowan is a true daughter of Clan Dacre. She has a gift, the likes of which even my sister admitted she had never seen before. My daughter has an affinity for the beasts. They understand her, and they respect her, and when they must, they fear her. I'm sure I don't need to recite her deeds since taking up the sword."

She pauses, and of course the crowd shouts that they want the recitation. And of course, Mom is prepared.

"The highlights, then, or we'll be here all day."

A chuckle ripples through the audience.

"First, she survived being taken by a gryphon, not once but twice. She had the chance to kill that gryphon but realized it was pregnant and knew that afforded an incredible chance for us to research the beasts. When the mother died, she raised the baby herself. When it became too big to stay, she took it to an aerie in the mountains, fighting monsters along the way. Then she headed into those mountains again to discover what was causing the beast migration. Dragons, or so it seemed at first. She went into the dragons' den *twice* and not only survived but impressed the mother dragon enough that it recruited her to fight the true menace. I believe the dragons owe us taxes for that."

She pauses for the laughter.

"Rowan faced six of those beasts with her warg and jackalope, while our hunters and Roivan soldiers took on another half dozen. The threat has been eliminated. The Roivans are happy and the dragon is, too, apparently. Oh, and on that excursion my daughter was also kidnapped—twice—and she killed a grootslang by . . . Well, I've heard a rumor that she jumped into its open mouth to save her companion and slew the beast from the inside, but I'll pretend that's not what actually happened, or I may never sleep again."

More laughter.

"Along the way, Rowan gathered human companions and beasts. There's Malric, of course. Also a jackalope, a pegasus, a chickcharney and a ceffyl-dwr." She looks at me. "That is the complete list, correct? I won't wake to find a jba-fofi in my castle?"

"Nah," Alianor calls. "Just a couple of young dragons who think she's the best playmate ever. Also possibly a young roc as big as the castle."

Mom gives an exaggerated eye roll. "Wonderful."

She goes serious then as she looks out. "My daughter has proven, over and over again, why she deserves to be the royal monster hunter. Why she may someday be the greatest one this country has ever seen."

"If she's not already," someone calls, and to my surprise, it's Wilmot, and my cheeks heat in pleasure.

Mom nods to him. Then she looks just below the dais. "Esteemed members of the Tamarelian royal council, I ask you to accept my daughter, as young as she is, as the head of our monster hunters. As the *royal* monster hunter. What say you?"

She turns to Liliath first, who gives enthusiastic approval. It goes down the line, one by one, as the council acknowledges me. The last is Heward, and when Mom says his name, silence follows.

That silence stretches for three heartbeats, and then a strange thing happens. A noise like a growl rises from the crowd as it ripples like a giant beast. The people's disapproval is palpable, and Heward doesn't miss it.

His jaw sets. Then he says, as if each word pains him, "I acknowledge Princess Rowan as the royal monster hunter of Tamarel."

A cheer goes up, swallowing the rest of the ceremonial words. My mother embraces me, and then Rhydd comes over, and the rest passes in a blur of relief so intense I can barely stand.

Before I know it, I'm walking down the dais steps as the crowd breaks up, the trumpets signaling the start of the festivities. Alianor and Dain run over, Jacko racing alongside them and leaping onto my shoulders. Trysten follows. Malric saunters toward me, taking his time, but when he reaches me, he pushes my hand for a pat. I scratch him behind the ears and he leans against me for a moment before standing straight. Jacko sounds his victory cry, and everyone laughs.

"You really are the royal monster hunter now," Dain says. "No one can take that away from you."

There's satisfaction in his voice. If I am the royal monster hunter, no one can take away his position at my side. No one will try, either, if I have anything to say about it.

I squeeze his hand, just briefly, and then Alianor says, "It's over, then. Just one more trial to endure."

"What?" I say. "I'm done my trials."

She shakes her head. "You forgot the most important one." She waves at the festivities unfolding around us. "You need to celebrate."

She grabs my hand and pulls me, laughing, as we all run and join the party.

Monsters

a field guide

PART. 4

Cockatrice

Legend says that cockatrices come
from rooster eggs. Of course roosters,
or cocks, can't lay eggs, but when hens are young, they
sometimes lay an egg without a yolk. In other words, they
lay an egg without the part that could become a chick.
People mistakenly believe these yolkless eggs have been
laid by roosters and that they'll hatch into baby cockatrices.
To be sure they don't, you're supposed to throw the egg
over a house without it touching the roof. When Rhydd and
I were little, we practiced throwing eggs over our house.
That's a lot easier when you don't live in a castle. We broke
a lot of eggs, and our parents made us spend the next
month cleaning out the henhouses.

Peryton

Perytons belong to the category of monsters Jannah called "animals with wings." Just as pegasi seem to be regular horses with wings, perytons look like regular deer with wings. There are differences, though, which are mostly in the skeletal structure. A regular deer (or horse) wouldn't get off the ground with wings—its body is too heavy. Perytons are more gracile than regular deer, meaning they're not just slightly smaller but all their body parts are thinner. Their bones are also lighter. These modifications, along with others, allow them to take flight.

KILLER PERYTONS?

I found a really weird "fact" about perytons in an old book. According to its author, when perytons are born, they cast a human shadow. If they kill a human, they get their own shadow back. I couldn't figure out what to take from this: Was the point that some perytons are driven to kill people to regain their shadows . . . or was it meant to be more of a warning that if a peryton has its own shadow, it's dangerous? Either way, I've never heard any confirmed reports of a peryton intentionally killing someone.

Bonnacon

ACIDIC DUNG

The most famous (infamous?) story about bonnacons is that they can fire lethally poisonous dung at their pursuers. They can't actually "fire" their dung. It is highly acidic, though, and will cause burns if touched. The acidity seems to arise from a combination of their diet and their unique digestive system. What makes the scat dangerous also makes it valuable, and people have been known to capture bonnacons to collect it. When properly treated, it makes an extremely potent manure for crops.

TOXIC EMISSIONS

Rhydd jokes that all the legends about bonnacons were clearly written by people with a five-year-old's sense of humor. I'll admit they were one of my favorite monsters when I was that age. Not only are they supposed to fire poisonous dung but the "wind" they pass is allegedly another defense mechanism. While the legends don't actually say it's toxic, they do say it smells so gross that, if emitted, it's enough to stop hunters from chasing the creature. I can't confirm that it *doesn't* smell really bad—I only know that the bonnacons we met didn't unleash it against us.

Nian

mane on both males and females

lion-like head

mane extends down back and over tail

boar-like tusks

ropy bull-like tail

body is more canine than feline

WHERE'S THE HORN?

The oldest accounts of nians insist the creatures once had a single horn, like a unicorn. There are many stories to explain the loss of it. My favorite tells of a pride of nians tormented by monkeys. The nians trapped the monkeys in a tree and then tried to shake them loose by stabbing the tree with their horns, except the horns got stuck and snapped off. One by one, the entire pride lost their horns. The monkeys then collected the horns and turned them into bugles, which they used to drive the pride off their land.

Kalabandar

RAISED BY MONKEY MEN

This story is true—it was reported in Roiva and fully investigated by their universities. More than fifty years ago, a three-year-old girl wandered away from her family's farm on the jungle's edge. Her village searched for months but found no sign of her. Ten years later, hunters were in the forest when they thought they spotted a human girl. Knowing this is a trick kalabandars play to lure people away from their belongings, the hunters didn't fall for it and sure enough, they soon had monkey men trying to steal from their camp. When the village found out, though, the girl's parents insisted on knowing exactly where this "girl" was seen. They set off into the jungle, where they found their daughter living among the kalabandars. She recognized them and came home, but for the rest of her life she insisted on living on the jungle's edge, and sometimes slipped back into the forest to visit her "other" family.

dark top and back of head
can look like human hair

prehensile
tail

dark lower
half looks like
trousers

fox-like snout

chest spots look
like buttons

hind legs smaller
than front

prehensile
hands and feet

Roc

Like the grootslang, the roc is one of what Jannah called the "monster monsters"—in other words, monsters of truly monstrous size. It looks very much like a giant eagle and appears to have no defensive or offensive "extras." It doesn't need them—it's an eagle big enough to carry off a full-grown cow for dinner. The only beasts that would pose a threat to it are grootslangs and dragons, and even then, an adult of either species would be evenly matched with the impressive roc.

A ROC RESCUE

There is a story about one of my ancestors, from the time before the clans united under ours. They say that a monster hunter was shipwrecked on an island while tracking a sea monster that had been terrorizing the coast. The island was the home of a roc. For a month, the hunter hid each time the monster came home to roost. Then he had an idea for how to get off the island: While the roc was asleep, he crept onto its back. The beast didn't even seem to notice he was there, and the next time it flew to the mainland, he went along for the ride.

Ramidreju

Most monsters are native to our continent. The ramidreju is an exception—it was introduced to Roiva hundreds of years ago. Some say that a few of the creatures stowed away on a ship. Others say that they were a "gift" to the Roivan queen from a suitor she'd turned down. In his country, ramidreju were horrible pests, breeding rapidly and destroying farmlands. He wanted to punish the queen by unleashing the beasts on her country, but the ramidreju quickly retreated to the mountains (which they liked better) and there, they became only a minor pest to border farms.

GOLD DIGGERS

With their long, thin bodies, curved claws and pig-like snouts, ramidreju are amazing diggers. Legend says that they dig so much because they are always in search of gold. One day, a farmer captured a ramidreju by accident, and when he realized what he had, he decided to keep it and send it out on a long rope, in hopes it would find gold and make him rich. Within a month, the beast had escaped, but not before digging under every inch of the farmer's crops, which collapsed into the ground. The man spent the rest of his life looking for that ramidreju, convinced it had discovered gold and fled with it.

Grootslang

elephantine ears
that rise like a
cobra's hood

note the faint pattern
inside the ears—these
can hypnotize its prey

tusks instead
of fangs

up to
50 feet long

A MISTAKE FIXED TOO LATE

Legend says that when the Earth and the Sky and the
Sea created all the creatures in their realms, they held
a competition to see who could build the most incredible
beast. They started creating monsters, beginning with
small prey beasts and gradually working up to terrible
predators, like gryphons and dragons. Finally, the Sea
created the grootslang, and when he saw what he had
done, he was horrified and begged the others for help
destroying this monstrosity. The Earth intervened, and she
split the beast into two, creating snakes and elephants.
However, it was already too late—the grootslang had laid
an egg, and from it another grootslang was born. A creature of the sea, the grootslang prefers the water, but in
retaliation for what the Earth did to its parent, it comes
onto dry ground to terrorize the inhabitants of her world.

Rowansaur

The proposed name is a combination of *saur* (meaning "reptile") and Rowan, because I'm the person who discovered it, at least on our continent. We know nothing about this beast beyond the observations made by myself and others during our encounter, which are detailed in my journal. King Estienne has promised to assign several researchers to scour Roiva's libraries for any mention of similar beasts in foreign monster guides, and I hope to join them, if only for the chance to *see* those guides. Where did the beasts come from? How did they get here? Why did they travel so far? These are all questions I hope to answer someday.

crown of feathers

thick head with a reptilian snout

dozens of jagged teeth

orange and yellow feathers

gills

wing-like front legs with talons

curved talon used for killing

powerful back legs with talons

Property of

Rowan